DIO

# Ham Martin

Black Rose Writing | Texas

This is a work of fiction. Names, characters, businesses, places, events, and incidents are either the products of the author's imagination or used in a fictitious manner. Any resemblance to actual persons, living or dead, or actual events is purely coincidental.

ISBN: 978-1-68433-622-7
PUBLISHED BY BLACK ROSE WRITING
www.blackrosewriting.com

Printed in the United States of America
Suggested Retail Price (SRP) $20.95

*Talk Radio* is printed in Garamond

For Karen and Gary Osbrey
who walk the walk at WINY

# TALK RADIO

The author has endeavored to depict a community of people on the Maine coast who care about one another. If anyone thinks she recognizes herself or her cousin or neighbor, consider it coincidence or that the archetype may simply be in the zeitgeist.

# Chapter 1
## An Institution

Ornaments of her nine o'clock rising: the flowered silk kimono and the tri-colored coffee mug with its thumb rest on the handle, gifts from Alan, her hints dropped by dog-earring magazines and catalogs. Thumb rest—rest from what? Vivien thought. None of my digits or any other part of me needs rest—unless maybe my whole self, a rest from me.

She arose because there was no sleep left in her. She sat with her coffee, plunked down in a Maine village of fishing men, sturdy working women, and schoolchildren, by now all well about their business—oblivious of her and she of them. None of the men knew that the guy with the silver German car was not coming back. None of the women envied her three-hundred dollar bathrobe. They had lives.

Above the long runs of white and golden granite countertop were electric outlets galore. A black radio and its skinny remote scarcely competed for space with her espresso machine and four-slice toaster. Yesterday she had discovered embossing in the chrome indicating the slot for one slice.

Sometimes Vivien left the FM music playing quietly all through the day and night. When on this September morning a man from NPR introduced a classical selection, Vivien found herself holding the remote that Alan had mostly managed. It was the human voice that had stirred her attention to the radio, and she put the volume up a little. But right away he was gone and piccolos started in. Somewhere in this thing there are probably people just talking, she thought. Cautiously she hit the AM button. Loud static. She didn't know the difference between SEEK and SCAN, but she hit another button and everything stopped on loud male voices. One of them said they were on AM 1420 in Frost Pound, Maine. Frost Pound—that's where she was too.

The fellow doing most of the talking in a deep, resonant radio voice sounded older. He spoke as though everything was funny and he was bringing the others along for the ride. Vivien moved to a leather tub chair with more coffee and listened in.

On-Air

*. . . a radio show's theme music fading out . . .*

Fred: We're back, and happy to have you along for the third hour of the *WNWT Talk Show*, where yours truly, Fred Boyland, daily from nine till noon, rips from the headlines the news of the day. I hope our debate in the second hour this morning shed some light on the bond issue for the Frost Pound Consolidated School District to pay for temporary classrooms at the Middle School. We can take that up again on Monday morning, if it is your pleasure. After all, this is the show guided and directed by you, the most informed listeners anywhere on the AM dial. But right now, okay, marvelous, here he is, out of his green scrubs. Grab another cup of coffee, at home or in your car, and, dear callers, if any of you are idling in the line at the Dunkin' Donuts drive-thru, a glazed stick for yours truly can be dropped off here at the station. Doc Fontaine, great to see you, yeah, right there, put that headset on, you know the drill, it's time for our weekly feature, *Focus on Wellness*, brought to you by your preferred healthcare destination, Frost Pound Regional.

Dr. Fontaine: Good to be with you, Fred. Can't believe it's been a week. We had hoped to send someone over from the blood bank, but they couldn't make it, so I'm afraid you've got me for a second week in a row.

Fred: We'll muddle through, though I had some wonderful universal donor stories lined up. No, we'll take anyone from our community's number one institution.

Dr. Fontaine: Number two, maybe. You, Fred, are number one, everyone says so, and now I learn you're O negative. Are there more surprises? How many years have you been—

Fred: —19 years, no, cut it out. Please cut it out. An institution—thank you, Doc. And perhaps we should keep the universal donor thing between us boys. Word gets out and everyone will want a little of Fred Boyland's blood. No—it's a long story—you're nice to ask. I was in a very successful life insurance practice with my brother-in-law up until the eve of the millennium, and then, hey, didn't we all want to try something different in the new century? Ha—

Dr. Fontaine: I finally got married.

Fred: —and, well, I guess something just clicked, and this little phenomenon that became *Ripped from the Headlines*, officially billed as the *WNWT Talk Show*, took off. An institution? I don't know, I'll leave that to others. Okay, here's what I'm talking about, Doc, we've got a call. Hello, you're on the air.

Male Caller: Am I on?

Fred: You're on *Ripped from the Headlines* with Fred Boyland and Doctor Armand Fontaine. Who's calling?

Male Caller: You know my voice, Fred. It's me. We talk every day.

Fred: You're on *Ripped from the Headlines*, what have you got? Give it to us.

Male Caller: My wife and I were down on the interstate this morning and I saw something that gave me an idea. Down near the New Hampshire border, there's a place selling huge prefabricated roof trusses, you've seen it. Roof trusses are not rocket science, you know.

Fred: I like it. Roof tresses—they're what?

Male Caller: You know, Fred. Where the rafters and the ceiling joists are all put together in a big triangle, all braced and everything—roof *trusses*.

Fred: Got it, roof trusses, I like it.

Male Caller: Just two-by material and a lot of plywood gussets. Well, the gussets are mostly sheet metal nowadays—we always made them from plywood scraps. Anyway, we've already got all these modular classrooms at the Middle School, right? Which I'm dead set against, as you know, middle school I mean. I've phoned in about that before. In my time, we had elementary, then junior high, which was seventh and eighth, then if you wanted to stay in school you went up to the high school, which was tough and more like what college is today. So, why couldn't we squeeze a few more modulars in among the ones that are already there, that's if the bond issue passes, which I oppose—I've been in those modulars and they're damn nice—and we get some of those trusses and knock together a big gable roof—volunteers could probably do it on a weekend, a little brickwork, you could make it pretty, and you'd have a new middle school.

Fred: I like it, George. I like it a lot. Call in Monday and we can kick this around. Right now, we're with Doctor Fontaine and our *Focus on Wellness* feature. I wonder what they're asking for those trusses?

Male Caller: Can't be much, snow's been gathering on them for three years that I know of. Hey, I'll call Monday. (woman's voice in background) Yeah, yeah, yeah, I got it, Hon. My wife's here, she sends her best, Fred.

Fred: Don't go anywhere. We'll be right back . . .

*. . . advertising . . . we've got to move two hundred pickups by the end of the month and no reasonable offer will be refused, yes, you heard it right . . .*

Fred: We're back with our very special guest, Dr. Armand Fontaine, with whom your host has been quarreling off-air about the definition of an *institution*.

Dr. Fontaine: That last caller's wife seemed to know you.

Fred: We were in high school together, which used to be like college, Latin, all that stuff—very rigorous. And George, the caller, was sweet on my wife. Are you married, Doc?

Dr. Fontaine: Yes, I'm married, but I rarely speak of it, sort of personal, if you get my drift. Getting back to wellness—we thought we'd talk to your audience about blood pressure. What it is, why we check it, the risks attending hypertension, what the average man or woman can do if their blood pressure is too high, all that good stuff.

Fred: This blood pressure thing's all the rage now, isn't it? Last week some volunteer ladies—I suppose they must have had some kind of training—these gals were set up in the bank trying to take everyone's blood pressure. You know what I'm talking about, Doc? You go in to quickly deposit your paycheck and there they are, calling you by your name and making eye contact, "Hey, Fred, would you like your blood pressure taken?" We're seeing lots of this pushing us to get healthy, live-forever stuff.

Dr. Fontaine: I concede that we may seem ubiquitous with our wellness agenda.

Fred: Not just that, but it's everywhere. It's the same with the flu shots, and the informational talks in the town halls, and then you see your neighbor holding those little dumbbells when she's power walking past your house—have you seen that, Doc? And senior discounts on everything. I can't keep up.

Dr. Fontaine: I think you sell yourself short, Fred. You're getting a lot of information out, just with the *Focus on Wellness* segment. So, did you have them take your blood pressure—the other day at the bank?

Fred: Oh, God no, I couldn't do it, right there in a public place. Hey, look, there's Fred Boyland from the radio, taking his sport coat off and rolling his sleeve up, and the bank tellers gumming up their line gawking at me, everyone thinking Fred Boyland is making a show of what other people do all the time—thinks he's a celebrity.

Dr. Fontaine: Can I guess that you are in your sixties, Fred? You'll forgive me. Being a doctor of internal medicine, I have had hundreds of patients and you get to where you know, within a few years, how old everyone is.

Fred: It's so true. Facelifts, hair transplants, make-up, tanning. They can't hide age, can they? No.

Dr. Fontaine: Have I offended? Speculating about your age? I apologize.

Fred: Mercy no—you'd probably be way off. So, what did the hospital people think we would focus on today, sending you over instead of the Draculettes?

## Off-Air

Vivien reassured herself that she had not from birth known what *ubiquitous* means. He's fun, this Fred, in his way, she thought. She could remember a man at a carnival in Springfield when she was little who guessed everyone's age and weight. The middle school stuff was dreary, but maybe, she considered, because she didn't know any of the background.

It was the moments when the people talking on the radio most seemed themselves that she liked. She knew about talk radio, knew it was a companion for millions of people who were alone. She got up and wrote on a Post-It, 1420—in case the fancy radio decided to take her back to FM where she belonged. Vivien thought she might listen to Fred again sometime. Tomorrow, or the next weekday, probably. She would check to see what day of the week this was. On this morning, though, she just listened on.

## On-Air

Dr. Fontaine: I have with me something pretty terrific, Fred. It's small and inexpensive and can save lives. We thought—I confess that ahead of time I discussed this with your boss, Mr. Hudson— that if Fred Boyland learned to take his own blood pressure, your example—

Fred: —Ha, that *institution* thing again.

Dr. Fontaine: Well, yeah, as an institution you might just inspire thousands of other people to monitor their blood pressure.

Fred: Whoa, what are you going to do with that creepy contraption?

Dr. Fontaine: What do you say? Can we take Fred Boyland's blood pressure live on the radio?

Fred: A live radio first, no doubt. Ha, what do I have to do?

Dr. Fontaine: I will attempt to describe the little routine for the benefit of your listening audience, but the directions on these blood pressure cuffs that you can buy in Walgreens are all pretty clear, and your doctor, or physician's assistant, can check folks out on their particular device. It's possible to frighten yourself with a false high reading if you're doing it wrong. Okay, so roll up that left sleeve like you *didn't* the other day in the bank.

Fred: You're making fun of the host. It's okay, comes with the territory.

Dr. Fontaine: (sounds of Velcro attaching and unattaching) So it could have gone on two different ways, but you want the rubber hose leading this way down toward your hand, the cuff just above the bend of your inner elbow, snug, but not tight; I think you could do this yourself next time, don't you think?

Fred: I'm pretty fit, wouldn't you say? We do all our own yard work. Would you say I'm overweight, maybe just a little, not bad for an old guy? Can you guess my age?

Dr. Fontaine: Are you in your sixties, Fred?

Fred: Seventy-two.

Dr. Fontaine: I was way off. We're going to hit this button—

Fred: Seventy-two. You're surprised. Whoa, it's like a boa constrictor, attacking Fred Boyland on live radio. (A small motor sound attends a constricting of the wrapping on Fred's arm, and then it stops.)

Dr. Fontaine: Okay, the worst part's over. We're going to have a reading in a few seconds, it's doing its thing (then, several seconds of silence).

Fred: What?

Dr. Fontaine: Okay, so that's how you do it. Maybe your listeners would like to talk about how we control blood pressure, just in a generic way, or any other questions about health, medical matters. I am at their disposal.

Fred: We need to take a break for AP network news, followed by the local news, but we will be back.

*. . . news, ads, bumper music potting up . . .*

Fred: We're back, and I see we have a call. Good morning, Caller, you're on *Ripped from the Headlines* on the *WNWT Talk Show* with Fred Boyland. Do you have a question for Dr. (pause) Armand Fontaine from a group practice, is that right, Doc, you're in a group practice, at Frost Pound Regional? Go ahead, you're on the air.

Male Caller: Am I on?

Fred: You're on the air.

Male Caller: Only thing is, even with a volunteer crew, are they doing it this weekend—I'm away at my daughter's in Albany this weekend, but I could help next weekend, but even with a whole gang of guys, you're still going to need a crane to lift those trusses in place, and that costs money.

Fred: Thank you, Caller. I expect you are right. We've moved on to our wellness feature, have you got a question for Dr. Gauthier—(click)

Dr. Fontaine: Fontaine.

Fred: We've lost him, but we've got another call, excellent, you're on the air with Fred and Dr. (a hesitation), go ahead, you're on the *Talk Show*.

Woman Caller: Am I next, the lady that answered said I was on deck.

Fred: You're up; what have you got?

Woman Caller: So, what was it?

Fred: What was what?

Woman Caller: What's your blood pressure, Fred? Everybody's sitting here wondering. What did the little machine say? There's two numbers, like with cholesterol, a big one and a smaller one, and your heartbeat. Look at the gadget you've got there, I think it says pulse, the third number at the bottom.

Dr. Fontaine: Thank you for calling, ma'am. Mr. Boyland's blood pressure is not so important as—

Woman Caller: —Mr. Boyland? It's Fred. Fred's on all morning and JJ and I listen to him fifteen hours a week and you set this whole thing up today to check Fred's blood pressure, and now you're saying it's not important.

Fred: Thank you, Caller. Thank you, and thank you and JJ the Jack Russell—this woman has a terrific little dog, Doc—terrific breed the Jack Russell—had one myself years ago, thank you for your loyalty, Caller. So, Doc, what was it? I think the top number was one eighty-something and I couldn't see the second number (silence).

Doctor Fontaine: (silence) In addition to monitoring our BP, we should annually order blood work for cholesterol counts, oh, and blood sugar. Our American diet is leading to an unfortunate epidemic of diabetes and pre-diabetes, not to mention neuropathy. We could do a whole program just on neuropathy . . .

# Chapter 2
# Moving On

Monday

*Talk Show theme music rising...*

Male Voice: Good morning, good morning, and welcome to the Monday edition of the *WNWT Talk Show*. This is WNWT news director, Rob Auclair, and I will be your host today. This is the talk show where for three hours every weekday morning you, the callers, set the agenda. I can certainly get us started. As I noted in the local news at the top of the hour, the Frost Pound Selectmen will open bids tonight for the purchase of a fourth snow plow. If the past is a predictor of the future, we may be in for an interesting evening. So, *The Gazette* had a piece in over the weekend quoting members of the taxpayers' association that were not very kind to the sitting Second Selectman, Mindy Tatem, who is new in town and new to the Board—okay, I think we have a call, if I press the right buttons (screeching feedback), sorry about that, this console is a little different from what I have in the newsroom—there we go, good morning Caller, you're on the *Talk Show*, hold on, I apologize, okay—

Male Caller: —the trusses for the Middle School—

Rob: Hold on, I couldn't hear you there for a minute, putting up the volume in this studio is a toggle deal and I was looking for a pot—it's like a big round dial—we hear you well now, sir, go ahead.

Male Caller: We've got a shoestring operation here with the *Talk Show*, don't we? Fred told me one time—my wife and I ran into him in town. It had to have been ten years ago anyway. The set-up for the *Talk Show* is not like in the big city stations. Fred is the host, and is also his own engineer and his own producer. He lines up the guests, screens the calls, minds all the controls, all for not very much money. I don't know how much Fred gets paid—I knew back then—but I don't know what he's getting now. You probably don't either.

Rob: No, but if I told you, I'd have to kill you.

Male Caller: That's a little rough. Anyway, Fred asked me to call today at the top of his show to discuss the proposal to erect pre-fab trusses over the temporary classrooms at the Middle School, and I'm sorry I don't have any cost estimates yet.

Rob: I'm sure that's not a problem, Caller—

Male Caller: I'm one of the regulars.

Rob: Thank you, Caller. I think what I am saying is that it may be premature to be talking about cost estimates for roof trusses. I've been reading through the fine print in the bond issue referendum this morning and the option for one more temporary classroom, which would be re-sold in due course, is only a small part of the overall project. I want to clear that up, you understand, that the bond issue is for a whole new building, not supplementing what's there temporarily.

Male Caller: Well, I talked to a lot of people around town over the weekend and putting a roof over the temporaries we've already got over there is an idea that has a lot of support—a lot of support. The Building Committee and the Board of Ed are going to have to explain to the people why those roof trusses down in Ogunquit should go to waste before they can ask the taxpayers to spend millions we don't have for a whole new building.

Rob: But, aren't I correct that there's nothing about roofing over the temporary classrooms anywhere in the proposed language?

Male Caller: Well, they've been talking about it on *Ripped from the Headlines* with Fred Boyland, so it's on the table. Is Fred going to be on today? Is he running late or something?

Rob: I'm hosting the *Talk Show* today, and I think probably tomorrow—

Male Caller: —I'll phone in on Wednesday. Fred has always been supportive of roofing over the temporary classrooms. I'll talk to him when he's in.

Rob: We've got another call, let me just (pause) bring it up. Good morning; this is Rob Auclair on the *WNWT Talk Show*.

Woman Caller: I've been holding for a long time. Fred never left me holding that long. Where is he, Fred?

Rob: I'm hosting today, ma'am. Did you want to comment on the issues of the day?

Woman Caller: You know, that's really not very nice. It's not the way I was brought up in the Catholic Church, but I guess everything has changed and maybe you don't even know what I'm talking about because everything has changed. I'm sure you are a nice young man. You sound young.

Rob: I am 31.

Woman Caller: I'm also a *yes* vote on the proposal to roof over the temporaries, but you can't make me talk about that this morning, because Friday some doctor took Fred's blood pressure on the air, and then they didn't have the decency to tell what Fred's blood pressure was—took his blood pressure then jumped right onto something else, and it wasn't the listeners' idea to take Fred's blood pressure, was it? No, it wasn't. It was just some kind of publicity stunt for the hospital, which I hear is probably closing. The government is against the small hospitals and wants us all to drive to Portland or Augusta. That's going to be really wonderful for girls in labor, isn't it, except maybe it doesn't matter because they've pretty much cut out labor, which was part of God's perfect design. That's the way I was brought up, but it's all Caesarean sections now. Do you think, young man, that God meant for all the beautiful new lives to start out that way—with a knife? Isn't that hard to imagine? You probably don't even know what I'm saying—everything has changed so much. Maybe you're what they call a lapsed Catholic. You have a French name, so maybe you were born in the church and left it like all the young people do.

Rob: I think you have a good idea for a future program. The statistical increase in C-sections versus vaginal deliveries.

Woman: I don't think we need to be so graphic, do you? Fred never speaks that way. So, you keep changing the subject. What is Fred's blood pressure and where is he?

Rob: I can only tell you I am hosting for a couple of days, and the previous host's blood pressure is his own personal business.

Woman: You people should have thought of that before you wired him all up on live TV. The previous host? It was Fred, what do you mean, *the previous host*?

Rob: Radio, I'm sure you meant radio.

Woman: Wired him up on radio, radio-TV, what difference does it make? If it's personal you should have thought of that before.

Rob: (long pause) Thank you for weighing in, ma'am. I expect you are right that it was ill-considered.

Woman: Where is Fred, is he back on Wednesday? Is he all right, Fred thought the blood pressure machine said 180. Do you know if Fred's a smoker? I can't picture Fred as a smoker.

Rob: The *WNWT Talk Show* is alive and well. You don't need to worry about that.

Woman: You are being very unkind, young man. What about Fred, Fred Boyland? He's a human being, isn't he? Maybe everything's changed and we don't have to treat Fred like a human being.

Rob: We need to get to the important issues of the day. I believe a new host for the *Talk Show* will be sought. I think as far as Mr. Boyland is concerned, the management would like me to tell you that we have moved on. We have moved on.

# Chapter 3
# Derrick Takes a Pass

Tuesday
Off-Air

On the Tuesday after Fred's stroke, Kathy and Austin Hudson had both, quite intentionally, come to the station in business attire for a hastily called meeting of all the owners of radio station WNWT: them.

It was four days since the Friday night that Fred Boyland had had his stroke when Austin Hudson, President of Frost Pound Broadcasting, with Kathy at his side, phoned his wife's twenty-eight-year-old nephew. Derrick's father had recently asked his sister, Kathy, if she and Austin could find an on-air role for Derrick at the radio station. His endorsement for his son was that "Derrick loves the radio."

When after a few minutes, a sleepy voice came to the phone in his parents' kitchen, Austin had said to the nephew, "An unusual opportunity has presented itself at the radio station, Derr. Maybe your dad has told you. Mr. Boyland, who has been hosting the *Talk Show* for many years, has had a serious health emergency. I'll come to the point. Your Aunt Kathy and I would like you to come down to the station to talk about you taking over." It had taken a moment for Derrick to realize that he wasn't to take over the whole radio station, but maybe just talk on the radio for part of the morning.

For Austin and Kathy, big programming bumps like this had been infrequent. The station had been on cruise control for years. It was in good shape. Kathy's father had made himself the best-known personality in the region, hosting the drive time with his stentorian bass and tireless affability, selling all the advertising, and single-handedly dictating the music playlist. In his lifetime, no one presumed to challenge his power, or even wanted to.

Kathy and her husband are more modern people (Kathy went to boarding school and fancy college in Massachusetts), but they are not tempted by the easy and profitable trend of filling up the broadcast day with syndicated programming. The license says it is *their* radio station, but in the ether something palpable disagrees. The little radio station belongs to Frost Pound, Maine, a small corner of the world not envious of the style and habit of bigger places, or for that matter, the other small places close by. Frost Pound likes its radio station, and likes itself, just fine.

"Today is not really, exactly, such a great day, you know, for me to come down. I was going to go to the mall with Shedder, you know my friend, Shedder, to get some stuff we need for his car," Austin said to his wife, mimicking his just-finished phone conversation with Derrick. Sitting next to her husband for the phone call, Kathy had even heard Austin make a second try, and was satisfied that the kid had surely understood and would not be coming in. It was as she had expected; her nephew was too busy with the friend who had taken the local word for a soft-shell lobster for a nickname. They'd done it. For the sake of her relationship with her brother, they had made the offer. It was rejected; the preposterous idea was out of the way.

Minutes later, through the glass partition that created Austin's office, they saw a young woman pass into the station lobby from the parking lot. It all happened very quickly, Vivien Kindler presenting them with a one-page résumé and a poised and articulate pitch. There had not yet been a formal announcement of an opening—it was on their agenda for this morning—maybe a small notice in *The Gazette*, or perhaps something kind of formal during their own afternoon programming—far removed from the *Talk Show*—out of respect for Fred.

Austin and Kathy had looked hard at one another when Austin, nodding toward their little glass studio said, "That's our news man doing the *Talk Show*. Fred Boyland has had a stroke. He is stable and is expected to recover, but he will not be returning—ever." They had not said even this much on the phone to Fred's wife, or to each other, but it was understood that the emergency, which according to Mrs. Boyland was seriously affecting Fred's speech, speech and walking, had with cruel irony presented an opportunity for an overdue change at the *Talk Show*.

Austin did not seem to mind that Kathy had leapt ahead and said, "It would be best to not introduce yourself as a permanent replacement, not for now. It might seem unkind. Fred's following, and folks that don't know the details of his condition, wouldn't understand."

When Vivien Kindler rose from her seat, the interview seemingly over, she asked, "Would it be all right if I don't use the *ripped from the headlines* thing?" Austin and Kathy looked at one another and nodded in assent.

Seated outside in her car, unsure even of which way her key should turn in the ignition, Vivien was quite certain that she understood correctly that she would be coming in on Wednesday at eighty-thirty for a short tutorial, and that she was the new host of the *WNWT Talk Show*.

# Chapter 4
# Baptism

Wednesday
Off-Air

Vivien Kindler reviewed that she had eaten a heartier than usual breakfast, had put her pencils and glasses in her jacket pocket, and was not, as she felt, completely naked as she stood just inside the radio station door. She was not at all sure that her careful preparations would arm her for the day she had brought upon herself by an unexamined impulse; she had heard the young news director say on the radio that Fred Boyland was not coming back, that they were "moving on." She had correctly assumed that Fred's job on the *Talk Show* would be filled by someone else.

She could not sit any longer by the fire in the lovely house that her husband, Alan, had said should rightfully be hers when he left her there alone six months ago. Sit there doing what? Doing what? For how many months or years in this mostly unfamiliar town? Doing what? Probably nothing significant because it had been so long since she had; was she even capable of breaking the pattern?

So, on this day, bolder than she thought herself capable, she had dressed up and driven herself to the radio station that she thought had hired her. A palpable fear told Vivien that she was still alive.

She was sure that 8:30 was what they had said, but three different busy workers scooted past her without speaking. She did not expect or wish a fuss over her radio premiere, but she was frightened, and hoping for—expecting really—reassurance from some quarter.

Two minutes early. I will bide my time, she decided. But they said I would go on the air at 9:06 when the popular morning drive-time DJ has finished his shift, and the national and local news have played. Vivien saw the empty chair where she would sit, right on the other side of the plate glass that began halfway up the carpeted studio wall. There was no one in the studio and *Bohemian Rhapsody* was playing in the lobby and out over the airwaves.

Vivien thought she'd better not just stand there any longer. She tapped on Austin Hudson's glass wall. He looked up, waved her into his office, and smiled politely.

Austin and Kathy had hired her, the only applicant after Fred's stroke. Of course, they had not even advertised the opening when this Vivien person had presented herself. On that morning last week, Kathy had reassured her husband that their decisiveness was a good thing, but as Austin looked at this woman now, a few minutes before her debut, he realized that he knew nothing about her, and that they had probably made a horrible mistake.

Austin led Vivien to the big swivel chair in the studio. "Put that headset on, Miss Kindler; what you hear in those phones is what's going out over the radio." The nuts and bolts of hosting a show was a baptism by fire for all previous hosts and jocks. It was cruel, but Austin knew it was the only way. He told her about the log, the way the monitor to her right would display the bumpers and ads, public service announcements, and the *Talk Show* intro, all cued up in proper order; and about the location of microphone on/off switches, and sliding toggles for volumes, and how to bring up the phone calls that most of the time an automated voice would have answered and put on hold, and how to cut them off. Rob Auclair would stand behind her for a while in the beginning, do it with her and be her backup till she got the hang of it. "Okay, here's the intro, I'll give you a signal when you're on."

## On-Air

*. . . theme music rising . . .*

Vivien: Oh, my, you are there, and I am here, and we have this wonderful gift called the *WNWT Talk Show*. It is Wednesday, or what the real radio professionals sometimes call hump day. For the foreseeable future, I hope that you will accept me as your host and facilitator of conversation, and, if you are a praying person, say a little prayer for Vivien who, this morning, is very nervous. I thought that on our first day we could talk a little bit about the beginning of radio, about how we (a hand appears over Vivien's shoulder and hits a button on her computer) got to where we are today and how an AM—

Woman Caller: Hello, hello, I think you're talking over me. Can't you see, miss, that I'm on? Isn't there a light or something that says there's a caller there for you?
Vivien: Yes, I apologize, Caller. I am looking at a dizzying array of lights and gadgets and a young man from the station, I don't

even know his name I'm afraid, has brought your call up and, well, I was not prepared.

Woman Caller: Where is Fred? Is it true what I heard in the grocery store? I tuned in at 9:06 and a woman's voice was talking about a hump day or something and I thought I had accidentally rolled off 1420, but I hadn't. Good morning, good morning, that's how Fred opens the show, and then we start the ripping from the headlines part.

Vivien: Yes, of course, that is what you are accustomed to, and I am sure that it was pleasurable for you. I will probably be a little different, and I hope that in time you will find that the program is still fun to listen to, and to participate in.

Woman Caller: Maybe it's station policy, they probably had a big meeting with their lawyers and somebody is afraid of being sued. When my son died, no one sued anybody. Nowadays, everybody would be after the money, or figuring how to hide the money from simple, common people, as if money could bring back the life of a teenager who just got in the wrong car after a dance, and now is gone. So, tell me, what is your name?

Vivien: I don't remember if I have even told you my name. This is my first day and I had written down how I wanted to begin. Please forgive me.

Woman Caller: Young lady, the way I was brought up, when a person says forgive me, they mean that they think that they have done wrong and are confessing that they have erred—erred, that's what they used to say, and they meant it. Is that what you mean?

Vivien: My name is Vivien Kindler and I had intended to tell you a little about myself, just to get our relationship started, and yes, I do ask some forbearance if only for the fact that I am off to a poor start.

Woman Caller: Forbearance. That's probably about the same as forgiveness. I think I am a nice person, Vivien. It has not always been easy to be nice, I can tell you, but I think I am still a nice woman.

Vivien: Please tell us your name?

Woman Caller: My name, why? Everyone knows me. I don't think that is necessary.

Vivien: That can be up to you. I just think that sometimes, that we may be more careful about what we say if, you know, if we put our name to it. Do you see what I mean?

Woman Caller: You sound like a thoughtful lady. I'll think about the name thing. Sometimes people have a radio name that's what they go by.

Vivien: Maybe accountability for our remarks isn't the most important thing. I'm thinking out loud about this. Maybe by our having a name for you, and hearing you speak it with your own voice, and at times speaking your name, there is more relationship: you with the other listeners, you and me, you and other callers. It's more like you are a real person, a friend perhaps, whom we feel we know.

Woman Caller: Fred Boyland was my friend—without him using my name. He knows about me and my husband, where we live and all that, which parish we're in, which Mass we go to, all of it. Fred was my friend and now he seems to be gone. You are replacing him aren't you, Vivien? And you seem like a nice girl, but you are speaking as though Fred was not here every morning for years and years, and now you want to be my friend. That's not very nice is it, Vivien?

Vivien: I think I understand how you feel, ma'am. (pause) See, there we go. I called you ma'am because I don't know your name and it just didn't seem right to me.

Woman Caller: It's all right, dear. I didn't think anything of it. Fred just called me Caller.

Vivien: Some modern women, if you call them *ma'am*, they think it is intentionally sort of patronizing. My father was a Southerner and he raised us all to say *sir* and *ma'am*, so it rolls naturally off my tongue, but I don't much like it.

Woman Caller: Modern women. I doubt there's anybody out there that would call me a modern woman. Is there something wrong with being old-fashioned? I don't think so, do you? The way girls dress today—I won't tell you—I think you know what I mean. Modesty, do you even hear that word anymore? I don't. And the way the kids talk among themselves. I hear it outside the convenience store where we get our gas. I wonder if they even know they offend old people like me. No, I guess I'm not very modern, am I? The F-bomb, that's what my husband says they are doing, "dropping the F-bomb," he says. I'm supposed to get used to that? Is that what being a modern woman means? I don't think I want to be that, do you? Do they want me to stop going to Mass every day? There's only a few of us that do, you know. I suppose to be a modern woman I'm supposed to stop loving the Blessed Virgin Mary and just stay home and watch Regis and Kathie Lee, but she's not even on anymore, is she? It's Regis and Kelly. Those two just laugh, and tease, Regis and Kelly, like Kathie Lee never existed, and Kathie Lee so brave when Frank died. They just move on, don't they?

Vivien: Is Kelly doing a good job? What do you think?

Woman Caller: Oh, don't ask me. I don't think anyone cares what I think, do you? No, if I think she's a bit of a tart you'll all just say that I am not very modern, and Regis knows what the big TV people want and he just goes along. Why does everyone just go along like Kathie Lee and Fred Boyland never existed?

Vivien: It does seem to me to be a cruel aspect of our humanity, Caller, that we are sometimes confronted with just how very replaceable we all are.

Woman Caller: Then how can you do this to Fred? You said it yourself. It's cruel. I know Fred is alive. Oh, I think he is alive and he's listening to the *Talk Show* right now. Is it legal for me to speak to someone out over the air? I don't care. What will they do to me, arrest me for not being modern? I'll do it—unless you cut me off.

Vivien: I won't cut you off.

Woman Caller: Fred, you know who this is. I have not forgotten you. Get well and come back soon. I hope it's not your heart, or a stroke or something. I think when they took your blood pressure on live radio the big number was 180-something and I asked around and everyone says 180 is dangerous, but I don't know why. What can be dangerous about a number?

Vivien: You are very kind. And you will not be arrested for it. I expect many of our listeners echo your high regard for Mr. Boyland.

Woman Caller: So, is Fred coming back? You are not answering me. If I was cute and all made up sexy like Kelly Ripa, would you have to take me seriously when I ask a simple question? When is Fred coming back? Fred, if you are out there, I asked her, I asked the new girl who actually seems very nice, when is Fred coming back.

Vivien: (pause) I will tell you what I can. Things can always change, but Mr. Boyland is not coming back here. He has had a medical event about which I do not know the details, so he would be out of work, out sick you could say, in any event. That said, I am his replacement. I don't know if the management here will find that I am good at this, or how long I'll last, but for now I am the host of the *Talk Show*.

Woman Caller: So, Fred is finished, then?

Vivien: You could say that, yes, he is not coming back as the full-time host.

Woman Caller: (small dog barking in the background) JJ and I need to go. I need to say goodbye, Miss Kindler. You told me the truth, anyway. Goodbye, Miss Kindler.

*. . . a commercial . . .*

Vivien: I think we have another call. Good morning, you are on the *WNWT Talk Show* with Vivien Kindler and I hope that you are not greeted by a loud screeching noise, and are not accidentally cut off, good morning.

Male Caller: It *was* a stroke.

Vivien: I'm sorry. Who is calling this morning?

Male Caller: I see no point in us changing everything Fred did that built this program up over the years. Ripping it from the headlines was working well. So, Fred had a stroke, is down for a while with a little slurred speech, and everything's turned upside down.

Vivien: Upside down may be extreme, but it's fair to say that I bring different ideas and a different style to the program, sir. See, I've had to call you sir. Not so friendly, is it, because you haven't told me your name.

Male Caller: Well, if you insist, it's George. You can call me George the Welder. There's a socialist that calls in from time to time and I happen to know he's also George, and I don't want to be confused with him if you get him to use his name, like you're doing with me.

Vivien: George the Welder. That's a fun and evocative handle, George. And thank you for your courage.

George the Welder: I don't think I've had any shortage of courage, Miss Kindler. Not in Korea, not when they were sawing my leg off, not when I gave up my only son, and not this morning. I just don't like change—change when it amounts to throwing Fred under the bus.

Vivien: I understand. And I expect that if I knew you better, I would know that you are a person of courage.

George the Welder: You might not like me. A lot of people don't like me. I'm backward. A guy called in to this program once and said that I was angry. Well, if hating waste and government foolishness, and sending boys to die in foreign wars is anger—then I guess I'm angry.

Vivien: All good things to talk about, today and on future programs, right? And I'm sorry about your leg. Did you lose your leg in combat, George the Welder? It's something I have never understood—that Americans know so very little about the Korean War. Mostly we know Hawkeye Pierce and Hot Lips Houlihan.

George the Welder: Who are they?

Vivien: From *MASH,* the TV show.

George: Diabetes. Losing the leg was no big deal. And having a stroke is no big deal either. The last caller—everyone calls her Catholic Lady—she said Fred was listening today. So, Fred, get well, Vivien is keeping the seat warm for you. Come back soon, buddy.

Vivien: Was there something else you wanted to talk about today, George the Welder?

George: Yeah, this. What do any of us really know about the protection of lobsters in the big lobster pounds along the coast?

Vivien: In what respect, George the Welder? I'm deliberately saying your name over and over so I'll learn it. I must tell you I love the ring of it. I can see blue sparks flying when you talk, little bits of hot metal. Do you think I should drop my face shield when you're talking?

George: Suit yourself.

Vivien: Suit yourself, Vivien. Right back at me.

George: A few years ago, they were talking about it, that the terrorists ought to poison public water supplies—like reservoirs and such—a good way to hurt a lot of people, but I haven't heard anything in a long time, till now.

Vivien: Has something happened?

George: How would I know what they're doing, if they're doing anything at all, but I know that our lobster industry is vulnerable and you rarely hear anything about it.

Vivien: And is there a new development on that front?

George: I guess some guys saw some suspicious people up near McLaughlin's big pound on Sunday. I don't have any details.

Apparently, they drove down the access road and were seen taking pictures. That's all I know.

Vivien: I love that place. The river is so beautiful, the shallow tidal expanse and all the pieces of island and peninsula. I have to keep looking at maps because I don't know what I'm looking at. The light and the colors change on a dime, and I find myself drawn down into that world, and thinking I would like very much to work there—in its richness among the wonderful, hard-working people. Was there something else that made the people seem suspicious—the visitors with the cameras? Was there a police report or anything?

George: They had New York tags.

Vivien: Oh, my. That is concerning.

George: I think your news department could phone the sheriff and ask those questions. They'd have better luck than the average citizen.

Vivien: Do you think our listeners all know what a lobster pound is? Can you take a minute to describe it, and where you think it is vulnerable to terror?

George: I'm not saying these people were terrorists. Can we even use that word? I know you can't say it in the airport.

Vivien: No, we're safe here. It's just us welders.

George: It could mean a commercial dock where a middleman of sorts has hundreds or thousands of lobsters submerged in the salt water waiting to be shipped, or in the case of McLaughlin's, a huge tank of circulating salt water full of banded lobsters. In some harbors, if there's a big rain, the lobsters have to be sunk because they'll die in the fresh water that sits on the top. In a tank a terrorist would just have to let a lot of fresh water into the tank and they'd all die—the lobsters.

Vivien: Thank you for that. I hope we haven't provided the terrorists with a roadmap.

George: You obviously don't take my concern very seriously or you wouldn't mock me. I know that just because people have sunglasses doesn't automatically make them terrorists.

Vivien: But they were New Yorkers?

George: They were followed back up to Moody's Diner. I guess they had breakfast and got back on the road. That's all my friend saw. If you don't think there's reason for concern, I can't force you.

Vivien: Thank you, George. I think I have another call. Good morning, you're on the *WNWT Talk Show*.

Woman: Hi, Vivien. This is Lorna Paige. I don't mind giving my name. I'm calling about the mums in front of the Frost Pound Town Hall. They're those dark reddish-brown ones, and some dark gold ones mixed in.

Vivien: I know where you mean—around the sign.

Lorna Paige: I'm pretty sure they buy them new every fall from a big chain store, and they look nice for a month or so, then they die. It's really a shame, don't you think?

Vivien: I guess they're propagating zillions of them pretty inexpensively. But they know they're mostly going to die. Don't they call them winter hardy, though?

Lorna: If they leave 'em there in the ground, next spring half of them will come back, but kind of weak, and the town will pull 'em up and get new ones next August or September. That's what happens.

Vivien: Interesting.

Lorna: I'm good with chrysanthemums.

Vivien: I like the smell of the leaves; I think the smell of mums evokes something from my childhood, something happy, but I don't remember the exact association.

Lorna: Then you probably feel same as me, that they ought to let me dig them up in a few weeks and take them home and heel them in good for the winter.

Vivien: You could go in and ask the first selectman what their intentions are. Maybe you could have them. Hey, I've got another call, Lorna, call again. Good morning, you're on the air with Vivien.

Young Girl: Now? (giggling) Me? You want me to talk to her, don't poke me, okay. I'll do it—hi, this is a bunch of us from the Frost Pound Marching Band boosters.

Vivien: And tell me who you are.

Young Girl: Our names, okay, there's Nate (giggle) who's an idiot, cut it out, and Jess and Haley and me.

Vivien: And what's your name?

Angie: Angie. Shut up, Nate.

Vivien: And what's up with you guys today?

Angie: We're at school and we got permission to phone in to ask people to please stop by the Frost Pound Marching Band's snack table at the football game on Saturday. We're fundraising for the Florida trip and we are offering several delicious choices of chips, soda, and candy at reasonable prices to help defray the cost of the trip. We will be grateful for all contributions. Thank you. (click)

Vivien: Makes you hungry, doesn't it? I'm falling behind, so stay with me till after a commercial break.

> *. . . Swift Flowing Waves, Frost Pound's premier hair salon, has moved to its new location on Route 135 . . .*

Vivien: We're back, and I see we have another call. (dial tone) Oops, I'm sorry, I think that was me. I cut him off. Please call back. (pause) Good, maybe this is the same person. Hi, this is the very poorly engineered *WNWT Talk Show* and this is your technologically challenged host, Vivien Kindler.

Woman: I'm sure she can have the mums.

Vivien: I'm sorry?

Woman: I was in the garden club with Hal and Vi Harrison, and Hal plants those mums at the town hall every year in Vi's memory. He's got plenty of money and wouldn't mind if Lorna dug them up. I'd wait till sometime in early December. If there's the least bit of bloom hanging on and she takes them, some a-hole'll raise hell and it won't have been worth it for Lorna, who's a good kid, and it would be a nice break for her to have Vi's flowers. I can't think of anything nicer. I won't give my name; I never call, but today I thought I would. (click)

Vivien: We have a riches of calls today.

Another Woman: Is it me, am I on?

Vivien: Good morning. You're on the air. Is there another way of saying that? I sound like a million other talk shows.

Another Woman: I was wondering if you heard about the new consignment shop opening up next week on the north side of town on the main road, on the left, after the convenience store?

Vivien: No, I have not, but I'm very excited. All my clothes are used. Well, I suppose after you wear something it is inherently used. I mean I buy lot of things from Goodwill, the Salvation

Army, thrift shops. I don't think I've seen the place you're speaking of. What's it called?

Another Woman: Well, they don't have the sign up yet. The guy's still working on the sign.

Vivien: And what do you think the new store will be called?

Another Woman: I heard they were calling it *Been There, Done That.*

Vivien: That's a very clever name. I get it: it's like the used hockey skate place, *Play it Again*, right? I'll be on the lookout for it opening up. Anything else?

Another Woman: No, that's about it. I just wondered if you had heard about it. Okay, bye.

Vivien: We're up against the network news, so please stay with me if you can. The *WNWT Talk Show* will resume at six minutes past the hour—

*. . . network news, local news, and bumper music (Vivien hits a button for her intro) Good morning, and welcome to another hour of Frost Pound's own Talk Show and your host, Fred Boyland, the show directed by you, the citizen callers. Join Fred now at 207–5 . . .*

Vivien: (music potting down) We're back. There I go again sounding like the other talk shows. Do you think at the end of the show I'll just say: Vivien out! I should learn some new expressions to fill up the dead air and set myself at ease? Maybe I can just learn not to be afraid of the silence. Will you still stay with me if sometimes I don't blabber while I am gathering my thoughts? I do hope so. It looks like we have a call already. Excellent.

Male Caller: The news fellow last week was talking about the bids on a new snowplow. I heard they were having a hard time deciding what to do and tabled it till their meeting next month.

Vivien: I don't know anything about trucks, Caller.

Male Caller: Neither does that new selectman.

Vivien: You should tell us which selectman you refer to, and your own name, too, if you don't mind, Caller.

Male Caller: Mindy Tatem. The second selectman, which is what we usually call the person on the board that did not run head to head for first selectman, but didn't get the fourth most votes. Then the person that gets the next most votes is the third selectman.

Vivien: And Mindy moved into town from Connecticut in recent years, didn't he? I take it from the little I read in the papers some people don't think he knows much about snowplows.

Male Caller: It's worse than that, what with so much money on the table. I'd say he's a fool.

Vivien: Those are fightin' words, Caller. I don't think I got your name.

Male Caller: It was down to the Freightliner and an International and the First Selectman, Milt Fossel, explained as good as he could why the International was a piece of junk.

Vivien: Then what happened?

Male Caller: Nothing. Well, Mindy from away insisted on taking the low bid and was insinuating that Milt had some angle in favoring the Freightliner, which he didn't. It's like this: the bid package asks for a price on a 7-yard body on a diesel truck painted Omaha orange, and the bids are all over the place because it's never apples and apples, if you know what I mean. So, nobody ever holds the board to picking the low bid.

Vivien: Would I be wrong in saying that "junk" may be an overstatement?

Male Caller: Okay, let's say lousy. Here's what happened. International got a jump on the competition a while back with government mandated emission controls, and they sold a lot of trucks, around here and all over. Sort of got a high profile in the market you could say. So, people think they're good, but now they're failing, motors breaking down and costing a fortune to fix. And this Mindy won't listen.

Vivien: Of course, I can't attest to your facts, Mr. (pause) So, did they vote?

Male Caller: They laid it on the table.

Vivien: Why didn't they vote? Isn't that how you solve the issue? Someone wins, someone loses, and we move on.

Male Caller: I guess the third selectman didn't want to stick his neck out and get people mad at him, so Milt saw they were at a roadblock, you might say, and they laid it on the table.

Vivien: I find the political aspect of it pretty interesting, Caller. Our listeners will come to their own conclusions, or might have more knowledge about the truck stuff. But why we act the way we do—that interests me. In this case: why did the second selectman not defer to what seemed like a more informed view from the first selectman; and, why was the third selectman so very cautious?

Male Caller: I'm not going to get into their heads.

Vivien: And you have such strong feelings, Caller. Why do you care so much about this decision? (click) Oops, I think we have lost that call, or perhaps something else has happened.

*. . . commercial break . . .*

Vivien: We're back, yuck—radio lingo, please tell me if I start doing a lot of that—with just a few minutes of today's edition of the *WNWT Talk Show*, and the panel is telling me to try to bring up another call. Thank you for calling Vivien—me.

Milt Fossel: Hi, Vivien. This is First Selectman Milt Fossel. I have not had the pleasure of meeting you. I know where you live and know some of your neighbors and they all say you're good people. Good luck with the show. It means a lot to the town and to good government.

Vivien: Thank you, Mr. Fossel.

Milt Fossel: Milt.

Vivien: Milt, it is. Did you hear my last call from the gentleman weighing in on the snowplow vote?

Milt Fossel: My clerk had the radio on and had me tune in. I heard the last of it, but that's not why I called.

Vivien: How can we expect the voting on the International versus the Freightliner to resolve itself next month?

Milt Fossel: It's much ado about nothing, I'm afraid. I wanted to let your listeners know that I will be contacting Lorna Paige, who we know very well—everyone does—to tell Lorna that she certainly is welcome to the chrysanthemums in front of the Town Hall. I'll be coordinating all that with Lorna and we probably will have one of the highway boys help her get them into her car. She's a good kid. Been through a lot, of course. I don't think he'll be bothering her for a long time.

Vivien: Thank you for the good wishes, and please call again.

Milt Fossel: Will do, go get your lunch!

Vivien: That is going to do it for today. I certainly am getting a flavor for what your program is like and (music rising a little too loudly) hope to be getting better at the controls as we go forward. Please join me again tomorrow.

Off-Air

That was pretty good, wasn't it, Vivien thought, as she gathered up her notes. She took her coat from the hook in the corner of the little studio and looked through the glass to Austin's office. Had he been listening, maybe for some of it, anyway? Surely, he'd be wondering how I'd do.

She was exhausted. Could this job possibly leave me so drained again tomorrow, tomorrow and Friday? We'll see. She had met Frost Pound: the Catholic lady, George who had his leg cut off, the woman who wants the mums, and the kids from the high school. Mr. Hudson would have liked the welcoming remarks from the first selectman guy. She looked toward Austin Hudson's office again, but didn't see him there. Anyway, it was over, for a day. Wow, she thought, I made it through the first day.

# Chapter 5
# Something a Little Different

*The following Monday*
Off-Air

From where Vivien sat at her kitchen table, she could have peered through naked oaks and birches all the way to the river, but today she did not. Her ex-husband, Alan, had enjoyed keeping track of the tides, and on high-tide evenings would chivalrously carry their drinks down a long path to the rocks. He had teased her about the way she could silently stare over the water for hours.

But on this morning, Vivien looked at herself, looked at the hands that peeled the brown shell from a soft-boiled egg, the hands which at 9:06 would adjust headphones, hit buttons, and slide toggles in a radio studio. Amazing. Maybe I am going to be good at this, she let herself consider. Anyway, I am off to a decent start and it's fun, fun getting to know people, if only over the phone. These hands will probably shake again this morning, rattled by the engineering tasks, but Rob Auclair will be there. He'll hold my hand for another day.

## On-Air

*. . . theme music rising, recorded intro . . . Good morning, and welcome to another hour of the WNWT Talk Show and your host, Fred Boyland, the show directed by you, the citizen callers. Join Fred now at 207–567–99 . . .*

Vivien: Good morning, welcome. I am happy that you are tuned in and choosing to spend some of your morning with me. I plan to do my best to facilitate an interesting morning for us—with your help.

As a starting point today, I would love you to think about your earliest, and if not earliest, maybe just early relationship with radio, and what that meant to you—then and now.

When I was a girl in Massachusetts, there were several Christmases in a row when I was probably between ten and thirteen, when my parents invited an older cousin of my mother's and his wife—I'm pretty sure it was Cousin Tusten who was the one we were related to—to join us for Christmas. (A phone call lit up on Vivien's monitor and she looked at it.) After these cousins died, I came to learn that we were their closest relatives and Mom was their heir. This was sad in retrospect because I was a cute little kid and they had never shown any interest in me. I would have gone over to their house to work in their yard or do a project with Tootie, that was the wife, if they had invited me, and I would have loved them. I think I have an ample supply of love and I can't imagine that *they* didn't need to be loved. I didn't tell you up front; they were childless. So, on one of the Christmases—

The station owner, Austin Hudson, opened the studio door a crack, waved his arms to get Vivien's attention, and held his hand to his ear, pantomiming a telephone.

Vivien: Oh, (pause) I think we have a call, good morning.

George the Welder: Yes, I've been holding.

Vivien: You're up now. It sounds like our friend, George the Welder. Am I right?

George: Yes, is that okay?

Vivien: Did you have a radio story to tell us? I was telling a special one of mine, but I've cut it short, I'm afraid.

George: The intro this morning said the *WNWT Talk Show* with Fred Boyland. For a minute there I was expecting Fred, which surprised me because I hear he's pretty bad.

Vivien: I hear disappointment in your voice George. I'm afraid no one has remade the intro bearing Fred's name during the time I've been on board. Sorry about that.

George: Did you see that they voted on a new Superintendent of Schools for the region?

Vivien: I did. It was on the front page of *The Gazette* this morning. Do you think that is something of interest to our listeners in Frost Pound?

George: Are you insulting me, Ms. Kindler? Maybe it is, maybe it isn't. The point is this is what's in the news and this is how we get a discussion going. After all, it's you people who think the answer to everything is talking it out.

Vivien: You may be too quick, George, in identifying me with a specific group of *you people*. What is your observation about that particular hiring that we should hash out?

George: Two things: They said they had a nation-wide search and the committee narrowed it down to three: a woman from Minnesota; a principal who supposedly roughed up a student at his high school job in Pittsburgh, which we shouldn't automatically hold against him, he was probably the best candidate; and the incumbent assistant superintendent. Guess who got the job after the exhaustive national talent hunt—the guy that was right under their noses all along. Isn't that a coincidence? The fellow is very capable, apparently, in purchasing supplies, holding down the costs of school lunch, and figuring out the most efficient bus routes. So how does that prepare him for curriculum stuff and teacher evaluation, or as a leader? I've talked to people, people in the area, and they are pretty angry about the whole thing. Pretty angry.

Vivien: If what you say, you know, the factual parts of your statement, are correct, I get why you would be suspicious. But he might be fine.

George: My facts are straight, don't worry about that, and they are going to pay him more than one hundred thousand dollars a year.

Vivien: It's a lot of money, isn't it?

George: In the private sector there would be incentives built into his deal. A new man is hired to head up a division, so in time, by some objective measure, production goes up, or costs are cut, or morale goes up. So, he's done well, and then he gets a raise. What's wrong with that?

Vivien: I'm afraid, George, the train has left the station on this one. You hear that the CEO of some drug company is getting three million a year and you think: wouldn't he do it for one million? Or, wouldn't he take one million and the company could lower the cost of the pills that they sell to poor old people? No, I'm afraid he won't take one million and, anyway, the savings on his pay would be a drop in the bucket. And if several millions of dollars a year is the price of getting a top man, what is the board of directors to do? You see what I mean?

George: Well, we're angry. Like that caller said about me that time, George the Welder is angry.

Vivien: The people on the school board look at a schedule of salaries and benefits offered to superintendents in other districts of the same size, and that's where the number comes from. Who's going to raise their head above the hedges, George? In Australia they call it being a tall poppy—nobody wants to be a tall poppy and try to structure the deal the way you're proposing, even if your way makes more sense.

George: Nobody?

Vivien: Maybe we should put our effort into things where we are pretty sure we can make a difference. I'm not saying you don't have valid observations. But is George the Welder's time and talent maybe wasted on issues like this?

George: So, that's it, is it? *Ripped from the Headlines* with Fred Boyland has just been a waste of time all these years. Please don't call me George the Welder any more. Please! It sounds like we're friends and as though you like me, but you don't, you have contempt for me, and today you have said it for thousands of people to hear. I'm wasting my time.

## Off-Air

The studio door opened and it was Austin again, this time glum-faced and shaking his head. Vivien wanted feedback from the bosses; she was getting it now. The good listening and gentle coaxing that had brought one listener some chrysanthemums, this morning devastated another. Austin *was* listening this time—and he was unhappy. Vivien did not know how long she had sat frozen at her microphone before she found a lifeline, her notes.

## On-Air

Vivien: So, on this particular Christmas, my mother's Cousin Tusten lifted from beneath his feet where he sat in my father's best armchair, a large tissue paper wrapped present and set it in the middle of the room. "It's for you, Vivien, used, but in good condition." It was a cream-colored Bakelite Cathedral radio. I don't know the brand, but those radios were topped with a gothic arch and it had two knobs and about three feet of antenna wire dangling off the back of it.

That radio was the finest gift I think I have ever received in my life. I bet that's not right, that there have been more important ones, but I loved it right away. I am sure that I was a thoughtless kid and never told my mother's cousin how much I used it, enjoyed it. I regret that.

It is probably not unusual for teenagers to feel alone and alien in the world. I was a loved child, I have no doubt of it, but many nights, as weariness crept over me, curled up alone in my cold upstairs room, a houseful of other humans under the same roof, I often felt alone—alone and sort of pathetic. The radio sat, for all the rest of the years I lived in my parents' house, on my bedside table, and I fell asleep every night with the external antenna wire wound around my left index finger. Quietly, clear signals from Cincinnati and Pittsburgh and Buffalo and New York City beamed music to my room. So, I was never alone.

I expect many of you had a similar experience when you were young. It feels to me pretty self-absorbed and foolish, but that's how it was.

### Off-Air

There are no calls on the screen and Vivien dares to indulge the dead air, to sit silent, and there is wetness on the paper log she keeps for the FCC, where she checks off the hour and minute that she plays station IDs and runs commercials, or plays a copyrighted song. She thinks she is crying; it can't be anything else, and she puts a hand to her eyes.

### On Air

Vivien: I want to apologize to George. I dearly hope you are tuned in. I do not think you have been wasting your time. I just meant that in this particular—no, I apologize without qualification. I'm sorry, George. And I apologize to the other listeners. The last thing I want ever to do with the privilege that the Hudsons and you have given me is to be unkind. Whew, this is excellent. Blessedly I have a call. You're on the air.

Male Caller: Slowed on my route this morning behind the yellow
bus,

Right, at Young's Corner past Dave Eddy's mowing—

Vivien: I'm sorry, Caller. I think you may have already started
speaking before I brought your call up. Can I ask you to start
over, I'm sorry. This is Vivien, good morning.

Male Caller: Slowed on my route this morning behind the yellow
bus,

Right, at Young's Corner past Dave Eddy's mowing and the giant
hay wheels,

striped cows grazing the new-shorn slope.

Right, at the milk parlor where intrepid calendulas bloom,

oblivious to autumn against the windowless concrete cube,

nourished by Holstein droppings scraped off the

slippery cement waiting room slab.

Right, at the lean-to shelter Ike built for his special boy after the
school quit the

scary-steep bus run to his cabin.

All right turns: modern, efficient, the quick way there!

The children through their windows see just one side of things.

To the right, to the right, to the right. Perfect sense!

The new young man at the school mapped it out and

leaders on the School Board nodded praise.

I, too, took all the right turns my elders chose for me,

and took too long to find my way to here.

Vivien: (a long pause) I think you have finished, you have, haven't
you, Caller?

Male Caller: Yeah, it's a little crude, but that's it.

Vivien: You have written us a poem. Does it have a title? (long pause) What is your name, Caller? I don't know what to say. It was very interesting.

Male Caller: You could call me Brownie. I need to go. I'm sorry. (click)

Vivien: He's gone, isn't he? Maybe some of you can help us recapture most of the poem. I was trying really hard—after I realized that what we were hearing was a poem, that he had written it out and was reciting it on the radio—trying really hard to process the lines. When we read a poem, don't we usually need to read it over and over to discern its meaning? Here we are at a disadvantage because it was spoken, and there's no written text to go back to.

There were place names, and names of property owners, farmers. I haven't lived in Frost Pound that long. Were they real people and places? I believe we have a call—someone helping the new girl in town?

Male Caller: Those are all real people. Dave Eddy. He got rid of his cows back in the Herd Buyout deal in '86. Ike Gardner is dead, but his son is doing pretty good in a group home. The concrete milk parlor was probably Hartley Wood's.

Vivien: Thank you, Caller. You may have a better memory than I. Would you like to take a stab at an interpretation?

Male Caller: Who, me? No, I don't know anything about pomes; I just was helping you out on the places the school bus was going.

Vivien: That's what I thought, it was unambiguous, wasn't it, that the poet, or perhaps just a fictional protagonist in the poem, was behind a yellow school bus? Do you think it really was this morning? Did this Brownie write the poem today? If he did, I'd say he's pretty smart.

Did you enjoy the poem, Caller? Hello, (silence) I think he's gone. Thank you for your help, sir. I think it's time to pay the bills; that's what they say on the radio just before the commercials.

*. . . commercial break . . .*

Vivien: I hope that you were with us a little while ago when a man phoned in and shared a poem—a poem set in Frost Pound. We have a call, good morning.

George the Welder: There was a thing in there about the guy that worked up the bus routes with all right turns. That's him, isn't it?

Vivien: Is it you, George? I think so; I hope so. I'm not following you, though. That's *him*, what do you mean?

George the Welder: The fair-haired boy at the school department that they're paying a hundred grand. Your poet put him in his poem. I've got to go, doctor appointment.

Vivien: We've got another call. Good morning, and thank you for calling. You're on the *Talk Show*.

Woman Caller: Yes, lovely.

Vivien: Who is calling?

Marie Scanlon: It's Marie, Marie Scanlon. I was an English teacher at the high school forever. I am retired. Retired from paid work, but I am still teaching.

Vivien: Why do you say that you are *still* teaching?

Marie Scanlon: One day a week I tutor at the county jail, working with the men, mostly men, studying for their high school equivalency examinations.

Vivien: How wonderfully brave of you, Marie Scanlon.

Marie Scanlon: Of course, that is an awkward mouthful. Why don't you call me Miss Scanlon, that's what the kids called me. No, not brave at all. Perhaps I deserve slight admiration for the effort, at my age, and with the requirement that I not have had a drink on the days I go to the jail, but it is a place where we are quickly made to feel very safe.

Vivien: I see.

Miss Scanlon: It's a liberating environment, really (clattering noises in the background). Damn, I'm sorry. I've broken something. Liberating—that's funny, isn't it? A jail a liberating place. Is there time for me to explain?

Vivien: Definitely.

Miss Scanlon: I think that it may be because in the case of the prisoners I work with, so much has been lost to them that it is understood that there's a great opportunity for growth, growth and renewal—everything is *up*, if you know what I mean. And, as for the teacher, the State is grateful for my services, so I give them my best without fear of reprisal.

Vivien: You sound very dangerous, Miss Scanlon.

Miss Scanlon: The danger is not in me, Miss Kindler, but in the poetry.

Vivien: You and poetry have had a relationship?

Miss Scanlon: We usually met without incident, but there were exciting exceptions.

Vivien: I bet you would like to explain. This interests me very much.

Miss Scanlon: Poetry was in the curriculum. In my time, quite a bit in the eleventh grade, actually. So, with considerable enthusiasm I taught the usual canon: Chaucer and Shakespeare, Dryden, Pope, the Romantics. But American poets usually were the ones who won the kids over.

Vivien: Why is that?

Miss Scanlon: Have you got a week? I'm teasing you. There is a consensus that it has to do with our bias in favor of the individual, and as such, less concern about fitting into a poetry tradition. Americans like to think that they can be new; I think that hasn't changed. I've digressed. I was making a distinction between introducing poetry in a walled and razor-wired prison, and a free public school.

Vivien: A vivid contrast.

Miss Scanlon: In the high school, a certain danger presented itself from time to time, not every year, but lots of times, to be sure.

Vivien: What happened?

Miss Scanlon: (clinking of glass and a long pause) An outrage: some of the kids fell in love with poetry. It always came as a shock to the administration and the school board.

Vivien: How did this create trouble?

Miss Scanlon: Mostly in the insidious way poetry diverted some of the kids from sports and cheerleading. And the boys staying after school for the poetry club, that was the worst of it. I was their advisor and some parents said that the boys were interested more in Miss Scanlon than in the poems. Maybe they were. There was no harm in it. I was pretty then. My fleeting beauty may have helped promote their interest in literature. I have no regrets.

Vivien: And no bitterness?

Miss Scanlon: Oh, no. To be fair, practical people in Maine know how precarious is our economic situation. The older generations have known extreme hardship. The school was there to prepare the young people for work. Just too bad they couldn't see the fun in musing on Frost while cutting their cordwood—that literature and toil can be friends. You have let me distract myself, Miss Kindler, from the reason for my call.

Vivien: Did I do that?

Miss Scanlon: You know you did not. The man that called in and recited a poem that we think was about following a school bus.

Vivien: Yes.

Miss Scanlon: There were interesting lines at the end. I liked the whole piece. What fun, really, Vivien, that we can do a community poetry interpretation on the radio. The last lines: we don't know if the author is speaking for another person he has known, or for a fictional character, or for himself, but he alludes to "doing what others wanted him to do," and that this, in his mind, has diverted—diverted him in a way that he regrets. I just wanted to tell you that I found the poem and others' reaction to it very fun, Miss Kindler. Good for you. I'm gonna run. (click)

Vivien: Please, do call us again, Miss Scanlon. We'll be right back.

*. . . commercials and a public service announcement about help for problem gambling, bumper music . . .*

Vivien: We're back and we have another call. Good morning, you're up.

Male Caller: I write stories.

Vivien: You are an author of stories?

Male Caller: My stories aren't like in a book or anything. I just write them for fun and keep them in a drawer.

Vivien: Please tell us your name.

Paul: I'm Paul. Most people in Frost Pound know me. I'm the piano tuner. I'm in the Historical Society and my family has been here for a long time. They've got an archive locked in the vault in the town hall, which is fireproof, so they'll take them from me if I ask them, keep my stories as a sort of record of this period in the town's history; they'll take them if I ask them.

Vivien: Do you have a short one there you could read? We've got time.

Paul: It's only a page and a half, and I've showed it to people before and they think it's pretty good.

Vivien: We're all ears.

Paul: Here goes. On the far eastern end of town, near where Camphert's ski area used to be, you can see where they live, two old swamp Yankees, in one of the oldest houses in town, a brick colonial that their mother left them. Surrounded by junk. They don't think it's junk and they won't part with any of it. From time to time some sharpie raps at their door, says something like, "I hope this is not an inconvenient time, but I was driving by and noticed you folks are collectors. I am too. I buy all sorts of things: old cars, gas pumps, metal signs, tools, odd farm implements. I was wondering if you are interested in selling anything?"

"Nope, we need everything we've got here. You'd better go away." They are the kind of Maine boys that are stuck in another time and are suspicious, maybe a bit fearful, of the modern world.

Other than somehow accumulating more stuff, you wouldn't say that they work. I know more about their affairs than I can say because I am their friend and they trust me. I help them with banking and paperwork for the government and the complications of life like auto inspections that rob peace and contentment.

They live in just two rooms of the beautiful, big house and heat with wood, mostly apple, cut from fallen limbs of the gone-by orchard that their father tended sixty years ago. They subsist on day old donuts and prepared food from a roadside stand—still good, but too old to sell.

If you have seen the brothers, it has been when they have driven past your house, always together, only one of them has a driver's license, perhaps on their way to the north cemetery where for years they sprinkled spent drain oil from Froehlich's garage to kill grass around the brittle little gravestones of the Civil War dead, keeping them clear so the selectmen can find the graves and stick in the American flags on Memorial Day.

Inseparable, they are. Hardly anyone knows their first names: they're just called "the Buck boys."

This morning the phone in my kitchen rang at seven a.m. I knew it was them, checking in, as is their habit. No one else calls me that early.

"Good morning, Buck," I answered.

The voice on the other end replied, "Bad news, Paul, one of us died last night." (an unusually long silence)

Vivien: Brilliant. A gem, and told so elegantly.

Paul: You think that's pretty good?

Vivien: Are you kidding? I hope your other ones are half as good. The bad news for you, Paul the Piano Tuner, is that it most surely is true. You can't sit down one day at a legal pad, pen in hand, and make that stuff up. It happened as you wrote it, didn't it, and stuff like this doesn't happen every day.

Paul: Yeah, exactly like that. But you'd be surprised. There are great stories everywhere, if you know people, really know 'em, are out with people, and paying attention.

Vivien: What is this I hear of sorrow and weariness,
Anger, discontent and drooping hopes?
Degenerate sons and daughters,
Life is too strong for you—
It takes life to love Life.

Paul: What's that, Vivien?

Vivien: It's one of the more famous poems from *Spoon River Anthology*, "Lucinda Matlock." I memorized it in school. Thank you, Paul. Will you call again with another story?

Paul: That was fun. I think I'm sort of published now. (click)

Vivien: Hello, you're on the *WNWT Talk Show*.

Caller: Yeah, you're the girl that's replacing Fred, right?

Vivien: Uh-huh.

Caller: Last night the power was out in the whole town, right? Well, it was. I drove up on the Sligo Road and found the downed tree in the lines, and Tom Gullickson's second kid's Camaro wrapped around the utility pole.

Vivien: Was the driver hurt?

Caller: Fine. Standing there laughing with the crew having a good ole time. The Gullickson kid and seven others. Point is, it took them three hours to get us fired back up when some of us are trying to make a living. This kind of crap is going on, and the new girl on the radio is putting up poems and stories. Is that where we're headed with this thing?

Vivien: I don't know. The poem and the story both came as a surprise to your host. (click) I think he hung up. I think whether there is more of such things will depend on the rest of you. We have another call.

Mindy Tatem: Thank you for taking my call.

Vivien: Actually, we take them all (laughing).

Mindy Tatem: I noticed. Poems. This is Mindy Tatem, the Second Selectman in Frost Pound.

Vivien: Good morning, thank you for calling.

Mindy: Aren't you going to say anything about me having a girl's name, and that's probably why I don't know crappola about trucks?

Vivien: I was coming to that.

Mindy: My parents gave me the name Normind, which is a family name, and I've been called Mindy from birth. In college most people called me Nevermind. Anyway, you didn't ask about college, which to my discredit, I did attend. You just wanted to know about the girly name.

Vivien: And you've come clean.

Mindy: I heard you stuck up for me the other day, and I want to thank you.

Vivien: I wouldn't say I stuck up for you, and no one should look to me for advice on trucks. Perhaps I was just slow to jump to the conclusion that you are a moron.

Mindy: Yes, well, the jury is still out on that. When I moved to Connecticut from New York City thirty years ago the local folks, not all of them, thought I was a moron. Now some here in Maine are coming to that same conclusion. I thought I'd call this morning and give you some advice that may spare you some trouble.

Vivien: Please.

Mindy: You're telegraphing your *from-away-ness* by the way you pronounce our town's name. It's Frost Pound—with the emphasis on Frost. Say it like *frost bite*, or *frog pond*. Can you hear it? Not like *Ezra Pound*.

Vivien: I can hear it, and I will practice at home. *You* have adapted well, but you appear to have chosen to die on the hill of the International truck.

Mindy: That's really why I called. I have told the first selectman, who was plowing snow before I was born, that I am prepared to accede to his superior judgment on the matter of the snowplow.

Vivien: My late father always said that discretion is the better part of valor. Does that apply here? It sounds good, but I never have known what it means, and I don't think my father did either.

Mindy: I have come off the International hill and it feels wonderful down here in Freightlinerland.

Vivien: Well, call again, perhaps about something less weighty, flowers perhaps. We have another call.

Catholic Lady: If George the Welder wants to call me Catholic Lady, I don't care. Do you people think that I'm ashamed to bear the name of the religion I was born into? No. I go to Mass every day and I love my priest.

Who comforted me when my son was killed? It was the nuns that weren't embarrassed to hold my hand, me wailing and shaking like the devil had hold of me. It was the Catholic Church that took care of me; so, no, I will not turn my back on them now.

Vivien: I'm sure that is the right attitude. I'm certain of it. It might sound gratuitous, me not knowing you very well, but I am so sorry you lost your son. It is unimaginable.

Catholic Lady: My husband is a good man, and I have JJ now, my little dog, but not a day goes by that I am not almost broken by it. Sometimes I don't know how I cope, how I fill up the day. Once I said that I wanted to die and go to heaven and be with Stevie. I said it on the *Talk Show* with Fred, and a Protestant woman phoned in and said that there was nothing in the Bible that when we die, we are going to be with the people we knew in this life. Can you imagine, Vivien, someone saying that to me, saying that to me when Father promised that Stevie and me would be together in Paradise? Oh, the Protestants are big experts on the Bible, aren't they? But maybe not so expert on kindness to an old lady whose son got in the wrong car on prom night and now is gone. Hardly anyone even remembers Stevie, but I do, even my husband doesn't talk about it, and I pray every day for Stevie's soul. Every day, and I muddle through. I guess that's what I do, muddle through, Vivien. You're probably a Protestant, Vivien, I'm sorry. I've got nothing against the Bible.

Vivien: You are brave to tell us all that. But you know what? I can't call you Catholic Lady. Please tell me something sweet I can call you.

Catholic Lady: How about JJ's Mom? That's my main reason for living these days. People call him cur and ankle nipper, but I defend JJ. (to the dog) JJ, they're going to call me JJ's Mom on the radio program from now on.

Vivien: JJ's Mom, it is. I haven't asked why you called.

JJ's Mom: I remember. It's about the flowers that woman is going to dig up at the Town Hall. Was there a legal notice or something saying that the Town of Frost Pound was making available to the public a certain number of asters or poppies or something, and you could put in a request, and maybe there would be a drawing of some kind—fair and square like. That's not what I'm hearing. I'm hearing that this one woman, Lorna, is getting the whole kit and caboodle. Does that seem fair to you, Vivien? It doesn't seem fair to me, no.

Vivien: I think the selectmen have just tried to respond kindly to one person the best they know how. That's all.

JJ's Mom: I would take some of those flowers to Stevie's grave if they were dividing them up fair.

Vivien: You know, you could help me and my family. We've got a bunch of mums that were given to us to decorate for a big family gathering and I've not known what to do with them. If you could come by the station, tomorrow right before my show, or right after, I'll have them in my car for you, okay. You'd be doing me a big favor.

JJ's Mom: Okay, Vivien, I don't drive anymore, it's not safe, but I've got a neighbor who will come for them. I don't mind helping you out.

# Chapter 6
# Farm to Table

Three weeks later
Off-Air

It had been Vivien's habit for the past few weeks to arrive at the radio station fifteen or twenty minutes before she went on the air at 9:06. In fair weather, she usually sat in her jacket on a granite outcropping next to the cinderblock Radio Station WNWT, the rock left not for its beauty, but because it was discovered to be attached beneath the soil to the entire peninsula—and probably the whole earth. From that perch Vivien rehearsed in her brain an opening monologue that she hoped would set the program on a course not ripped from the headlines. Vivien treasured the small slice of water view to the south and west, the perspective enhanced by the distant islands and endless vast sea.

It was unusual for Austin Hudson to speak to Vivien at all, but on this day, he came all the way outside, and met her at her rock.

"Vivien, Kathy has a new advertiser who thinks it would be fun to do an hour with you on the *Talk Show*."

"Please tell him that I'm pleased to have him on, and maybe he could give me some prompts about what we could talk about."

"Actually, he's here now and I'd like you to take care of it this morning. Okay?"

*. . . theme music rising, recorded intro—Good morning, and welcome to another hour of the WNWT Talk Show and your host, Fred Boyland, the show directed by you, the citizen callers. Join Fred now at two o seven, five six seven, nine, nine . . .*

Vivien: Good morning, good people of Frost Pound and environs, and guests visiting us from sad, less-lovely places in the lower forty-seven. I am kidding—sort of. As I have told you, I have lived in lots of other places and I have been more or less contented in them all. One of the things that distinguishes our corner of the world is the great variety of unusual, risk-taking ventures popping up all around us, businesses that enrich us, many of which are food and drink related. One such enterprise is the somewhat newly opened, is that right, Marcus?

Marcus Deloitte: It's been about nine months.

Vivien: The Loca, Locovore Restaurant in Camden. Good morning, Marcus Deloitte. You have to put that headset on. Tell me if the volume is okay.

Marcus: Thank you for having me on the *WNWT Talk Show* with Fred Boyland.

Vivien: Yes, of course, the intro, it holds a nostalgic place in the hearts of many of our listeners.

Marcus: As it should, of course.

Vivien: Have I pronounced your name correctly? My husband's people came from Beloit, Wisconsin, and I am saying it like that.

Marcus: You've got it.

Vivien: Our boss, Austin Hudson, wrote your name and the name of your establishment on a note for me, and it did say *Locovore* with an O. Is there significance to that, Marcus?

Marcus: Yes, and I am at risk of making trouble with the movement. Let me explain to your listeners. Some of you have read or heard about the localvore movement, which sometimes is spoken, locavore, without the second *l*. It's about a commitment to purchasing and consuming food grown near home. Some, rather arbitrarily, have stipulated one hundred miles as local. That's neither here nor there.

Then there evolved what is an easier construction: farm-to-table. Oh, the name of my restaurant—Locovore. I switched out the *a* for an *o* as a nod to the craziness of launching a restaurant on the coast of Maine. Not so much crazy because it's Maine, but because it's so damn hard. I must be loco. Get it?

Vivien: We have a call, Marcus, and I've learned to take them right away or they become surly. Good morning, you're on the air with Vivien and Marcus Deloitte.

JJ's Mom: Good morning, Vivien. This restaurant fellow, is he tall and handsome with a head of beautiful black hair?

Vivien: I would say that's a fair description if I were one to notice such things.

JJ's Mom: Ask him, Vivien, if he grew up in Waldoboro. Well, never mind, I'll ask him. I think you know me, restaurant fellow, I'm Stevie's mom, are you from out on the Neck in Waldoboro?

Marcus: Did I ever pay you for those pumpkins we squashed, Mrs. D? These days I am making a nice, cold curry soup from pumpkins. Please come by Locovore with your husband, as my guests. I mean it.

JJ's Mom: Vivien, your Marcus Deloitte is Mark Elliott from a very nice local family. Where ever did you get that fancy name, Markie?

Marcus: After high school I went out west for a while and wherever I lived I usually ended up waiting tables or cooking. As wonderful as my family was, is, Mrs. D, something made me want to reinvent myself, and now you've blown my cover. I loved food and decided to apply to the CIA and it was in those years that I tried out Marcus Deloitte. I became Marcus Deloitte, and the rest is history.

JJ's Mom: Were we really so boring up here in Maine, Markie, that you had to change your name and become a spy?

Marcus: No, there was nothing wrong with you or Maine. It was something in me. And now with the restaurant, I'm afraid I am too busy for intrigue.

JJ's Mom: You be careful, Markie. God must love you, Markie. He took Stevie and left you with us, so you be good. I'm hanging up now, Markie. I'll tell your mom I spoke with you.

Vivien: We have another call. Good morning, you're on the *WNWT Talk Show*—

Fred Boyland: —with your host, Fred Boyland, which m- m- makes your intro very f- fitting, doesn't it, Mrs. Kindler?

(Vivien knows that it truly *is* Fred Boyland on the line, made even more unmistakable now with the small, shaky voice.)

Vivien: Is it you, Mr. Boyland?

Fred: What with your g- guest speaking about me at the opening of the show, and hearing from my old friend, Catholic Lady, I could not resist phoning in to my own radio program; that's kind of funny, isn't it? An in- indus- dustry first: radio host phones in to his own show. I know many people have been asking about me and are w- wondering how I am feeling and when they can expect me back on the air. (Fred's voice was so shaky and weak, Vivien considered asking him to speak up, but she did not.)

Marcus: Hello, Fred, this is Marcus Deloitte, and I am a fan.

Fred: Hey, cut it out.

Marcus: No, really, I am. I want to tell you that you have been missed and to wish you the very best in your retirement. Surely, you have earned it.

Fred: I'm sure you can under- understand, Mark. If you were to never crack another egg, it would not be your style, and it's n- n-not mine either.

Vivien: I'm afraid, Mr. Boyland, you have me at an awkward disadvantage. Did someone at the station tell you that you would be coming back on the *Talk Show*?

The studio door opened a crack, Austin Hudson made eye contact with Vivien, shook his head, and pantomimed a *hang up the phone* motion.

Vivien: I'm sure you, as a seasoned pro, Mr. Boyland, will understand that I need to go to a commercial.

### Off-Air

Marcus said to Vivien, "Are you all right? You look like you've seen a ghost."

"That *did* take my breath away. I really thought this matter was behind us, but it obviously isn't."

After contending with the faded radio star, easily vamping through another twenty minutes on the challenges of farm-to-table cuisine, five minutes on the storing of root vegetables from Marcus's own garden, a discourse on seasonality, and ten minutes on the local sourcing of seafood, with particular attention to the soft-shell clam, the hour went by.

## On-Air

*. . . local news and weather, some public service announcements, Fred's theme . . .*

Vivien: And we've another call all queued up. Good morning.

Caller: Is that you there, Fred? (in a thick down east accent)

Vivien: And who is calling?

Caller: Folks hereabouts mostly call me Old Sabe and I don't know why. Fella from the restaurant that changed his name got me wondrin' if he's doin' anything with the freshwater lobsters they're raisin' up Sligo way.

Vivien: Fella that changed his name's left the studio, but I believe *Locovore* has a website with their menu posted there. You could look for—what is it? Freshwater lobster.

Old Sabe: Fella has a web something; if that's got to do with technology, you're talking to the wrong man.

Vivien: That is a wonderful way of talking you have there, Old Sabe. I'm glad the charming Maine dialect is alive and well. Where is your home?

Old Sabe: Our people, intermixed you might say with the Sanfordsen clan, has pretty much stayed put on the Sligo Road since the seventeen hundreds, 'cept when a few of the boys went off to Ticonderoga with young Knox. Still talkin' about it, quite a winter that one, hadn't built the Mass Pike yet.

Vivien: I've forgotten why you phoned the *Talk Show*.

Old Sabe: Shellfish of me, I reckon. Thought we'd have some better markets by now. Few years ago, Sally Sanfordsen was drivin' past the orchard where the pond comes close to the Sligo Road, bringin' that second shift paycheck home to Sandy and the girls. She was awful tired and going awful slow like she always does. Sally thought she saw something crawlin' across the road. Sally got out and was the first to see in person what we had long suspected, a great procession of three- and four-pound lobsters crossing that road and walkin' through the public beach and into the pond.

Vivien: Is that possible?

Old Sabe: You're prob'ly wondrin' about the inland part of the pilgrimage, gettin' from Frost Pound through woods and fields, and into the orchard.

Vivien: Not just that, but yes. Arduous, for sure.

Old Sabe: There's been some more recent nocturnal observation, and it seems like the lobsters been takin' some rest there in the orchard, and eatin' some Cortland drops. May be having some effect on their adaptability to the fresh water.

Vivien: Have you asked the folks at the Darling Center to study it, the so-called Cortland effect?

Old Sabe: You're a bright girl, Vivien. Ought to have your own intro someday. (click)

Vivien: We have another call, good morning, you're on the *Talk Show*.

Caller: Am I up, okay, good, that's all bullshit, that whole freshwater lobster thing, and that guy's accent, he made it all up. It was bullshit. (click)

Vivien: Thank you, Caller. I know some people near where I live talk in that way, and I do love it. Old Sabe may be more of a *Bert and I* knockoff. It's a wonderful premise, though, don't you think? Big lobsters coming overland to fresh water? We have another call. Good morning, you're on the air.

Caller: My wife and I go out every other Saturday night and she wanted to try that *Locovore*. Well, I can tell you what's *loco* about it—the prices. It's that new fixed price deal, seventy-five dollars a meal, extra for wine and drinks. Anyway, next available reservation was in five weeks. So, I don't know why the guy's even advertising—maybe just a swelled head wanting to hear himself talk on Fred's show.

Vivien: I hope you found Fred's show today interesting on some level. Fred's doing the best he can. (click) Good morning, you're on the *Talk Show*.

Brownie: This one has a title:
    Soft Shells
    Stay on your toes, weight forward, rubber-booted hunters.

Weary, muscle-stretched and pride-strained you must be.
To the shuck shack on the State Route you take them to
where the piece-work girls ply their farm-to-table trade.
Before the district judge I confessed:
So what, yes, it was I, Brownie,
Who fell in love with Sarah Jane
whose hands rolled and turned,
sleight of hand I could not see though sidelong
I watched her doing what all the others did,
faster and lovelier than the rest.
A pint, a quart, a gallon, twelve, tallied with the chalk.
A new pile of the boys from their warm bath,
resting unawares on a crushed ice bed.
One-by-one, Sarah Jane's knife separates them from
their pearly home, and with a magic twist
Frees them from the horrible black rubbery sheath.
That vile thing,
tossed to the waste never to see the tartar sauce.
Your Honor, a machine came to our little corner of life
and they said it was faster than Sarah Jane,
bigger profits to be made.
I stole in one night with the key
one of the girls had left for me under a stone.
Unconflicted, the stone and I smashed
the hideous thing the corporation had named *Sheila*.
When the replacement parts came all the way from China,
Brownie lost the package en route, a perfect crime.
But I had forgotten all about the tracking code
and I was done for.


Vivien: (silence) Brownie, (click), Brownie, I hope you can hear
me, Brownie. What wonderful fun, thank you. As they say, I

needed that. We have a call, we have several calls lined up, oh, my!

George the Welder: I was phoning in about the fixed price dinners, and I heard that poem. I don't know anything about poetry. I mostly steered clear of that sort of thing, but that damn thing made me laugh. I think it was about shucking clams. Is that right, that it was about clams? You've got other calls. I'll let you go.

Vivien: You're on with Vivien Kindler.

JJ's Mom: I liked the poem, I have to admit, but why do they have to make everything so sexual nowadays. Am I old-fashioned? I guess I am. Do you think the fellow really did smash the electric shucking machine?

Vivien: No, but he may have loved the girl. (click) Let me bring up another call. You're on the *WNWT Talk Show*.

Caller: How about an old song?
    You get a line and I'll get a pole, honey, honey
    You get a line and I'll get a pole, babe, babe
    You get a line and I'll get a pole and we'll go down
    To the crawdad hole, honey, oh baby mine. (click)

Vivien: Thank you for that, Caller. Who has shared that classic with us this morning? (silence) I think our vocalist is gone. Today we have had poetry and a song. I'll take another call.

George the Welder: I think he's right.

Vivien: Who is right? I am happy to have consensus, but I'm losing the thread—my fault.

George the Welder: Not the guy that swore; the one that sang the song. He's saying that we already have freshwater lobsters—crawdads, crayfish. And the man with the fake Down East accent, he's just pulling the leg of the new girl—you.

Vivien: I suspected as much. And if they take some gentle potshots at Vivien in the interest of creativity, I can take it. So, what about you, George the Welder? Do you sing, or write poems, or tell *Bert and I* stories? Maybe you are one of the mad geniuses that weld salvage and found objects into fanciful steel creatures.

George: I don't know what you mean.

Vivien: I've never stopped, but I've spotted such things in Bremen and Waldoboro and Tenants Harbor; I'm sure you've seen them.

George: I'm mostly at home now. I don't drive. I still am pretty much up on what's going on in the state, from the papers mostly.

Vivien: You knew about the roof trusses on the side of the highway in Ogunquit. Maybe Mrs. George drove you down to New Hampshire. Never mind that. Are you welding?

George: I'm done with that. Eight years ago, I quit the shipyard. And I'm glad of it. Everything had changed, and not for the better. Anyone would say that who worked down there in my time.

Vivien: Is there something that you especially enjoy doing?

George: I don't think the *Talk Show* audience is interested in me.

Vivien: I am interested in you, because you care about this program and make a contribution, and because you are George the Welder.

George: I take care of my yard. It's small. It's mostly behind the house, fenced in from the neighbors. It's flat ground with smooth granite dust paths for my chair. I told you I lost a leg, and I have a shed of tools and supplies and I fuss around out there in the afternoons most of the year. People drop off odd plants and little trees and shrubs, sometimes rocks and broken bits of crockery.

Vivien: Do you think it is a canvas for the creative side of George the Welder who no longer welds? I won't put words in your mouth. Or is it a retreat of sorts? I can say about myself that I have tried to build safe places in my life and, truthfully, that urge, or need, or whatever it is, doesn't seem to go away.

George: I'm just telling you how I spend my time and you're trying to put me on a couch.

Vivien: I will not invade your privacy, George, but—

George: —A few weeks ago, no one knew my name, and now they know about my backyard and my wheelchair. I think you've tricked me into enough information about myself.

Vivien: I would like you to believe me about something important. It may just be Vivien and some odd minority of people like me, but I think that a man fashioning a walled garden in Maine, from trees and shrubs and stuff people have brought him, is more interesting than which snowplow the town is going to purchase. So, let's forget about your motivation for now. Just tell us more about the place you have made, and how you have done it. Is that fair?

George: We'll have to disagree on whether it's interesting—interesting to others. I go out there every day after my lunch. Do you need to know what I eat? I like sardine sandwiches, sardines with raw onion and mayonnaise. The big features are Japanese maples, they're about twelve feet high and spread very horizontal. You'd say they are sisters, the copper color, which I like better than the red. I have one small cut leaf one also, red, and it has never fit in too well with everything else, and I don't know why. I have three kinds of bamboo that serve as fencing in spots where there's a skip in the fence. My neighbor knows that when the bamboo sends shoots his way, he's free to hack the new growth back, or leave it if he wants—it's his land.

Vivien: Do you hire people to help you with digging and such? You once mentioned a son.

George: You mean because of the one leg I must need help. That's okay. I do everything myself. I am strong and can get myself in and out of the chair. I grub around on my hands and knees—dig holes even. You wouldn't want to see it.

Vivien: Do you consult books?

George: No. I stare at it. It's a small area. I stare at it in every season for hours and hours. I know every branch and root. If a small tree seems like it's not quite right, I'll sometimes bend a branch with a guy wire, or wind wire right around it to curve it to what looks right. There have been many experiments and many of them have failed and been redone. I have no son. I crawl around and weed into a peach basket and in the fall, I rake leaves and debris with a short-handled rake and keep a compost pile in one corner of the lot. Table scraps go in there too, and there are huge night crawlers.

Vivien: Do you think it's beautiful?

George: I have tried to train other things in my life and they have not worked out. The garden suits me, and plants can't talk back. I sit there for hours every day. At five o'clock if I am still out there, my wife brings a blanket for my lap, and my glass of bourbon.

Vivien: You have drawn it well enough for us to picture a peaceful place, and to imagine that you have made something finer than what was there before—before there was a George the Welder.

George: I'll go now.

Vivien: —and we'll take a short break, too.

*. . . soft instrumental music . . . the scent of our own roasted parsnips and turnips and Swiss chard. Monkfish with pea tendrils on a bed of today's polenta. An ambience you and your special partner will not soon forget. Call us at Locovore about the next dinner availability . . .*

Vivien: You're up, welcome to the *WNWT Talk Show*.

Old Sabe: Fella talkin' about his garden put me in mind of the couple got in a heap of trouble up in Lincolnville.

Vivien: Caller, are you the gentleman that told us about the freshwater lobsters up on the Sligo Road? Old Sabe.

Old Sabe: Sounds familiar.

Vivien: Go on, then.

Old Sabe: Husband and wife went into the bonsai business. Summer people were right excited about it and there was some heavy traffic up the Benner Road for the three or four weeks the establishment was operatin'.

Vivien: I definitely would have stopped in there, probably would have bought something. But it would have died. So, what happened? The business was short-lived?

Old Sabe: Got the girl to do all the dangerous work. She'd drive a van up north into the mountains after dark, go up near the tree line, 4,000 feet, and pull up small spruce and fir trees by the roots. Hundreds of 'em in a burlap bag each trip.

Vivien: Horrible, Old Sabe. Can I call you that?

Old Sabe: Husband was the brains. Mail ordered couple hundred Japanese lookin' glazed pots—shallow like—customers were partial to the blue ones, and the two of 'em planted the gnarled, weather-beaten little trees from Katahdin in the Japanese pots and sold 'em as bonsai. Hardly needed any pruning—just sold 'em pretty much as they come off the mountain. Folks liked 'em just fine.

Vivien: What happened?

Old Sabe: That first two hundred bonsai sold out mighty quick, but they were under obse'vation by the sheriff after that, and couldn't replenish their stock. Kind of a shame. Hadn't put a dent in the native fir tree population and they had themselves off the State pove'ty programs. Heard the husband is locked up in Thomaston now. Where's the economic sense in that? Don't quote me on the jail part, though. Don't like to gossip. Dead set against it.

Vivien: Of course. I'm curious as to whether the little trees survived, transplanted into small pots and moved to a different climate.

Old Sabe: I can't answer for that, but some wise folks say that every species does best if it just stays where it belongs, leaving things as they was, if you get my meaning. You're from away, aren't you, Miss Vivien? (click)

Vivien: We have another call. Good morning, you're on with Vivien.

Marie Scanlon: Miss Kindler, it's Miss Scanlon, the schoolmarm. The just-completed tale of the larcenous couple, bless their hearts, who harvested the dwarf evergreens from up near the tree line. Do you think it qualifies as literature?

Vivien: That's above my pay grade, as they say. But not yours; what do you say?

Marie Scanlon: I say, yes. It works pretty well as satire. It's quite impressive, especially if the guy just told it extemporaneously. And the metaphor at the end is quite charming—if mean-spirited.

Vivien: The metaphor?

Marie Scanlon: The little trees from Mt. Katahdin planted in Japanese pots trying to survive down here. Moved too far from their native environment, just like the talk radio host.

Vivien: I didn't get that.

Marie Scanlon: I could be mistaken. Where are you from? You *are* from away? I just assumed you were.

Vivien: Massachusetts.

Marie Scanlon: Yes. I was liking the satire. The unkindness of it should not have blunted my admiration, but it did. And, of course, others may have different interpretations, as they should. We bring different experiences and sensibilities. I'll let you go.

Vivien: It's okay, Miss Scanlon. We'll take culture wherever we find it. Gotta run, dear friends, see you all tomorrow.

# Chapter 7
# How We Got Here

Early winter

*... theme music rising, Good morning, and welcome to another hour of the WNWT Talk Show and your host, Fred Boyland, the show directed by you, the citizen callers. Join Fred now at 207–567–99 ...*

Vivien: Thank you for tuning in this morning to Frost Pound, Maine's daily talk program on station WNWT, broadcasting on 1420 on the AM dial.

A brief history from a lifelong lover of the radio, me, Vivien Kindler. In the early 1900s inventors and tinkerers made the fantastic discovery that through the marvels of electricity they could put the human voice out into the air, and that a device called a radio could locate and home in on that signal, and that a man, woman or child hundreds or thousands of miles away could sit at the device and listen to the voice of a far-off stranger.

What followed was (Austin's part-time secretary whose phone also displays Vivien's calls, is waving at Vivien through the glass that somebody is on the phone.) a scramble on the part of the federal government to regulate the new technology. But very quickly the airwaves were becoming clogged with too many stations on too few frequencies. Our government had to really hustle to conceive new public policy for issues that mankind had not previously even considered. An impending chaos had to be dealt with; there was no way around it. I think that that intervention of government in the Radio Acts of 1912 and 1927 and the Communications Act of 1934 was one of the wisest applications of government power in our nation's history.

So, what does that have to do with us, sitting here today in Frost Pound, Maine. Well, the government first had to come to one very foundational principle that everything else would be built on, one that we now take for granted: the radio waves belong to the people. Without that sweeping claim, how could the federal government begin to ward off the chaos? (The young ad salesperson/secretary is waving at Vivien again, but Vivien goes right on with her lesson.)

The right to broadcast on the AM frequencies began to be allocated to entities that applied for licenses and the applicants needed to demonstrate that by holding such licenses they would serve the public interest, convenience, and necessity. When our current boss's father-in-law first applied for the right to broadcast on this frequency, it was that to which he attested, and that to which we lay claim with every renewal. (More smiling waves from the front lobby, and Vivien thinks, geez, cut it out. Let me finish what I spent hours working on. If I let them in here, they'll never let me finish.)

Vivien: Licenses were granted to applicants allowing varying degrees of power measured in wattage. Some got to broadcast with huge power, and with a promise of no competition on their wavelength. Those are the so-called "clear channel stations."

Some of the licenses stipulated directional broadcast, in other words, the signals might aim a certain way to not step on the signal of another station on the same frequency. And some licenses like ours here at WNWT allowed only daytime broadcast.

And then, the holders of the licenses got to pick call letters. East of the Mississippi the stations all started with a W, to the west they start with a K. The Pittsburg powerhouse KDKA is a notable exception.

So, this is our birthright. And I think it safe to say that broadcasting a program like the *WNWT Talk Show* securely qualifies your local station as serving the public interest and, as such, the renewal of the license every eight years for this station is nearly assured.

Many people ask, do the call letters stand for anything? Usually, no. You pick four letters starting with W that no one else has picked.

Caller: Am I up, okay, good. Did you see the story in the paper this morning about re-routing traffic around downtown Wiscasset?

Vivien: See what I mean.

Caller: What?

Vivien: Never mind, Caller. I was arguing with myself. Yes, I did read about the Wiscasset deal. I believe this is the twentieth or thirtieth installment on that subject since I moved to Maine. Did my little talk on the history of radio interest you not a bit, or perhaps you have been on hold, for some reason unable to hear my monologue? (click) Oops, we've lost him and lost, perhaps a chance to ponder the imaginings of the people on the long line waiting for a lobster roll at Red's Eats. It appears we have another call. Good morning, you're on the *Talk Show*.

Fred Boyland: (in a weak and quavering voice) I think that after that little history lesson, the fact that people began phoning in about the tr- traffic issues in Wi- Wiscasset ought to be a wake-up call, Miss Kindler.

Vivien: *People* didn't begin phoning in about traffic on Route 1; one person did, and my feelings will be hurt if the homework I did in preparation for today's show proves useless.

Fred Boyland: It's unfortunate that your own needs seem to make it hard to see the other man's point of view (silence).

Vivien: Are you still with us?

Fred: I'm, I'm f- fine. That caller was simply 'ripping it from the headlines' and you had your own agenda and decided to mock him. You seem to have a need to control the direction of the program.

Vivien: To whom are we speaking this morning?

Fred Boyland: I think you know who I am. (voice weak and shaky) Perhaps now you will try to control *me*.

Vivien: I don't wish to discuss the running of this program with you, Mr. Boyland.

Fred Boyland: (In the background can be heard a woman, "Come have your tea, Freddie.") Don't discuss it with me. You don't have to. It's all right there in the intro, the program where you, the public, set the agenda. I hope that still means something down there.

Vivien: Hang up, Mr. Boyland, hang up or I will disconnect you, and don't call this program again as long as I am in this seat. I hope to control things just that much. I will attempt to keep the previous host of the program, the host who had the privilege of several uninterrupted years, to keep him *off the air*. If that makes me a control freak, I plead guilty.

*. . . commercial break, and Vivien hits buttons to play some ads not even in the log . . .*

## Off-Air

Vivien needed a minute to gather herself. How can I let one man get under my skin like this? What am I going to do? I'm alone in this. Why don't the Hudsons come to my aid? Has Austin listened to any of this from in his office? And isn't the fact they've been too lazy to record a new intro—isn't that part of the problem? Does that damn intro give Fred encouragement that he's coming back? No, probably he's just nuts. Worse than that, he's a terrible human being. Looking at the digital display, Vivien saw that her stalling tactic had run out.

## On-Air

Vivien: We're back and have been talking about the history of radio and this one station in Frost Pound, Maine. Is there any meaning in the call letters, WNWT? We have a call.

Caller: Am I on already, okay, good, yeah, WNWT, it has something to do with newts, salamanders and such, don't you think?

Vivien: You may be on to something. That would explain the giant plywood cutout of a Komodo dragon on the roof of the radio station.

Caller: I'm outside the station right now and I don't see a Komodo dragon up there. Anyway, I think a Komodo dragon is a lizard, and a newt is an amphibian, and a Republican.

Vivien: What are you doing outside the radio station, Caller?

Caller: Oh, I was just in the area and I saw the station and got the idea to phone in. Can you see me, I'm the older dark red Mazda? I'll wave, okay, I'm waving.

Vivien looked out the big plate glass window of the studio and saw a small red car. Creepy, she thought. There he is, pulled off the road on the far side. Maybe I am not as safe as I would like to think I am in this big chair, talking with poets.

Vivien: No, I'm afraid I can't really see very well out of here, sir. (She lied; she could see just fine.) I wish you well on your morning errands. I think we have another call. You're up.

Caller: Obviously named for Newt Gingrich. Thought they'd do conservative talk radio—very successful format—then they changed their minds and hired Vivien. What were they thinking? Just kidding, Vivien. You're doing fine. Hang in there, kid!

Vivien: Thank you, Caller. Let me take another call. Vivien on the *WNWT Talk Show*—hanging on by a thread.

Paul the Piano Tuner: I told you I had other stories. Is there time for a short one?

Vivien: Yes. Is it Paul the Piano Tuner, can I call you that?

Paul the Piano Tuner: Sure, why not.

I titled this one "Great Expectations." In the 60s a fellow from Rhode Island and his wife bought that red cape across from the Prichard Realty, up near the crossroads. Bill Smith had never owned his own place, even down in Rhode Island, and he was all excited about having that 18th-century house with the wood roof sloping down so low in the front that the wall was only six feet high. The place had foot-wide punkin' pine floors that Smith was fixing to sand down and varnish up all bright-like.

Smith and the wife both had jobs at the credit card place up in Camden, and it was August, so they hadn't lived through a Maine winter yet, and didn't know how they would suffer with drafts and the winter air dried by the wood stove that the previous owners had left for them. You might say their lives were all promise and expectation.

On one of those first days, the homesteader walked into Wheeler Cardin's Store. It was more like a general store than the Variety that's there now. There was a gas pump in front, full service, and in the summer Wheeler even dipped ice cream cones. He'd pump regular gas, check your oil, and dip you one scoop of coffee on a sugar cone without a beat. They said he was the biggest Sealtest seller in Maine. Folks came from far and wide for ice cream, but no one ever ate the cone. (long pause)

It was one of Smith's first days as a real, grown-up property owner when he opened Cardin's creaky door that never latched quite right. Smith nodded agreeably to the taciturn old gent setting in the grease-stained, oak armchair behind the counter.

Smith set his few housekeeping items on the counter. Wheeler Cardin surveyed the Brillo pads, light bulbs, a steel dust pan, toilet paper, and a Snickers bar.

"Six dollars and twenty-five cents," Cardin said.

Smith wasn't cheap exactly, but he'd grown up without much. You would probably say he was frugal—not in a miserly way—just careful. "It's Mr. Cardin, isn't it? I'm Bill Smith and my wife and I are in the old Griffin place. Mr. Cardin, six twenty-five seems just fine, but I'm wondering. You don't have a cash register, or an adding machine, and you haven't added up my items with a pencil and paper. How do you know that it's six dollars and twenty-five cents?"

Cardin composed himself and looked the homeowner in the eye. "Well, mistah, the way I see it, this is my store, and my merchandise, and if you want it, it will be six dollars and twenty-five cents." (silence)

Vivien: That's it, isn't it, Paul the Piano Tuner?

Paul the Piano Tuner: Yup. Do you need me to say, The End?

Vivien: No, the way you presented it was just right, just right in so many ways. Another gem. You honor us.

Paul the Piano Tuner: There's a bunch more.

Vivien: Please, don't hang up. You told us that to have good stories, you need to be out with people. How is Paul the Piano Tuner out with people?

Paul the Piano Tuner: Apart from piano tuning?

Vivien: I would have thought you needed to do that all alone.

Paul the Piano Tuner: Sometimes I linger and chat while they write the check. (pause) And I know lots of people from the fire department, and through the kids.

Vivien: Wonderful—you're a fireman.

Paul the Piano Tuner: Not exactly. I'm one of the chickens. (pause) Before my time somebody started calling the guys that don't go to the actual fires *the chickens*. For public consumption they say they call some of us that because we grill chicken for the fundraising barbecues and support the fire department that way, but that's only half of it. I don't care—I really don't mind telling you. I'm afraid of going to fires, not so much because I would quake in my boots, but because I don't think I'd have good judgment and would probably just be in the way.

Vivien: I see. So, alone in someone's parlor, you strike E flat or C sharp and you know to tighten or loosen a string. There, under the lid of the Steinway, or alone with one of your stories, you have perfect pitch. So, you do what you know you do well. (She can hear that he has rung off.) We hope that in time we will hear them all, brave fellow. We've got another call. Good morning, you're on the *Talk Show*.

Caller: Now we're talking!

Vivien: How's that, Caller?

Caller: When we get good stuff like that on Vivien's program, we say, Wow, Now We're Talkin'!

Vivien: Thank you, and thanks to Paul the Piano Tuner. We're up against the news at the top of the hour, but please join us again in the second hour of the *WNWT Talk Show*. (Vivien hits some buttons.)

*. . . AP news, music rises to the network's tone that marks eleven o'clock on the dot . . .*

Vivien exhales, and throws her head back in the big chair.

*. . . (theme) Good morning, and welcome to another hour of Frost Pound's own Talk Show and your host, Fred Boyland, the show directed by you, the citizen callers. Join Fred now at 207 . . .*

Vivien: I hope some of you were with us before the news to hear Paul's quintessential Maine story. It may be presumptuous of me to make such an assertion, that I know what is a Maine tale when I've only lived in the State a short time.

I am just thinking out loud. Correct me if I'm all wet. It seems to me that what the storekeeper in the story typified was an individual who knew who he was, knew what he believed, was in no way insecure in the way he conducted his affairs, and was not tempted to change his ways and bend to new or foreign influences. Many of us find something reassuring in that, don't we? Do you? We have a call. Good morning.

Caller: Now we're talking. (click)

Vivien: I think that was a man who called a little earlier. We have another call.

JJ's Mom: I don't know, Miss Kindler, maybe it's just me and I don't see things the same as everybody else. I don't care. What can they do to me for seeing things different when the whole world's upside down? I've been listening this morning—I listen for three hours every day—and I heard the piano tuner's little story. I know Paul, and he knows me. Everybody knows me. He's been over here to tune the spinet we bought for Stevie. It sure doesn't seem right—those other men in the fire department making fun of Paul. No—poking fun at a decent human being like Paul—that's not right, is it, Vivien? No. Those Smiths in the story, they moved away after two years in town. She was very nice, but she hated Maine. Don't you suppose Wheeler Cardin did the numbers in his head? When we were in school all the bright kids could do sums like that in their head. The kids today all have machines for it. That's not progress is it, Miss Kindler? I don't think that's progress.

Vivien: I think I'm on your side on this one. I bet when you were in school you were made to memorize whole long poems, passages from Shakespeare, things like that. I think that's all gone now and it feels to me like a loss, but I can't say why exactly.

JJ's Mom: Maybe God needs people that are good at remembering things. I remember everything that the callers to the *Talk Show* say—like this morning. That fellow that called twice: he said, "Wow, now we're talking." Maybe it's just me, but

I thought he was saying, now we're talking, that that was where the name of the radio station came from, WNWT—Wow, Now We're Talking. Isn't that it, Miss Kindler? Now we're talking?

Vivien: Now we're talking. Are you saying NWT stands for *now we're talking*? Do you think so, JJ's Mom? That's what the guy was suggesting? Wow.

## Off-Air

Vivien went silent in the swivel chair. She didn't know for how long. It was probably only seconds, and Austin banged on the studio glass from the outer office. Rob Auclair, the news director from his adjoining studio banged too on his side of another glass wall and Rob pointed at his watch. She had zoned out through the top of the hour and failed to hit the button for the network news. JJ's Mom had talked right over the Associated Press.

Vivien hit a button and into the air "*. . . airstrikes are reported to have severely compromised a Taliban basecamp near the Afghan border with . . .*" She frantically grabbed her coat from the hook in the corner of her studio, swept up her papers, scrunched them violently into an outside pocket, and wrestled with the door as though she were fleeing an intruder in a scary movie.

She was rushing off-balance to Austin's office; she had to talk to him—confront him—about Fred Boyland phoning her program—*the* program—it was out of control. Fred Boyland was out of control.

From the parking lot entered an entourage of smartly dressed men and women, obviously coming for some kind of a meeting. Doctor Fontaine was among them, and a big fellow that Vivien thought was her state senator, and a distinguished older guy in a business suit. Marcus Deloitte, the restaurant guy, was poking and teasing with Kathy Austin. The whole entourage felt alien to Vivien, their spirits so jaunty and high, and she under assault from that horrible Fred Boyland.

Vivien slid sideways past the huddle, forcing a fake smile, and achieved Austin Hudson's doorway where she met him face to face.

"Mr. Hudson, did you hear it? Did you hear him on the phone near the end of my show, Mr. Hudson? We need to talk about this."

Austin said, "You can see I'm tied up right now, Vivien."

"I'm not able to go back in there tomorrow without knowing what to do."

"I understand, Vivien. Come in early tomorrow and we can have a talk."

"Did you hear him though, Mr. Austin? He thinks he's coming back. Why does he think that? No one has made a new intro for the show—he hears his name on the radio several times every morning."

"Of course, that could be misleading. I agree completely. We can talk about the intro, for sure we will talk about the intro." He looks over her to Kathy and Marcus Deloitte and the others. "Tomorrow, will that be good?"

"I want to know where I stand," Vivien forced it out. "I'm doing the best I know how, but I shouldn't have to live with the dread of him calling."

"Tomorrow at 8:30, I must ask you to excuse me."

"The dread of him calling and talking like he's coming back any time."

Vivien put her head down, parted the little assembly, and made what they all could see was a tense escape.

# Chapter 8
# The Town's Snow and God's Birds

The next day
Off-Air

"I apologize for that assault on you yesterday, Mr. Hudson," Vivien said.

"It didn't seem like that to me. And call me Austin. That meeting with the politicians and the hospital people was going to be a big deal and I couldn't take the time with you—not just then—I'm sorry."

"Do you listen to the *Talk Show*, Austin? Can you listen, you know, and do your work with it in the background, at the same time?"

"Mostly I'm not much of a multi-tasker, but that I can do, probably because radio has become so much of who I am."

"The music, and the rhythm of the speaking voices?" Vivien asked.

"You give me too much credit. I probably just get used to the radio voices as a sort of comforting static. I listen to syndicated talk in the middle of the night with headphones."

"Does your wife love it, too, love the radio?"

"You'd have to ask her that yourself." Austin makes an ironic smile. "The station was her dad's—you knew that—before it was ours. You'll have to tell me what she says."

Vivien asked him, "Did you listen to Fred's show much? I didn't, actually. True confessions."

"Yes, I listened to it—maybe let it wash over me."

"Did you like it?"

"Here's the dirty little secret, Vivien. I'm mostly running a business that Kathy and her father dropped in my lap. We thought we would do it together, but—never mind, you're going to ask her about that. I like the business aspect of it and I'm scared to death of messing up what is really Kathy's, so I'm focused on the business side. And I don't know what I would do with my life if not this."

There was a long pause. They stared at one another. It was the first time she had really seen him. On the day they hired her she had been so nervous and on her own agenda, sticking to her script. Their other encounters had always been brief and animated by some little crisis. Vivien saw that Austin Hudson's features were nice, a good bone structure to his dark head, a tightness about his mouth, and eyes that were working very hard at betraying nothing. Not a great pleasure to look at, but she was trained on him still.

"You asked me what I thought of Fred Boyland's program," Austin said.

"Yes."

"There's a guy on my sports channel in the middle of the night. He's a real idiot, obnoxious, and I used to ask myself why I could listen to someone who so regularly offends me. It has probably been like that with Fred. Not just for me, but for his audience locally. It may be something about talk radio more generally. I think we get attached to the familiar, so we hate change."

"I'm sure you're right. I hear from his following almost every day, less now than at the beginning. Now I mostly hear from his biggest fan, Fred Boyland himself."

"He phoned yesterday, didn't he?"

"He sounded frail and shaky—I'm sorry that he has health problems—but he proceeded to criticize the way I do the show."

"Yeah, that's not fair."

"—and he said that I was a control freak. It's unsettling, Mr. Hudson. Wouldn't anyone in my place be upset? Yesterday I was so shook up I could almost not function for about an hour. A nice caller bailed me out with a cute story, and then I accidentally let Catholic Lady talk right into the network news."

"The FCC must never know about this," he smiled.

"I'm going on the air in fifteen minutes. What will you do to help me, Mr. Hudson?"

"Austin."

"Austin. I can't deal with it by myself."

"You just won't take his calls anymore. I'll back you up on that 100%."

"How will I do that?"

"I can get the monitor to show the caller ID data. You'll see his number and just won't take the call."

"That would work."

"I'll get on it."

"What about the intro? Why do you still have his name on the intro? I came here in late September and today it's five degrees and snowing. He really may think you're keeping the seat warm for him. Isn't it logical that he could think that?"

"Of course, you're right. I've been meaning to get to it."

"I have an idea for it," Vivien said.

"I'll probably just put Vivien whatever—"

"—Kindler," and she helped him with her last name.

"—in where Fred's name was," Austin continued.

"Wow, Now we're talkin'."

Austin said, "How's that?"

Vivien said, "While I'm here at least, can we call the show, *Now We're Talkin'*? Radio station *WNWT*, *Wow, Now We're Talkin'*, after the call letters of the station—WNWT. People will like it. It's funny.

Austin Hudson said, "Okay, now we're talking, or as you say, *talkin'*. I'll have it for Monday—promise. For today and tomorrow, it's still Fred's show," and he got her to smile.

Maybe this is the start of a relationship, Vivien thought, hoped. This is better.

"And you need to do something for me. The hospital, they're big advertisers, and Kathy's on the Board. We need to put their weekly hour back on, *Focus on Wellness*.

"*Focus on Wellness with Fred Boyland*—just kidding. They're sending somebody over tomorrow for nine o'clock. They've been gun shy and beating it to death in their board meetings since the blood pressure debacle. We're lucky we weren't all sued."

"We? I only heard about it, and swooped down on the poor guy's job."

"So, you'll do it. Good kid. Let's get it off to a fresh start, right?"

There were big clocks on the walls everywhere, all reading 9:04. Vivien knew that she was going to be all right.

On-Air

*Network news, local news, and bumper music (Vivien hit a button for her
intro) Good morning, and welcome to another hour of Frost Pound's own
Talk Show and your host, Fred Boyland, the show directed by you, the
citizen callers. Join Fred now at 207 . . .*

Vivien: Good morning. This is Vivien Kindler and I am happy
that you can join me for a while this morning, Thursday,
December 11th. I am happy to tell you that the intro you just
heard played will only be heard five more times. If you want to
record it for some historical purpose, or as a fan of the previous
host, you have only today and tomorrow to grab it for posterity.
So, friends, it is my purpose and goal that at some moment this
morning, you will be moved to say, in the privacy of your car or
your home, "Wow, now we're talkin'." (And she sat quiet, today
buoyed by her meeting with Austin Hudson and unafraid of the
silence—hoping that some power in the show's new incarnation
would sink in, into the imagination of her listeners, that
something even spiritual might happen.) I believe we have a call.

Caller: They done it again.

Vivien: I can't believe it.

Caller: I didn't say what they done.

Vivien: I'm outraged, anyway.

Caller: You're kind of cheeky, Vivien.

Vivien: I apologize. It was an attempt at humor. I failed. Someone
challenged me once with the principle that real humor is when

you can make people laugh without hurting or diminishing anybody. So, what have *they* done?

Caller: I spent an hour this morning shoveling my driveway including where it meets the street, and I spent half an hour shoveling around my mailbox where the mail lady pulls off the road to put mail in our box. So, the town comes along and puts town snow right in front of the mailbox and the driveway.

Vivien: I don't know, Caller. You know, if you tell me your name so I don't say "Caller," because we have another fellow we call "Caller," we won't confuse the audience.

Caller: I'm Larry.

Vivien: I don't know anything about the law—the law or even common practice in Frost Pound on such things.

Larry: Well, it can't be the law that the guys they hire in big storms can put the town snow in people's driveways.

Vivien: What is the town snow?

Larry: The snow from in the road.

Vivien: So, there's a guy in a big truck out there in the cold—cold and dark a lot of the time—and he's hired to plow the road. Isn't the primary responsibility to make the roadway safe and passable?

Larry: Sure, but they just go along blocking me in my driveway with the town snow like I don't count for anything. (click))

Vivien: We'll take another call.

George the Welder: That last guy's name is not Larry.

Vivien: Perhaps we should just call everyone "Caller," or call everybody "Larry," and we could rename the town Lawrence.

George the Welder: Or Lowell.

Vivien: Now we're talkin'.

George the Welder: He used to call in all the time. I thought he had died. I know his real name, but what's the difference—he's wrong about the snow plowing. Those guys are out there in the big trucks and they're just trying to see where the edge of the pavement is and move the snow off the road and not tear up curbs and sod and stuff. Unfortunately, they're also putting down tons of salt and sand and trying to pay attention to where they're putting it.

Vivien: Good morning, George the Welder. Is your beautiful garden put to sleep under a blanket of new snow?

George the Welder: Good morning, Vivien. I've mulched what needed mulching and left it tidy, I guess.

Vivien: Can you go out there in the winter months?

George: With my handicap? Yes, I keep a path shoveled to get to the compost and we feed birds.

Vivien: I begin to imagine it. So, what's unfortunate about the road sanding?

George: You're the one who told me to stay out of the things that I can't control.

Vivien: I guess I did.

George the Welder: And this is another one. The town and the state have gradually given in to the idea that the road needs to be practically bare and safe to drive on at normal speeds, all the time. The public, lots of people anyway, won't stay in when it snows and they think they need to get out and shop or eat or visit or whatever they want, and they just do. They go out on the roads when years ago they would have stayed in.

Vivien: I've been living in other places. You think you've seen a trend?

George: It's about the insurance. The town is afraid of the liability if someone gets hurt or killed, and with half the people on one side, and half on the other side, what politician is going to skimp on the plowing and the sand when somebody might get killed out there?

Vivien: I see.

George: It's another train that has left the station.

Vivien: What about you feeding the birds?

George: My wife loves them.

Vivien: I'm going to get in trouble. Truly, I don't know the answer to this: would those titmice and juncos and nuthatches find other food, were it not for your feeder?

George: My wife thinks they would die. Has this got something to do with the snowplowing?

Vivien: I told you I was going to get into trouble. Is it possible we are creating a dependency? Are there unintended consequences—like, could they lose any of their natural foraging skills—say over time?

George: It gives her pleasure. I think it was you, Vivien, who said that we should disregard the issues when the train has left the station.

Vivien: —and I am talking through my hat. We have experts in the area, folks from the Audubon camp. It would make a good subject for another day, and we could have experts in the studio. I'll drop it for now.

George: You'll drop the birds, but you still have to fill up three hours.

Vivien: So, what is the answer to the matter of the town snow blocking people's driveways?

George: Do you want me to answer your question so you can make fun of me? I'll be the butt of a joke for the benefit of your radio program.

Vivien: Try me out, George the Welder. What's the answer for the guy dealing with the town snow?

George the Welder: There's no answer. The guy either keeps shoveling or hires somebody to plow it for him. The town can't custom plow with different little maneuvers for different people based on their complaints. Everybody knows that—and deals with it.

Vivien: There's a word for a broader principle. I'll think of it. The idea is that we take on a civic responsibility for the public land adjacent to our own place. I think the point is that by taking care of what is nearest us, we split up among lots of people a large public burden, and in a logical way, among the people most directly affected.

George: Probably from the Greek city states, or maybe from the Talmud. It just makes sense.

Vivien: You're a smart guy, George the Welder.

George: Hm-m.

Vivien: That's not a strong endorsement. (silence)

George: I'm here. I had a good brain. I had a football scholarship to go up to Orono.

Vivien: Did you attend? Were you a wonderful football hero, George?

George: No, I didn't go.

Vivien: Did you want to? Was it a disappointment?

George: No one cares. It was a long time ago.

Vivien: Some don't care, maybe even most don't care—I don't know. But some do, and everyone should. I care. It's your story that you lived and know. Maybe your story can help people think through issues they're dealing with right now. Why didn't you go to Orono?

George: We were a big family and didn't have much. Dad was drinking and running out of pep and he said he needed my help with the household expenses—to help him and my mother—so I went to work. It sounds rough, but I didn't think so at the time. Lots of people were in the same boat and I accepted it—wasn't even surprised.

Vivien: Was your dad grateful? Did he tell you he was grateful for your sacrifice?

George: Men didn't say things like that.

Vivien: Was he proud of you in sports?

George: Probably, but he didn't say. There was not much softness to him. I think even my football clippings were a challenge to him—

Vivien: —to his integrity, to his security or something?

George: I probably only figured it out much later. He thought that if I went off to college, I was going to change so that he wouldn't know me, and I would be lost to him.

Vivien: And so, you went to work to help your mom, and he had you close by.

George: It was only a short time before he died.

Vivien: You think now that his insecurity was wrong, but you seem gracious about the working to help the family. You've probably tried to put yourself in his place. We sometimes are foolish. We hope that we can learn.

George: I learned and it still did no good. I made up my mind to be different than my father and I helped my son into a bigger world than my own, and he rejected it—rejected the opportunities dropped right in his lap, and rejected me.

Vivien: How old is your son, George?

George: He's dead. He's dead to me.

Vivien: It is a horrible grief. I can tell. It's terrible. (long silence) So you went down to work at the shipyard in Bath to help your folks.

George: Not at first. This isn't interesting, Vivien.

Vivien: It is to me. Where did you go to work to help your family?

George: A guy my dad knew with the state got me on with the DOT and I worked with the mechanics in a highway garage. An old guy there taught me everything he knew about metal work. I liked the welding and was good at it. It was all stick welding back then.

I think somebody said the money was better in Bath, so I went down and caught on at the shipyard. I liked the idea that I was building ships for my country's Navy, which I was. And I thought the river, the Kennebec, was beautiful. That was probably a draw, too.

Vivien: I love a river. I love the Sheepscot and the Damariscotta and the gentle Medomak.

George: I never travelled the Kennebec beyond Phippsburg or up past Richmond, but in my mind, I rode those cruisers we built, sailed them down the river and to the Atlantic Ocean.

Vivien: You are a poet.

George: Not really. I am George the Welder, tender of a small garden.

Vivien: Can you stay on the line till after the break, George? I am interested in the Navy ships.

George: Yeah, sure, if you want.

*. . . ads for the Chrysler dealership down Route 1, two different banks, and a spot about the hospital giving appeal . . .*

# Chapter 9
# Welding

### Back from the Break

Vivien: We're back. I think George is still with us and we were sliding down the ways aboard a space-age destroyer to the great blue sea.

George: Am I on?

Vivien: Thanks for holding, George.

George: I've been gone from BIW for eight years. I missed the ships you're talking about. Those are the Zumwalt class destroyers, which are sort of cruisers, really. Toward the end of my time, they were starting to bring in and prepare steel for them at Hardings.

Vivien: What is Hardings?

George: It's a site in Brunswick that belongs to Bath Iron Works, to General Dynamics, where lots of steel work, even building sections of the inner bottom of the ship, takes place.

Vivien: Were you working at this Hardings place?

George: At the end.

Vivien: Was that okay?

George: I knew I wasn't going to be around long and I was getting kind of ugly.

Vivien: Is that a Maine expression, getting kind of *ugly*?

George: I don't know.

Vivien: Do you remember why you were getting ugly.

George: Sure. The safety stuff was ridiculous, face shields and ear protection when you didn't need it. And everything was going over to metric. You couldn't even bring a tape or rule on the work site if it was in American. Everyone was angry about it— not just me.

American Navy ships built in metric. And they had done away with welders' helpers. It was an economy measure.

Vivien: Was it wise?

George: Maybe, but you have to remember that I was having trouble with my leg and not getting around very well, so I had to chase around the yard after tools and material where before your helper would do that for you, and if you were close to losing a leg you could sit down and rest for a spell.

Vivien: I see.

George: At Hardings I was welding on the flat, on the flat and indoors in a controlled environment, but it was boring—doing the same task week after week, welding bulkheads and T-bars on the panel line. They put me on stuff that was beneath my training and skill level. Humiliation—it was the tool they could use to force you out. They couldn't force me out exactly, Local 6 wouldn't let them, but there's something called *right to assign,* which means they can put you where they want on whatever job they want. So, if you were me and a 1st Class welder, that's a grade, and they've got you doing mundane tasks, it's hurtful. College kids that couldn't carry my tools, watching me like I was some kind of idiot.

Vivien: Was there a lot of supervision?

George: I had the seniority to get the shift I wanted and Mrs. George the Welder wanted me to work 1st shift, to be on her schedule so we could have a normal life together. How could you refuse that, even if it meant working daytimes when there were way more company guys around?

Vivien: Were the company guys jerky to men in your position?

George: No, they really were okay. Some were really good guys, to tell the truth.

Vivien: Well?

George: I didn't like being under them. I was smarter than most of them, but under them. It ate at me.

Vivien: I get that. I think I understand. But you gave us those other big ships, too, didn't you? The ones before the Zumwalt. Thanks for that, George the Welder.

George: I worked on the FFG's, fast frigates, and mostly on the DDG's, the Burke Class destroyers. Lots of them.

Vivien: We're up against a break, George. I'll let you go now. Thanks for all that, and for your service.

# Chapter 10
# Re-Focus on Wellness

## Off-Air

There was, as always, a long break at the end of the hour and Vivien gathered herself for a segment with guests. The hospital had sent over Dr. Armand Fontaine again, and through the glass Vivien saw that Kathy Austin, her boss, and Marcus Deloitte, the restaurant guy, were there, too.

Smiling and childishly jostling one another, they slipped into Vivien's little studio as the news and weather played.

Kathy said, "Armand needs extra encouragement to get back on the horse after giving Fred a stroke, so we're coming on with him for a few minutes, just to put him at ease."

"You can go, guys. Ms. Kindler probably won't let me give her the pneumonia shot on the air, anyway," Dr. Fontaine said, playing along with the nonsense.

There were three chairs and three headsets and three mics in a row to Vivien's right, though she had never had more than one guest at a time. Kathy knew how they worked and helped Vivien by getting everyone wired up. Vivien switched on the microphones and leaned across the big monitor to where she could reach the volume controls. She felt that she had begun to own it all.

## On-Air

*. . . another hour of Frost Pound's own Talk Show and your host, Fred Boyland, the show directed by you, the citizen callers. Join Fred now at 207 . . .*

Vivien: Welcome to the third hour of the WNWT Talk Show. I am your host, Vivien Kindler, and this morning I am pleased to be joined by Dr. Fontaine from the hospital, for what has been called *Focus on Wellness*. And joining the good doctor today are his emotional support team, Kathy Austin, who with her husband owns and manages this radio station, and is, as such, my boss.

Kathy: Thank you, Vivien, but actually, we are at the mercy of the ratings, so the Frost Pound audience remains master of us all.

Vivien: And from the hospital board, am I right, Marcus? Marcus Deloitte, who listeners may recall has a new farm-to-table restaurant called Locovore.

Kathy: Crā′-zee (in the melody of Willie Nelson's song)—

Marcus: Go ahead, Mrs. Hudson, it's your station. Sing us just a few bars. She's actually quite good.

Vivien: Somebody recently put it on our music playlist. I heard Patsy Cline twice yesterday.

Kathy: Thanks. I'll just keep practicing in the car. We'd better get on with focusing on wellness. Keep us on course, Vivien, and watch out for Marcus. He's a cut-up.

Vivien: Noted.

Marcus: Dr. Fontaine has planned some dangerous medical procedures he would like to perform on the air, and we are here, sort of like a rescue squad.

Kathy: See?

Vivien: I don't think I'd be very helpful. Be that as it may, yes, we should get on with it, you are all very welcome. Dr. Fontaine, how would you like to start things off this morning?

Dr. Fontaine: I want first to say that with this esteemed team, I am sure nothing can go wrong. That really has been the emphasis in most of our discussions on the radio—the simple preventative things that many of us can do. What we want to talk about this morning is atherosclerosis. It's what used to be commonly called hardening of the arteries.

Marcus: Ahh, cholesterol, the silent killer.

Kathy: Is cholesterol the silent killer? I don't think that's right.

Vivien: Neither do I. What is it? I haven't heard that expression in a while.

Dr. Fontaine: I think the silent killer is high blood pressure. (All four of them go quiet and look at one another with clenched teeth and scrunched mouths.)

Marcus: Yeah, what could go wrong?

Vivien: Hardening of the arteries. What is it, and how can we prevent it?

Dr. Fontaine: When plaque, which is fatty deposits, much of which is cholesterol, builds up in your arteries, it clogs them. It happens in different areas of the body, different ways in different people, and with varying results. The plaque may partially or totally block blood flow in arteries in your heart, brain, legs and arms.

In past generations, many more people died prematurely from this stuff than they do nowadays because we know so much more, and because there are well-understood and readily available treatments.

Vivien: How does the clogging of the arteries manifest itself?

Kathy: We're doing better now. Vivien has her cue cards.

Dr. Fontaine: If the clogging causes reduced blood flow to the heart, what is called angina, or chest pain, can occur. If a blocked artery supplies the heart or brain, a heart attack or stroke may occur.

Vivien: What can people do to head this off?

Kathy: She didn't even have that one written down.

Dr. Fontaine: The first and safest measures are just about healthy eating. I think it's fair to say that the research on the consumption of dietary cholesterol is still evolving. There is LDL in our blood, which is the bad cholesterol, and HDL, which actually offers protection from heart disease. The current research points to fried foods, fast food, processed meats, and desserts as being harmful.

Kathy: Marcus, don't you serve desserts at Locovore?

Marcus: Vivien, make her stop.

Dr. Fontaine: Of course, these things are always a matter of degree.

Marcus: I think it's added sugar that's bad. We rely heavily on the natural sweetness of locally grown fruit, and local dairy. And cinnamon is good, right, Doc?

Vivien: This may be off the subject. I haven't gotten into good habits about breakfast. Isn't that typical of lots of Americans? We eat a lot of toast with butter, and breakfast cereal with sugar.

Dr. Fontaine: Try oatmeal, and put fruit in it, and almond milk. A lot of people like smushed avocado on toast, no butter. It's pretty good.

I had in mind that we'd tell people about testing for cholesterol, and about common drug treatments. Adults should have the blood serum analysis for LDL and HDL counts done every four to six years. If LDL levels are too high, a doctor may recommend that his patient get on a regular prescription for a statin drug. Lipitor is one of the names we commonly hear. There are several of them. There has been discussion in recent years as to whether the statins are being over-prescribed. It's an ongoing argument, but too complicated for us today. There's no question, though, that these drug therapies, used appropriately, are saving a lot of lives.

Vivien: We've had a call on the line for a while already, would you all mind if we took it? Good morning, you're up on our *Focus on Wellness* segment.

Caller: My question is more general. I want to say something about how they're treating us at the hospital. You guys are from the hospital, right?

Kathy: We are. Mr. Deloitte and I are on the Board, we're just volunteers, and Dr. Fontaine is on staff.

Caller: Okay, so hear me out on this.

Kathy: Go ahead.

Caller: You know how when you have an appointment, a girl comes and gets you and takes you to one of those little examining rooms?

Vivien: Yes. With the wonderful laminated illustrations of body parts.

Caller: I think you're trying to distract me from my point. Do you want me to just hang up?

Vivien: No, please go ahead.

Caller: It used to be, not that many years ago, that you'd sit there in a johnny—freezing—and the doctor would eventually come in. Then we were told that it was cost efficient for a physician's assistant or a nurse to see you first, take your blood pressure, and then the doctor would come in. So last week it changed again. I got to meet two nice young people before the doctor came in.

Dr. Fontaine: We are all having to adjust to the new realities.

Caller: I wonder if that's why they call us patients? We're just regular people who are sick, and they are doctors—so, of course, we should be patient. (click)

Vivien: I think we have another caller. Good morning, you're on *Focus on Wellness*.

Caller: I was trapped in one of those little rooms for about twenty minutes recently.

Dr. Fontaine: That's not acceptable. I hope someone apologized and explained the reason for the delay. Sometimes the doctor is called away for an emergency and the schedule gets jammed up for the whole day.

Caller: That's okay. It's just boring. I kept looking at the boxes of rubber gloves. They have small, medium and large. At first, I was just trying to decide which size fit my hands. I thought probably the medium would be right, then I thought about Johnny Cochran in the OJ case, "If the gloves don't fit, you must acquit," but I decided I really wanted the large ones. So, this is my question. Do you think I was just bored and playing mind games to get through the long wait, or do you think I was really close to stealing a few of those gloves?

Dr. Fontaine: I don't know. Maybe we should send in a psychiatrist next time. I'm kidding, of course, because I think you are kidding us, right?

Caller: Only sort of. I'll think about it.

Vivien: We need to take a short break, and then we'll be back with our guests from the hospital.

## Off-Air

They all take off their headphones. Dr. Fontaine has done most of the heavy lifting, but appears only a little rattled.

Marcus said, "Well, show business is exciting."

Vivien said, "I'm sorry, Kathy. You can see how it is. We just take them as they come."

"It's not your fault," Kathy responded. "You couldn't have done anything differently, and Marcus encouraged them with the *silent killer* business. They call in and talk about what they want to talk about. And a latex glove fetish is funnier than cholesterol, anyway, isn't it?"

## On-Air

*. . . commercials play . . .*

Vivien: We're back on the *WNWT Talk Show* and our *Focus on Wellness* feature. Good morning, Caller, you're on the air with Kathy Austin, Dr. Armand Fontaine, and Marcus Deloitte.

Caller: Am I on?

Vivien: Yes, good morning. Whom are we speaking with?

Caller: I'll tell you one thing. I wouldn't get that pneumonia shot for anything.

Dr. Fontaine: I understand that people are naturally reticent.

Caller: I don't know what that means, but I've heard enough horror stories. Get the pneumonia shot, get pneumonia. Fella in town went deaf in one ear, almost deaf in the other, all after getting the damn flu shot a couple years ago.

Kathy and Marcus are squirming in their seats and suppressing laughter.

Dr. Fontaine: Yeah. I'm afraid we can't practice medicine on the radio. Not knowing the case, I can't really comment except to say that this man's experience is anecdotal. Probably the flu and the hearing loss were unrelated, but I can't really know from here. You understand? (silence)

Vivien: I think we lost him. We have another call. Shall we take it?

Fred Boyland: (there is a fumbling of papers and a woman's voice that sounds like it is not close to the phone, and eventually a slow, shaky voice comes on.) It wouldn't be the f- f- first time you practiced medicine live on the radio. Ha!

Vivien: Who is calling, please?

Fred: I want to thank all the people that have asked about me, and the friends who have phoned me at home to ask when I am coming back on the show.

Kathy: This is very awkward, Fred.

Fred: I apologize for my voice, but it's getting stronger every day, thanks to the whole team of local medical professionals taking care of me. I want to assure Dr. Fontaine that I bear no bad feelings about the incident we had live on the radio with Fred Boyland's blood pressure. It was an honest mistake and we will never know for sure whether my stroke was a direct result of the on-air test.

Vivien can see that Austin has come out of his office. He apparently had been listening. She assumed that Fred's embarrassing appearance coaxed him from the safety of his office and she expected a signal from him.

Kathy: Fred, this conversation is probably inappropriate.

Fred: Ha! Remember how we used to talk about setting up the seven-second delay, Kathy? Don't worry. I would never swear on the air. Guy that called before said the curse word for darn. There goes the license renewal.

Vivien saw that Kathy had whispered something to Marcus and that a tête-à-tête briefly distracted them from the on-air drama. Out in the lobby, six or seven feet on the other side of the glass studio wall, Austin was looking not at her, Vivien, but at the backs of the other two. And he was frozen. For an instant

Vivien thought that this is what shock looks like—that Austin Hudson was in shock.

Fred: At least Ms. Kindler has learned this from me: whether we are r- ripping it from the headlines, or doing the hospital segment, the show belongs to the callers, and we have to just let them s- sound off, even if sometimes they miss the mark. That's live radio, isn't it?

Kathy pulled herself up in her seat and made a chopping motion with her hands that Vivien took to mean she should cut Fred off. Vivien looked past her to the hallway and Austin. He was the one who told her to do just that the next time Fred phoned in. The audio of the live broadcast plays throughout the building, but Austin seemed not to even hear it, Fred again wreaking havoc with her program. His eyes were not meeting hers and there was only a blank, dead stare.

Kathy: Fred, we are on the subject of healthcare this morning. I suggest you phone the office at your earliest convenience and have a talk with Mr. Hudson. I know he will be glad to hear of the great progress in your rehabilitation.

Fred: Mr. Hudson, that's rich.

Vivien: We're going to have to let that caller go, friends.

Vivien disconnected the unfinished call. She had never done it before. Vivien looked over the heads of her guests to where Austin had stood. The others turned and looked to see what Vivien was looking at, but there was nobody there.

Vivien: I think we have time for one more call before the top of the hour. Good morning, you're on the *Talk Show* with Vivien.

JJ's Mom: That's who I phoned, so I don't know where else I would be.

Vivien: How is my friend, JJ, today?

JJ's Mom: We are sad. Is that all right to say on the radio, for people to hear so they feel sorry for you?

Vivien: Sure, it is.

JJ's Mom: Don't pity me. I have suffered plenty for years and years and the Blessed Mother has comforted me. But that doesn't mean that hearing Fred struggling to talk on the radio—when he was so strong for all those years—that doesn't mean that it's not sad to hear him now.

Vivien: I see.

JJ's Mom: I don't know if you do, Miss Kindler, maybe you do, maybe you can guess what it's like to lose the thing that's the most important thing in your whole world. I heard it in Fred's voice. Did you, Vivien? You probably didn't. JJ heard it. We were sitting right here by the radio at the kitchen table and when Fred spoke. JJ cried, not tears, but a little whining cry. Sure, JJ knows Fred's voice—everybody does.

Vivien: I believe you that JJ cried.

JJ's Mom: Fred, if you are still listening. I don't think you should phone in anymore. Vivien is a nice girl and she's doing a good job. I'm going to hang up now, Vivien. I'm tired and Fred has made me sad this morning. Goodbye, Fred. Goodbye, Miss Kindler.

The guests looked at one another. There was a collective nodding and a quiet acknowledgment that by grace something good had happened. Vivien pointed to her watch, there was half a minute left and there was another call hanging. She takes it.

Vivien: Good morning.

Caller: Wow, Now We're Talkin'!

There was a long pause before Vivien hit the button for the twelve-noon tone and the network news rolled. The guests pulled off their headsets, rose from their seats without speaking, and through the little door slipped into the hallway.

# Chapter 11
# Her Own Show

Monday Morning, Nine-O-Six

*A new recorded intro, "Everybody's Talkin'" from Midnight Cowboy ...
(and then, in Austin Hudson's voice), where 1420 on the AM dial skips
over the ocean, like a song. Thank you for tuning in to the WNWT Talk
Show with your host, Vivien Kindler, taking your calls and hearing the
concerns of our listeners in Frost Pound, Maine. So, let's all in unison, and
with great enthusiasm, once again this morning say: (louder) Wow, Now
We're Talkin'. Lines are now open at 207 ...*

Vivien: Wow, now we're talking, indeed. Thank you, Mr. and
Mrs. Hudson, for that wonderful new introduction. And it
appears to have induced a call already this morning. You're on
the *WNWT Talk Show.*

Caller: Is it me?

Vivien: Yup. Whom are we speaking with this Monday morning?

Caller: Can I ask a question without saying my name, who I am?

Vivien: It's up to you.

Caller: Okay, yeah, well, I was listening to the show last week when those guys were on from the hospital. So, I was just wondering something, and maybe you know about this, and maybe you don't.

Vivien: Try me out. Sometimes I will even expound on things I have no knowledge of. I believe it's called "talking through your hat."

Caller: I think you're pretty smart; I know I couldn't do what you're doing. Oh, so this is what I'm supposed to ask—what I want to ask about—ask you about. The man that's on the board of the hospital, well—

Vivien: —who was on the *Focus on Wellness* segment last week?

Caller: I guess so.

Vivien: Mr. Marcus Deloitte.

Caller: When you are on these big boards, do they put you on there 'cause they expect you to give them a lot of money? So, I guess what I'm asking is, does that guy Marcus have a lot of money?

Vivien: You've sort of asked two questions. No one has ever asked me to be on the board of anything, and I have never had much money, but I was once married to a fellow who did have pretty much money, and he was on some boards, and I think I was as smart and capable as he, so maybe it was the money that did it.

Caller: But what about the restaurant guy, he must have spent a lot of dough to get that fancy restaurant going, so if he's giving a lot of money to the hospital, he must have a lot of money?

Vivien: I can't disagree about the cost of launching a new business, but really, I think it's none of our business how much money this particular man has. I suppose if a person's wealth has come from illegal or otherwise immoral activity, that would be fair game, but even that would be so difficult to substantiate as to make it foolish for you and me to speculate about it on a radio talk show.

Caller: I don't know how a young guy like that has so much money—that's all.

Vivien: A person could have family money, or a wealthy backer, or borrow from a bank—I don't know and I don't care. Why do you care, Caller?

Caller: Maybe they shouldn't put people who have gotten their money from illegal stuff on the hospital board, unless maybe he's giving them a load of cash.

Vivien: Let me be clear that I did not suggest that Mr. Deloitte obtained money by illegal means. The hospital probably publishes a list of their large donations someplace. I'm all for transparency in these things, but about this man's affairs, I'm not very interested. I'm just glad that people give what they do. We all should be grateful. (long silence) I think you have a cynical attitude, Caller, and I find that very regrettable. If you phone in again, we would like you to bring a more generous attitude, and give your name.

Caller: I've just got one more thing written down. Maybe he gets on boards to meet girls. I heard he was a big ladies man.

Vivien: I am going to hang up on you, young man, unless you hang up first. You're way out of line. (click) Good. This is not a place where we go about maligning the character of people we don't know. And I don't imagine running a restaurant leaves much time for a private life, anyway.

Austin had come out of his office and Vivien could see that he was looking through the glass at her. He had his elbows at his ribs and palms up, made a bemused expression, and a what-can-you-do-about-it shrug.

Vivien: I apologize to Mr. Deloitte and to our listeners and to the management of this station that I left that kid on the air for as long as I did. It was unwise of me. Let's go to a commercial.

# Chapter 12
# Freshwater Lobsters

*. . . commercials play . . .*

Vivien: We're back and we have another caller on the line. Good morning. Who's calling?

Old Sabe: It's your friend up on the Sligo Road.

Vivien: With the wonderful Maine accent. Old Sabe, isn't it?

Old Sabe: I guess so. Up here on the Sligo Road we're what you might call tight knit. When you want to say something to another fella, you don't need to know the other fella's name, you know him by sight, though outsiders think we look awful alike. We just move our lips and words come out and next thing you know, we're talking to another fella without even saying his name.

Vivien: You speak mostly of *fellas*. Do you have women and girls up there?

Old Sabe: Some. Not sure how many. Never did an actual count. Keep pretty close to home. Sally Sanfordsen gets out and about more than she prob'bly should.

Vivien: It sounds a little cultish.

Old Sabe: That would not be accurate, Miss Vivien. Some folks say we're like a sect, or a church, but that would mean we subscribe to some kind of doctrine, which we don't, unless just wantin' to be left alone is a doctrine.

Vivien: You've mentioned Sally Sanfordsen and I believe you said your clan had intermarried with the Sanfordsens quite a lot, but I don't think you've told us *your* surname?

Old Sabe: You don't need to call me Sir. Like I said, just move your lips in front of the microphone and we'll be talkin'—which is what I heard this show is all about—talkin'.

Vivien: I'm sorry. I meant, what is your last name? I'm thinking, if I knew some of the last names I might know your people when I meet them, like in Hannaford's or the hardware store.

Old Sabe: You prob'bly won't meet us. We keep to ourselves though we're out more than usual on account of marketing the FWLs.

Vivien: The fresh water lobsters, and our listeners are fascinated by them—but about your people—do you think you are in some ways fearful of the world—not that I would much blame you?

Old Sabe: Skittish, wound a little too tight, you might say. If you met any of us, you'd know what I mean. We run to small, wary, and most of us with unruly hair. Some of our leaders feel a need to protect our way of life, and have taken *measures*, you might say. You seem to want to know all about everybody else—our security measures, how we support our clan, but you never tell us much about yourself, Miss Vivien.

Vivien: I'm just thinking it might be healthy to connect with the broader community a little more. Telling our listeners about the fresh water lobsters is probably a good start.

Old Sabe: We're on that pretty good. Before you moved up here—you're from away, aren't you, Vivien—we had already opened up considerable about the FWLs—what with the trail and the museum and all.

Vivien: The trail and the museum?

Old Sabe: I told you that some of our boys went with Knox after those cannons at Ticonderoga. Young Knox had been a bookseller, way before David Goodine. Went down to New York City first, took in a few musicals, loved *Hamilton*, then up to Lake Champlain after them cannons, which by the way, were never fired against the Brits down in Boston. Redcoats turned tail and went up Halifax way. Cannons are in mighty good condition to this day, I can tell you—kept a few. Seven Sanfordsen men and six Spaldings, my people, on the Noble Train of Artillery, so you'd understand how us marking the original route of the fresh water lobsters from Muscongus Sound into Sligo Pond was an idea that came kind of natural.

Vivien: So, there is such a trail?

Old Sabe: Maintained pretty well for a few years by the Crustacean Trail Trust, but mostly grown back in now. Trail markers are still up, but there's a two-mile stretch where you're better on your hands and knees. Hiker might still meet a few stragglers—better at night.

Vivien: Stragglers—other hikers?

Old Sabe: No, fresh water lobsters.

Vivien: And there's a museum?

Old Sabe: There was—more like a laminated display they let us put up in the apple store. Pictures of Henry Knox and Dorchester. Henry was the first freshwater male taken into captivity, seven pounds—gave us a terrible fight. Had to respect him, fightin' like he did—so, Sally took a snapshot of him and we let him go. Nearly got hit by a Subaru gettin' to the pond. And Dorchester was the first blue FWL, which was sort of an exaggeration since most of them are sort of blue-green, but children liked the idea of it—a blue lobster. Just them photos and some xeroxed trail maps that folks could take with 'em.

Vivien: Between training the militia and selling the freshwater lobsters, it sounds like you're busy boys.

Old Sabe: Not so. Them big saltwater fellas squeezing us out of the market. Not right is it Vivien, with a soft-shell FWL selling for a dollar a pound less than marine, and tasting almost as good—sorta like bass. Big money boys and the Canadians sticking it to us pretty good.

Vivien: Mostly soft-shells?

Old Sabe: All soft-shells.

Vivien: I'd love to try them. Where would I come if I wanted to buy a few freshwater lobsters, say three two-pounders?

Old Sabe: Most generally we have no retail location per se. Sally Sanfordsen would deliver them to your house, sort of like pizza, except we don't take credit cards. Cash, and always even dollar amounts. We do the math and always round down to the nearest dollar. That's the way we are. What's your address, Vivien? They're out of season right now, but we should have product in a few weeks. Sally'll bring them to you—probably will run you six or seven dollars.

Vivien: A pound?

Old Sabe: No, total. I've got a pencil. What's that address, Miss Vivien?

Vivien: I think I'll put in an order when I know I'm having company and need a special treat. Sally can deliver here at the radio station.

Old Sabe: Now you know all about us, and we don't know much about you, only that you had a rich husband. Don't seem quite fair, does it? (click)

Vivien: Isn't it fun to learn about the charming local people? We'll take a break and "be right back," as we say on the radio.

*. . . commercials play . . .*

Vivien: We have a call. You're on the air.

Caller: That guy's smart, but he ain't funny. He's threatening you, ma'am. Even tried to get your address. That's all I want to say. (click)

Vivien: We're okay, and there's another call. You're up.

Brownie:
    Social Conventions
    Sometimes my van takes too big a half
    of the winding Maine road,
    gorged with wine-of-the-month,
    Mrs. Meyer's dish detergent,
    and do-it-yourself gourmet dinners for two.
    Oncoming strangers and I steer our hurtling tons of steel,
    but have learned what we humans do:
    The tired, the bored, the senile—and hurried Brownie too—
    all stay in our own lane.
    So much depends upon it. I trust them and they trust me.
    The coq au vin and the Côtes du Rhône must get through.
    Are the Amish in Whitefield safer in their
    horse-drawn buggies?
    Matters of trust: Spring will come to Maine and
    we will be warm again in April, or May, or maybe June.
    Husbands hew to their wives, and wives to their men.
    Tired, bored, drunk, senile, hungry—

we accept the social conventions.

Funny how we sit in restaurants, arranged at small tables,

ours among others occupied by total strangers—

close enough to reach out and touch.

You dare to speak to one: "Your halibut looks lovely."

Am I diminished by adherence to customs?

We call it order, we call it culture.

It is what humans do—

go places where we know other humans will be.

Someone notices me. I am clean-shaven and all dressed up.

A stranger smiles at me and I am reassured.

Is a restaurant still a restaurant in the day with no one there?

No pretty boys and girls in black and white,

weaving among the crowded tables with farm-to-table kale

and Brussels sprouts delicacies.

The restaurateur moving through the empty room must say:

"This is not fun at all; it is just a big room.

Give me life, give me warm humanity."

But there is no time for a private life.

Vivien: Brownie, thank you.

Brownie: It's a little rough. Gotta run.

Vivien: Stay in your lane, dear Brownie. (pause) I think Brownie hit on an interesting thing about us people. Unlike Old Sabe and some of the folks up on the Sligo Road, most of us do like to be where there are other people. Oh, I've got an example. Try this: go to a beach town in New Jersey—Wildwood or Atlantic City, or to Ocean City in Maryland. On every boardwalk you'll find yourself in a throng of people, mostly happy people—thousands of them. From Ocean City drive to the Assateague National

Seashore, miles of beautiful, undeveloped beach. Wonderful quiet and natural beauty. And you may find that you are completely alone. Where are the other humans, where are the wild ponies? We have a call. Good morning.

Marie Scanlon: Hi, Vivien. It's the old schoolmarm. I admired the poem. I felt like it may have tried to say too much, but I was relieved that the poet resisted the temptation of rhyming "halibut" with "hell-of-it." It's overdone, don't you think, Vivien?

Vivien: Ogden Nash?

Marie Scanlon: I think so. Of the too many things Brownie attempted to cover, for me the most interesting is our need to feel alive, to feel significant. I think it may be one of our less well-explored characteristics as humans: the craving for significance. I confess I have it. (pause). I'll go. Perhaps others will weigh in?

*. . . commercials, several of them, all in a row . . .*

Vivien: We're back and have a call. Good morning.

Caller: She's got a craving all right. A craving for booze. They booted that old bat from the school—drunk in the middle . . .

Vivien disconnected the call.

Vivien: I'm sorry, listeners. That is truly horrible. We have another call. Maybe something nice.

# Chapter 13
# Golf

*Another day*

Vivien: You're up, friend.

Paul the Piano Tuner: The following will appear in the paper in the obituaries this week.

Bold heading with his name, Stuart Atwood, like they always do, and a recent picture.

**Stuart Atwood,**
*ornithologist, 76, of Bremen Long Island*
*passed peacefully on Friday.*

Do you think that I did not know that you all thought me a fool? What kind of man would join an expensive golf club and never play a single round? Bob Williams played as my guest one day and never told me about it; what contempt he must have held me in to even have gotten the notion. There was much laughter at Stu Atwood's expense. Word spread, and soon I was hosting hundreds of you with my membership. But do you know what? I didn't care at all. You see, I have always taken the long view.

You were right that I would not be walking into the clubhouse to catch you at your game. You thought that "Crazy Stu" was out on the water, and I was. Patience was always my special gift. I was ill-equipped for most ordinary jobs and with the fortune from my father's polluting textile mill, I did not have to work. So, I did what came quite naturally to me: I patrolled our islands and kept a careful scorecard of eagles and birdies. Monday, 17 June – 27 Black Guillemots, 0 Roseate Terns, 2 Storm Petrels, 1 nesting Great Bald, 14 clowns with multi-colored bills. All alone in my small boat I was content and certain that my counting was useful. Year after year, I kept and signed a careful tally—never cheated.

And you, great man, do you remember the July morning off Eastern Egg Rock when you rolled your pink sofa into the sea? Do you remember that for a minute the fog lifted and you thought that I saw you, and you reconsidered jettisoning the big television set that only got two channels. Surely, it was the good in you that imagined the couch a cozy resting spot for the fat ocean sunfish.

Do you recall the quiet little man in the pro shop that made change for the soda machine? I helped my wife's cousin, Gussie, get that job and he wrote down all your names and kept the list for me these many years.

I took the long view, but my time is up and my patience is at an end, and now I shall have my say.

In lieu of flowers, one hundred dollars a golf round, you sports, and ten thousand for the sleep sofa, checks made payable to: The Puffin Project.

(silent pause) That's it.

Vivien: Paul, what is this, it's hysterical? Is it a story you wrote yourself?

Paul the Piano Tuner: No, it's not made up. It's my friend's actual obit. He'd written it himself when he got real sick. I helped Stu polish it up and it'll appear Wednesday. They didn't change a thing.

Vivien: Did this man, Stu, really die?

Paul the Piano Tuner: Yeah, he just died last Monday, and that's his obituary.

Vivien: Wow, now we're talkin', Paul the Piano Tuner.

*. . . commercials play . . . "Everybody's Talkin'" from Midnight Cowboy. . . where 1420 on the AM dial skips over the ocean, like a song. Thank you for tuning in to the WNWT Talk Show with your host Vivien Kindler, taking your calls and hearing the concerns of our listeners in Frost Pound, Maine. So, let's all in unison, and with great enthusiasm, once again this morning say: Wow, Now We're Talkin'! Lines are now open at 207. . .*

Vivien: I am so excited about my new intro; you'll forgive me if I play it a lot for the first few days. That line about not hearing a word you're saying, it doesn't really fit, but so what—I think you know I'm listening—and the skipping over the ocean part is so lovely, probably written just for Frost Pound, Maine, where we are surrounded by ocean everywhere. I believe we have a caller. Good morning, I promise to hear every word you're saying.

Caller: Am I on, am I on the radio?

Vivien: Hi, yes, you're on.

Caller: I hope that your listeners will all turn out Friday evening at 7:00 pm for the annual Home School Concert at the Grange Hall. Paul the Piano Tuner's kids are all in it—they always are.

Vivien: Does Paul have several children?

Caller: Six or seven, anyway.

Vivien: And they have their father's musical ability?

Caller: Some more than others, I'd say. They're all sweet kids. That's all I had. Hope folks turn out for the children. It's free. You know, donation if you want. Thank you, Vivien. (click)

Vivien: You're on the Talk Show.

Caller: That guy telling you all that stuff about freshwater lobsters, crossing the Sligo Road by the orchard, that's a lot of BS.

Vivien: I thought it was pretty funny.

Caller: It might be funny except he's making fun of you—like you don't belong here. He and his buddies belong here and you don't. That's what he's saying. He's got no right to talk that way to you, ma'am.

Vivien: I can handle it, I think! Maybe he'll get used to me. I hope so, anyway.

Caller: He won't. I know him—everybody knows him. I should have told you that up front. I know him and he's always been an asshole, and he won't change.

Vivien: Leopard who won't change his spots, huh?

Caller: We do get some funky lobsters sometimes. That's why I called in. Did you ever hear of a calico?

Vivien: A calico cat?

Caller: No, lobster. Dennis Creamer caught it last summer and it was in the paper, a picture of it.

Vivien: In the obituaries like the ornithologist?

Caller: I don't know?

Vivien: I apologize; I couldn't resist. We had another wonderful story already this morning about something else that's going to be in the paper. What's a calico lobster?

Caller: It's one in thirty million. It looks like a calico cat, like with big patches of orange and black and white. Another thing is, it has no sex. You flip it over and where we look for them little flippery things that are different in the males and females—that's just one way of telling the difference—well, there's nothing there at all. Blank!

Vivien: Do you think they're sterile? Calico lobsters?

Caller: I don't know about that, but it's weird.

Vivien: Was it big?

Caller: Legal, same size as most of the others.

Vivien: Did you see it?

Caller: I banded him and crated him up separate from the other ones. Took the picture with my phone that went to *The Gazette* and to the Darling Center.

Vivien: Him?

Caller: You are funny sometimes, ma'am. It. I banded *it*.

Vivien: You are Dennis's stern man, then?

Caller: Yeah, I was my brother's stern man till he took his boat out for the winter. In the Spring, Dennis can get somebody else if he wants and I'm shit out of luck.

Vivien: He'd do that to his own brother?

Caller: Sure. Done it lots of times.

Vivien: Why would he fire his own brother?

Caller: We fight. I can't haul some morning 'cause I'm getting a tattoo and he thinks he's God, and fires my ass, and we have a fight.

Vivien: A real fight? Blood and everything?

Caller: Oh yeah, blood.

Vivien: Did anyone eat the calico?

Caller: No way. There was no way anyone was going to eat that thing. Even before he'd been handed all round the dock for all the summer people to take pictures with him. That was one tired freaking lobster. Don't know how he would have made out in a crate with all the others, or in the tank at the restaurant.

Vivien: The others would bully him—her?

Caller: For sure.

Vivien: We hear about blue lobsters—that's more common, I imagine. And I've always wondered if they get eaten by tourists.

Caller: Same thing, but not as much. Blue lobsters get handed around a lot for pictures, sort of like pets. Wouldn't seem right to eat them, I guess.

Vivien: Thank you for telling us about calico lobsters. One in thirty million. I hope to see one myself someday.

Caller: Sure, maybe we'll get one next summer. (click)

# Chapter 14
# Calico and Siamese

Same day

Vivien: Hello, you're on *Now We're Talkin'*.

JJ's Mom: Oh, I don't know, Vivien. That takes some getting used to.

Vivien: Good morning. What takes getting used to?

JJ's Mom: The "now we're talking" business. I've been phoning this number since you were a little girl and it was always just *The Talk Show*, and for a lot of years, *The Talk Show with yours truly, Fred Boyland*. Maybe I'm not good with change. Do you think that, Vivien, that some people just don't like change?

Vivien: I think so. It seems to me that these days there is a trend toward seeing all change as good, as progress. I have to admit I'm skeptical about that. If JJ's Mom is a little stuck in her ways, I hope she won't worry about it. I think you're fine. By all means, just keep calling it the *Talk Show*, and maybe the other part will grow on you. What would you like to talk about today, JJ's Mom?

JJ's Mom: Stuck in my ways, is that what you think? Maybe because I'm not very interested in the sex of that Siamese lobster. I'm here at my kitchen table in Frost Pound, Maine, sitting here with my friend, minding my own business, and it looks to me like the whole world's gone crazy, people poking around at the sex organs of a lobster. I'm sure when my husband and I were picking a lobster, we never thought about if it was a boy or a girl.

In my time, the folks living down by the water spent their free time knitting gloves and hats for the fishermen, baking beans for suppers and praying for safety for the boys on the water. I don't know, Vivien. Maybe I am, maybe I am stuck in the past, like you say, JJ's Mom, poor old lady stuck in the past. I don't know.

Vivien: I would have liked to have lived here during those wool hats and baked bean days. I've read the books by Ruth Moore, have you? One called *The Weir* is my favorite. Of course, we risk romanticizing a time when everyday life was very hard. Can I go on?

JJ's Mom: Are you asking me?

Vivien: I think what comes through for me in those books, and which I hope is faithful and true—it's the strong sense of place—place and people who were very grounded. And I like to think that most of them loved their neighbors. (long silence) And I want this program to have some of that—of helping us quiet ourselves and listen and understand one another, because we belong to one another. I think that that is what Mr. and Mrs.

Hudson are thinking with their commitment to local programming. In every era, life remains hard, but in new and different ways. (long silence)

JJ's Mom: Am I still on?

Vivien: Of course.

JJ's Mom: I hope your life hasn't been very hard, Vivien. I don't expect you have lost a child. Maybe people think that I stopped living when Stevie died, that that was when I got stuck. Maybe I should have cried more. I don't know. It seemed like I cried forever. I need to go now, Vivien.

*. . . several commercials . . .*

Vivien: We're back. I think we have another call. Good morning, you're on the *Talk Show.*

Old Sabe: You pretty good down there at that radio station, Miss Vivien?

Vivien: No, I'm not, actually. Sometimes sitting here, down at the radio station, I am confronted with things that nearly break my heart, and I am caused to question whether I am the cause of another person's pain, or if it was there all along. I don't know the answer, but at the moment I am very sad, and sometimes have more than an hour of show left to host, so I can't go home.

Old Sabe: Some of us were sitting around here thinking 'bout the lobster family—thinking about how they must feel when one of their own has to give birth to Siamese lobsters.

Vivien: Painful, of course—and thank you for so seamlessly changing the subject for us. But the previous caller may have misspoken. In referencing a lobster that resembled a cat, she said "Siamese" when she meant "calico."

Old Sabe: Perhaps. Thought she prob'ly heard about the Siamese five-pounder they brought in yesterday afternoon from out near Monhegan. Not ten pounds total, just two, two-and-a-half pound keepers, stuck together.

Vivien: Very unusual, to be sure. Are you sure it wasn't just two lobsters hanging on to each other, perhaps in a fond embrace? They have those pincer things for grabbing stuff, fighting, and presumably, hugging. Might that be what they were observing?

Old Sabe: No, saw it myself. It was definitely a Siamese. They're one in six million. See 'em every couple years.

A Second Voice: (in the background, quieter, but still distinct) Tell her to fuck off.

Vivien: Do you have friends with you this morning, Caller? I think I hear another man who would like to be on the radio. What's his name? I'm sure everyone— (a click as Old Sabe rings off) —that was fun, but we've lost our call and we're up against the news, anyway.

> *. . . ping, the network news at 11:00 am . . .*
> *the President will address a joint session . . .*

# Chapter 15
# Chivalry is Not Dead

Same day at 11:06

*. . . Good morning, and welcome to another hour of Frost Pound's own Talk Show and your host, Fred Boyland, the show directed by you, the citizen callers. Join Fred now at 207 . . .*

Vivien: Oops, looks like the events of the last hour have thrown me off my game. Played the old intro. If you're curious about how this happens on my end, all these short things, bumpers, intros, station IDs, the weather, public service announcements, are listed and displayed on a computer in front of me, and I click on them to play them, and one called *Talk Show intro* has not been deleted. It's obsolete and I hit it anyway by accident. I apologize. Good morning, you're on the air with Vivien.

Fred Boyland: No need to apologize. (a faint and halting voice) Your ham- ham-handedness with the te- technology aside, there seems to be a larger issue of the public n- not enjoying your work.

As long as I have been properly introduced, I thought I'd take this opportunity to— (click)

Vivien: There we go, that was quite adept of me, I would say professional. My fingers and my brain are working better now. Now we're talkin'. Good morning. You're on with Vivien Kindler.

George the Welder: I'm so sorry, Vivien.

Vivien: Thank you, George the Welder, I'm all right. I have been provided assistance in recognizing all of the emeritus talk hosts, but I haven't yet mastered it. I am comfortable now. You needn't worry for me.

George the Welder: Oh, no, not Fred. Forget that. The men with the cleverness that can't disguise their nastiness. The one that shouted the profanity is a stooge and a pathetic fool, but it is your caller, Old Sabe, who I would like to see in person. I know who he is. I know voices you see, and I invite him to come to my garden where I will show him what a man is.

Vivien: It's all right, George. I am grateful. No one has defended me like this for a long time—maybe ever. And you've got troubles enough of your own.

George: You are remembering that I have one leg and move about my garden on my hands. Maybe you are wondering how I could fight another man, a younger man, strong from daily labor in people's kitchens and bathrooms. I can tell you. Our previous talks have had me thinking. In a sense, I am stronger and braver now than I was when I was young. It would make sense if you thought that physical courage in an old man comes from not giving a darn, but when we get old, we still care, but we begin to concentrate our caring on things that we think are important. Today I would like to concentrate my caring on a certain local tradesman, and beat the coward for treating you so badly. I think if he comes to my back gate—he knows where it is—we can meet face to face, I will drag him down to where I am on the ground, and since he will have bravely come here on his own, the sheriff will not very easily charge me with assault.

Vivien: Hmm! This is a new one, isn't it, George the Welder? My first instinct is to say to you that even though I rather respect your thinking, and would even like to talk more about it, the sparring had better stay on the radio. Let us have at it with words, with grunts and groans, gasps and guffaws, with silences, and with self-edited profanities.

George: And I respect your rules, too, Vivien. But my invitation to the local tradesman stands. He won't show and I won't have gotten you or Mr. Hudson in trouble. The coward won't take his chances with the one-legged welder.

Vivien: Well, good. (long silence) I am interested in that matter of bravery—courage. If a one-legged man is not afraid to drag a two-legged one onto the ground in a Japanese garden to pummel him, are we speaking of physical courage mostly—I don't know—I'm thinking out loud—that's what we do on talk radio.

George: I think so, yes.

Vivien: Are you sure you weren't always that way? You were a big football player with a scholarship to Orono, and you probably kept up your physical toughness crawling around the shipyard. Is that fair to say?

George: I was defending you and going to get bloodied up doing it, and now you're saying I'm just being myself. (George laughed at his own remark)

Vivien: (Vivien laughed, too.) Cheap shot by Vivien because I was coming around to your idea about older people learning how to concentrate their courage. I like that a lot. I'm going to put words in your mouth: you are wiser with age and you are more certain about what's important. That's what you think, right? In this case, the intersection of wisdom and physical prowess might culminate in a brutal act of chivalry in a Japanese garden.

George: (laughing, as Vivien had never heard him) I should be flattered that you take me seriously and want to make a big deal out of me backing you up with those jerks, but I doubt if it's interesting to the listeners.

Vivien: It will be to some, and not to others. It's interesting to me. Do you believe me, George the Welder?

George: I'll ask my wife when we get off, she's usually listening. See what she thinks. I wanted to talk about the gifted program in the elementary school, but today I'm going to go along with Vivien, maybe because you've earned it, taking bunk from people that don't respect you for just trying to do your job best you can.

Vivien: Thank you, George

George: Now I have a question for you. Do you have courage? I think you do.

Vivien: In some things.

George: I think you are not afraid of surprises. I can say it better than that. You are not afraid of the unknown, the unexpected. You have put yourself in a situation where for several hours every day you don't know what is coming your way. Fair?

Vivien: Yes, I think so, and thanks for noticing. I've thought about it, recently, I should have given it more thought before I asked for this job. Can I say what I think is the basis of the courage you think you have noticed?

George: Go ahead.

Vivien: It would have been better if you had pried it out of me because it's going to sound self-serving. Anyway, what you have observed is probably either just confidence that I will bring to the microphone a consistent philosophy, a way of seeing people and the world, and that I will react to the callers in a constructive way. (pause) Or maybe I'm just too big an ass to be afraid. I hope it's the former.

George: You are always nice, but it's not the only way to do the program; do you agree with me on that?

Vivien: Of course, but if I was going to put in all the time that this requires, for pretty small remuneration, I think I should do it my own way.

George: Courage or arrogance?

Vivien: Now we're talkin', George the Welder. (laugh) If you knew me better, I think you wouldn't think me an arrogant person. So, I vote for courageous; that's settled. But here's a great question for all our listeners. If we act a certain way that may be, let's say, appealing, or humorous, or somehow noble, and we do so because it comes naturally to us, can we be pleased with ourselves?

George: Maybe I should get off and give someone else a crack at your question?

Vivien: No, please stay.

George: So then, if I agree that you're mostly just being yourself, I would then ask, what *are* you afraid of? What requires more than just being yourself? Now we're getting personal. Want me to ring off?

Vivien: I'm thinking. (silence) I want to give you a straight answer and it is not coming readily to mind. Do you think I've been blocking? I'm kidding, but maybe I should think about it more. Well, this isn't very nice, try this, I am a little afraid of being broke, poor.

George: Have you been broke? I have and it can be terrible. Young people today, and I know this too well from personal experience, don't understand that. They don't know where our prosperity came from and they think they can do whatever they want and they'll always have everything they need. Don't get me going, Vivien. I can make myself crazy.

Vivien: Those young people might argue that they are right, that they're getting everything they need.

George: They're young and not saving anything for leaner times, and not making mortgage payments, and a lot of them have parents subsidizing them. It's a fantasy. They're going to end up on the government.

Vivien: Probably some of them, yeah. And they're probably right in assuming they'll be helped when the you-know-what hits the fan.

George: So, you are smart and hard-working, right? And you admit you're afraid of being poor, and we've got people coming along who are not afraid of poverty at all. What happened? (an indistinct voice heard in the background) I'm all right, it's okay. That was my wife. She is listening to us on the radio in the kitchen and is worried about me.

Vivien: Should we continue this another day, or maybe drop it.

George: No, what were you going to say?

Vivien: It's not like I'm in mortal fear. I'm more saying that it may be a weak spot in my personality that has affected my life.

George: How so? I'm asking the questions now.

Vivien: I've never said this before, even to myself. I have been married to a very nice man, not anymore, very nice in almost every way. That's how I got up here. His work brought him to Maine and I came along, and after a time, we drifted apart and he has gone away and left me here. Not deserted, just left me alone in a small town where I don't have family or old friends.

George: I don't know what your point is, about courage.

Vivien: I said that I was afraid of being poor. I married someone for money, for security would be a kinder way of putting it—someone for whom I was not suited. It was a mistake caused by a lack of courage. There you have it, George the Welder.

George: I think that's kind of harsh. You don't strike me—me and I'd venture most of the listeners—as a selfish person.

Vivien: I hope not. (Vivien laughed) George, have you ever been cold, uncomfortably cold, for months at a time? I have. It was when I was a teenager in western Massachusetts and we were living in an old rented duplex. We had heat, old steam radiators. They'd come on with a racket and you'd be warm if you were near one of them with your skin cracking from the dryness. Then they'd cut off, and you might be reading a book for your homework, and the draft in the room would literally flutter your pages. I'd sit there and count, January, February, March—three more months till I'll be comfortable again. I think I could accept having much less clothing, and less food—I *should* have less food—but I don't want to be cold ever again.

George: I could beat him up for you, when I'm finished with Old Sabe.

Vivien: Who?

George: Your husband.

Vivien: Oh, no. He doesn't deserve a licking.

George: For walking out on you?

Vivien: It wasn't like that. It was mostly my fault, and he left gradually, and left me in a beautiful house by the river. There's an empty place, I think, but not because I lost someone I love like another dear caller, but from something that never grew in me.

George: I think you'll be fine.

Vivien: I think I am working on it, and you are helping me. (quiet) You've suffered, too. I know that you have, because you told me so another time.

George: I need to go now, feed the birds. (click)

Vivien: Tuppence a bag. We'll take a break . . .

# Chapter 16
# A Brief Word Picture

### Winter wearing on

*... commercials ... There are still two more months of snow on the Mid-Coast and we've got a huge selection of Fisher plows, ready for quick installation on your truck. You'll be popular with the neighbors when you dig them out of the next big blizzard ...*

Vivien: Good morning. You're on the *Talk Show* with Vivien. I'm happy to say I have plenty of fuel oil and plenty of food. I try to be grateful. We have a call.

JJ's Mom: It's me again. I won't be on long. Maybe you have one of those talk show rules about only one call a day, I don't know, Vivien. I could call Fred as many times as I wanted. Why do they make rules about things like that when there's people out there robbing houses and selling drugs to kids and stealing your identity? Go ahead, steal my identity if you feel like it. I'm not sure you'd like it very much, being me.

Vivien: We've got a few minutes. What's on your mind?

JJ's Mom: We were wondering what you look like. You've never said, and it's radio, not TV.

Vivien: I've never even considered describing myself—that anyone would care.

JJ's Mom: Why wouldn't we care, Miss Kindler? We hear you on the radio every day. What if I'm sitting here thinking you are a blond, and you're not. I know what Rush looks like, and Glen Beck, and when I listen to them—I don't listen to them much anymore, I used to, but I'm not much for politics—it's helpful to know what they look like. You just told George that you eat too much. I hope that's not a problem for you, Vivien. I read somewhere that there were a lot of fat people in the radio business. Maybe it's from just sitting in one place for hours at a time. That can't be good, can it? Maybe you bring a snack in that little room with you. I can see how that could be a problem, a bag of M & Ms or chips. Maybe you're talking and you think, I'll just have a nibble, what harm could it do, and next thing you know you've put on a few pounds.

Vivien: I brought the end of a Dunkin' Donuts breakfast sandwich in here one time when I was running late. Just that one time—that's it, I swear.

JJ's Mom: Please don't swear, Vivien. We've had enough cussing, haven't we?

Vivien: I'm overweight for sure—probably 15 or 20 pounds. Five foot five, medium length brown hair, a little round all over, not horrible, but round enough that you'd notice. Pleasant looking, I've been told, getting some grey. Is that enough?

JJ's Mom: I hope you won't starve yourself, Vivien. What the girls do to themselves these days to make a big hit in show business. Maybe you're going to leave us for a big job on television and they'll want you to be all skin and bones and blond hair with dark roots. Do they think we don't see the dark roots? Fred promised one time he wouldn't leave us if they offered him a big show in Portland. "Do they think Fred Boyland will chase the money? Well, they don't know Fred Boyland," is what he said. People liked that about Fred. You told us today you had a weakness for money. I hope you don't go anytime soon, Vivien. I heard there are plenty of overweight people on the radio. What difference does it make, anyway, Vivien? You're doing a good job.

Vivien: Thanks. If they think I'm giving up my potato chips and ice cream, they've got another think coming. We've gotta go and—

*. . . ping, twelve o'clock . . .*

On that late winter day, when Vivien Kindler ended her shift at noon, Austin Hudson caught her as she was leaving the radio station for her car. "That was quite a show. Have you got a minute? We need to talk."

Austin nodded toward his office and Vivien knew where he would like her to sit in the glassed cubicle. She said, "I'm sorry about the guy swearing. He wasn't even the guy I was talking to. It came out of nowhere."

"No, that's not a problem, unless, of course, you're upset by it."

"I'm not upset by the swearing, and I really don't think I mind if some people hate the show. It goes with the territory, doesn't it?" She caught herself. "Except if lots of people are really hating it, I don't want to tank the listenership and hurt your business, I really don't."

"I have a sense you're holding your own. That said, I have to say it is different. That whole exchange this morning with George Dessert about his bravery, it gets pretty personal."

"Is that his name? You know him?"

"It's a small town," Austin replied. "His handsome son married a girl from a family that is close to Kathy's, a little younger than us."

"Dessert, like ice cream and cake?" she said.

"Yeah, probably *des-say* the French way, but I've always heard it as dessert. Kathy says you're Delilah on steroids."

"I'm what?"

"Delilah on steroids. Delilah is a woman with a popular syndicated show. She mostly plays songs she dedicates to callers. You hear a few seconds of somebody's sob story, and Delilah empathizes. It's nice, but pretty superficial."

"I've heard her late at night on the big clear channels," Vivien replied.

"I set you up with the new thing displaying the caller's phone number. Have you used it?"

"No, I'm sorry—you mean about Fred sneaking through our defenses. I was still rattled by the F-bomb when he called."

Austin said, "We've never set up the seven-second delay."

Vivien said, "No, don't bother on account of that one idiot, unless you really have to. I doubt I'll have much of that sort of thing."

"I'm sure you won't. And you won't be hearing from Old Sabe for a while, I'd venture to say."

"Why do you think that?"

"He's stuck his neck out too far already. People know who he is and he's got a business in town. He used to advertise with us."

"Probably easier for me not to have known all the history before I started here. Friends of Kathy's family, old advertisers, I'd be scared to say anything," Vivien said smiling.

"You're fine, and I heard that small remuneration crack. I'm upping your pay $75 a week. It'll never be a real job, but it's what we can do. Oh, Kathy wants to put Marcus Deloitte on again, about his restaurant. I think you can get her to come along for hand-holding one day next week."

# Chapter 17
# On Beauty

Another day

*The new recorded intro, "Everybody's Talkin'" from Midnight Cowboy ...*
*(in Austin Hudson's voice), where 1420 on the AM dial skips over the*
*ocean, like a song. Thank you for tuning in to the WNWT Talk Show*
*with your host, Vivien Kindler, taking your calls and hearing the concerns*
*of our listeners in Frost Pound, Maine. So, let's all in unison, and with*
*great enthusiasm, once again this morning say, Wow, Now We're Talkin'!*
*Lines are now open at 207 . . .*

Vivien: Good morning, Frost Pound, Maine, and all the beautiful
nearby places. We have a call.

Lexie: Are we on the radio.

Vivien: Sure are. Who's calling?

Lexie: We called right away at 9:00 o'clock. I guess there was no
one else ahead of us.

Vivien: I'm sorry that I can't tell you that there's a prize.

Lexie: That's all right. There's four of us in the room here—in the principal's office so we could use her phone, but no one else wants to talk. (From the background a boy's voice says, "Tell her your name.") Oh yeah, I'm Lexie Simmons.

Vivien: Good morning, Lexie Simmons. You have a wonderful, big family. There are Simmonses near me.

Lexie: My Nana lives near you.

Vivien: Giant yellow house?

Lexie: You see her picking up bottles and cans.

Vivien: And staying so fit.

Lexie: U-huh. Well, the eighth grade goes to Washington, D.C., every spring and we are raising money. We are asking Frost Pound residents to drop off already rinsed, redeemable bottles and cans at the public school this Saturday from ten to four. Eighth graders will be there to assist you.

Vivien: What about Nana's bottles?

Lexie: I got them already, don't worry. There was $243 worth.

Vivien: What will you do in Washington, Lexie?

Lexie: I don't exactly know. They haven't told us much yet. I know we get to visit our Congressman, which is a woman right now. They always do that. I'm supposed to say that we're all excited about it, the trip, and we actually are.

Vivien: Of course, you are. Maybe you will see the cherry blossoms. They're planted around a lake at the Jefferson Memorial. You'll have a wonderful time, Lexie. It's beautiful, but a different kind of beautiful than what we have here. What we have right at home is the best. Please promise to come back to Frost Pound. Tell that to the others, too. Learn all that you can, but then come back. We need you here.

Lexie: That's all. Thank you, Ms. Kindler, for the opportunity to promote our project on your radio program. Goodbye.

Vivien: I believe I have lots of green glass. Let's take another call.

Brownie: Here's a new one. Okay—

Mistake

I had the prettiest girl in town,

and that was her misfortune.

Do you think that she discovered her beauty a curse

that attracted stupid boys like me

who thought they loved her, but were only in love?

My sweet father was so pleased because

he had chosen her for me

and thought I had not discerned his plan.

It was hard for all of us, my mother too,

learning to match the bride's family's manners and style and putting on the dog at the reception at Stu Atwood's golf club.

They say that He gave us our beauty to spur our mating.

There was that, and I gave myself to it avidly at first,

her slender loveliness coaxing me on.

But there was no propagation.

Her physical perfection, the fabulous mortgaged house,

the job with its wonderful future,

and an entrée into the local politics;

they gave me no pleasure.

And after a time, the perfection of the girl and the flawless plan

could not salvage the whole.

My fault, all of it, realized before incurable ugliness inside us both

could take hold.

I freed her, and the beautiful woman freed me.

And do you know what was the miracle of it all?

She forgave me.

But who will heal the disappointed ones?

(silence)


Vivien: Thank you, Brownie. I'm very glad you listen to our program, and I like to think you are happy out there somewhere. (click) And you're off, aren't you? Hurtling to your next stop. Wonderful. We have another call.


JJ's Mom: Yes, good morning.


Vivien: Thank you, and I hope you and JJ are well.


JJ's Mom: I think you like that Brownie best of all the callers. Anybody can see that. It's okay, no, really, it's fine if you play favorites. That was a nice poem, I have to give that to him, but I don't know, Vivien, do the young people today just walk away from their vows when things get a little rocky? I guess Brownie's not thinking about being alone because he's split up with that beautiful girl, when horrible things can come his way. I'm not wishing trouble for him, no, but life can be very cruel, very cruel, I can tell you.

Vivien: I think the gift of poetry may be to get us to think about things that we might not otherwise have considered. So, even though Brownie writes the poem as if it's he who has married the prettiest girl in town, it doesn't mean that he's writing about himself. He's just put it in the first person. Do you see what I mean?

JJ's Mom: If he didn't mean it was him he was talking about, he could have written it different. I don't know, Vivien, it's no use explaining to me all that college stuff. I guess I'm too simple for poetry. I just thought he was writing about getting a pretty wife, and a skinny one too, probably because last week you told us that you were a little heavy, and so what, no one cares about that, Vivien. We really don't.

Vivien: See, you are smarter than you think, and college has nothing to do with it. I think you are right on this point. He may have gotten the theme of the limits of physical beauty from a brief discussion last week when someone wondered what the host of the *Talk Show* looks like.

JJ's Mom: You're too hard on yourself about your weight, Vivien. I'm sure it's not that serious, and besides, it's no one's business what you look like.

Vivien: I guess you're right. Thank you for that. Anything else today?

JJ's Mom: No, I can't stay any longer. Someone's hungry.

# Chapter 18
# Monks and Dogs

Another day

*. . . skipping over the ocean like a song. Good morning . . .*

Vivien: Please be with us at the top of the eleven o'clock hour for another in-studio visit from restaurateur, Marcus Deloitte.

There was a lively, non-stop succession of calls:

A long-time resident is angry that a rich, new fellow in town claimed that he owns right down to the low tide on his waterfront, and ran off some kayakers.

An explanation of the netting of pogies (menhaden) and their value as lobster bait. And a subsequent call on the early use of fish oil in house paint, and that the paint today is "excuse me, shit" and so's the pine the lumberyards are selling for house trim. "The old growth was good stuff."

Traditions in the naming of working boats, often for wives and daughters onshore, for whom the sturdy, brave men toiled on the water—nowadays unappreciated.

Recycling thoughts, ending with a heated argument about the carbon footprint cost of getting a peanut butter jar clean enough to bring to the transfer station.

*. . . local news . . .*

Vivien: We're back, as the radio professionals like to say, and I will be joined in just a few minutes, there they are, my boss, Mrs. Hudson, and the dashing farm-to-table-atarian, Marcus Deloitte. We have time to take another one of your calls while they're settling in, good morning.

Brownie: Here's a new one—a little rough. I rushed it.
    Love Practice
    Will I someday know an annealed love?
    And know the places in another,
    worn out and broken beyond mending,
    and still other places where faith abides
    and tomorrow is benevolent?
    I know a woman who has the loving way,
    forged by daily practice
    like all the kinds of work that make us good and strong.
    It was her choice.
    Good that she made it when loving him was easy,
    when he was tall and beautiful and moving up in the world
    that needed his competence, strong legs, back, and brains.
    Today she will bring tea to him in his garden
    and spread a quilt on the gravel path where he is trimming.
    He will hesitate to meet her eyes.
    He thinks he is unworthy of her persistent ministrations.
    He sees the French girl who grew him a home and a child,
    who on other blankets met his passions with her gifts,

like the couple I startled this morning practicing
behind the clam shucker's white delivery van.


Marcus Deloitte and Kathy were already seated in the studio
with headphones on for Brownie's contribution. Vivien was, as
before, anxious that things be easy and fun for her boss and her
boss's friend. She had learned to manage the off/on of her own
mic, to chat with others in the studio, to listen to a caller (in this
case Brownie), and to mind the board—all at the same time.

At the end of the poem, she had looked over and seen in the
face of each of them—a certain fright. They quickly looked at
one another, Marcus, Vivien thought, kind of surreptitiously.
Vivien thought she heard Kathy say softly, "Let it go."

Vivien: Thank you, Brownie. We are joined in the studio by
Kathy Hudson and her friend from the hospital board, the owner
and executive chef of a new restaurant in the area, Locovore.
Good morning, guys.

Marcus: Who's the poet? (Kathy looked to be trying to get his
attention)

Kathy: Let it go.

Vivien: He hung up. The caller—he may have a delivery route of
some kind around here. He has said that we can call him Brownie.
When he calls in, he goes right into a poem, without introduction,
which I think is cool. (no response) If you think about it, if you
are reading a poem from a book of poetry, there usually isn't a
short paragraph ahead of the poem giving you context, or hints
for your reading and interpretation. So, our friend simply reads
his composition—I always have had the impression that the

poems are new, composed almost on the fly from observations along the road—and then he just hangs up. He may be too busy to chat, or he may just want the poems to speak for themselves.

Kathy Hudson: I'd rather talk about food, and I expect your listeners feel that way too.

Marcus Deloitte: It can be rather hit-and-run, wouldn't you say, his not hanging around for your response. I'm not sure I like it, Ms. Kindler—

Vivien: Vivien, please.

Marcus: And Vivien, I've heard you ask your callers to give their name. Why should a poet like your Brownie not respect your rule?

Kathy: Maybe poetic license?

Vivien: I have always expected that he was phoning me from his work and didn't want to get in trouble. But I do let callers speak without identifying themselves, and some have made-up handles. There's no hard and fast rule. Anyway, I'm surprised to hear that you don't like Brownie's calls. I've had the impression that a lot of the listeners do. Anyway, food for thought—food for thought.

Kathy: I shouldn't think it would be that hard to find out who he is and who he works for.

Marcus: That would probably put a stop to his mischief, wouldn't it?

Vivien: Mischief, really? To my way of thinking, I've found them, the poems, lovely. Gentle and lovely. Usually, even today, they bring me close to tears.

Kathy: Wow, really? Let's put that aside for now. We don't want to depress our audience. I've been close to tears from the grilled monkfish at Locovore.

Vivien: I believe that's what in the radio business we call a segué. Should we take the call that's holding, or would you like to set things up with the monkfish first?

Marcus: Take the call, by all means.

Vivien: Good morning, you're on the *Talk Show*.

Caller: Now we're talking. (silence)

Marcus: I'm sorry?

Caller: Now we're talking. That's what Vivien likes to say, "Thank you for calling *Now We're Talkin'*."

Marcus: Of course, I see. So, what's up with you today. I'm sorry, I didn't catch your name?

Caller: Frank, I didn't say my name, but I don't mind. What am I afraid of?

Kathy: It doesn't matter. As Vivien said before, either way's all right. What would you like to talk about, Frank?

Frank: We get them in our traps from time to time, monkfish, small ones. I been throwing them back, them and the small cod, wormy—lots of them.

Vivien: Wormy, really?

Frank: Hey, them segways—wife and I went down to Boston and we were walking around down by that Faneuil Hall Market, and I rented one.

Vivien: It looks fun. What'd you think?

Frank: I got the hang of it pretty quick, but mother's a little top-heavy and was scared. You can't really go off by yourself on the thing and leave your wife back in the crowd alone on her first time down there, can you? So, I didn't use my whole hour. Anyway, you guys brought it up and I thought I'd put in my two cents. They're fun. I recommend people go down to Boston and try them out.

Vivien: Thank you, Frank.

Kathy: I think we had a misunderstanding.

Vivien: It doesn't matter, does it? He was a nice man.

Kathy: Probably someone will call in with a poem about it. A woman tried to make a clever rhetorical transition and was run down by a stand-up scooter.

Marcus: Now we're all vamping. I begin to see how the program can get a little off track.

Kathy: I couldn't resist.

Vivien: Don't apologize. We take them as they come, don't we? No producer, no call screener. Mostly it's pretty fun.

Kathy: Hm-m-m.

Vivien: I do think our listeners would love to hear about the yummy stuff you are preparing on your marvelous wood-fired grill.

Marcus: Thank you, yeah, someone mentioned monkfish. As long as I can get them, and they are in considerable demand right now, very popular, we will have grilled monkfish. They are native in the Gulf of Maine. If you ever saw one, you would remember. They're a homely critter. That they're so delicious, therefore, is a wonderful irony.

Vivien: You could give that entrée the name, on the menu: *Wonderful Irony*.

Marcus: We tried that, but customers thought the fish would be irony, sort of like smelts.

Kathy: You two are too clever for me, but I guess this is what live radio is all about.

Vivien: Tell us about the cheeks, Marcus.

Kathy: Please, no, Vivien. Don't get him started.

Marcus: The choicest flesh is in the so-called cheeks; they're small nuggets in the head, just south of the eyes–usually not enough of it to offer as its own menu item. The whole tail section is wonderful.

Vivien: Am I right in remembering that the monkfish has been called the poor man's lobster?

Marcus: I see you've done your show prep. That's right, a lot like lobster, but sweeter. Oh, you've got a call, don't you?

Vivien: You're learning my job. I may ask you to fill in for me sometime. Shall I take it?

Kathy: Sure, we love poetry.

Vivien: You're on with Marcus and Kathy and Vivien.

Caller: It's the same thing as a sand shark—monkfish.

Marcus: You're close, caller. You're thinking of dogfish—but that's an understandable mistake. A sand shark is a dogfish.

Caller: Maybe, I'll look it up on the Internet and call back (click).

Vivien: It's all out there on Google, isn't it? Let's take another call. Good morning.

Caller: You know what they call a whole school of monkfish?

Marcus: No, what? Is this from the Internet?

Caller: A monastery. (click)

Marcus: How about that Mrs. Hudson, classic live radio. We've got another call.

Caller: It's me again. I've got it. We were both right. Monkfish, dogfish—they're both edible. You could just as well be serving sand shark in your restaurant. I'll ask around down on the dock where you could get it. If I can get one, I'll bring it in. What time is there somebody there, at the restaurant?

Kathy: You'll have to remember, Marcus, when dead fish are dropped off at your door, that you sort of asked for them the time you were on the radio with Vivien.

Marcus: Thank you, friend. Come any day but Monday, after noon.

Vivien: Shall we take another call? (palms up, as if to say, why not?) Good morning, any other seafood cuisine thoughts?

JJ's Mom: I don't see why you young people need to make fun of religion, just because you aren't believers yourself. Maybe someday you'll need God. I hope He won't have turned his back on you, I really do. I guess most of the monasteries are closed up now. Convents, too. That's very sad to me. When we were young a lot of the girls that were my friends went to the nuns, a lot of the nicest girls. Maybe I should have, too. You never hear of that anymore, do you? No.

Vivien: I had a friend who went on retreat to the Trappist monastery in Spencer, Massachusetts.

Kathy: See what I mean, she encourages them.

Vivien: You know what, JJ's Mom, we really should talk about dining out in this segment, it's why our guests are here. You understand?

Marcus: It's all right, we can come back to that.

JJ's Mom: I don't want to get you in trouble, Vivien. No, I don't expect anybody else feels like me, no, not nowadays.

Marcus: I've known this nice lady all my life and I respect her choice to believe passionately in whatever she chooses. I expect it's been good for her, too.

JJ's Mom: Thank you, Markie. Stevie always liked you, Markie, and that's good enough for me.

Marcus: This lady probably thought I was a jerk when I was a kid, and I was. She probably is surprised that I amounted to anything. What happened is I found something that I really loved, my passion you might say, food—not very impressive compared to God—but that's the way I'm built, I guess. I'm passionate about food.

JJ's Mom: I didn't think you were a jerk, Markie. I guess I was just worrying for Stevie, and you were so flashy with all that wavy black hair and all the girls after you. I don't know, maybe that was just in my head that you were dangerous. I was thinking about Stevie. I hope you can forgive me, Markie.

Marcus: Hey, forget it, it was all a long time ago. And as for the hair, I'm losing a little of it, but a measure of savoir faire doesn't hurt in the restaurant business.

JJ's Mom: I wish you well with your business, Markie, really, I do. No, I won't be coming in. I wouldn't even know what to wear. I'd probably need a credit card, wouldn't I? I'm going to go now, Markie. You take care of yourself, okay. God loves you, Markie.

Kathy: High praise for Marcus Deloitte.

Vivien: Let's take a break.

. . . *commercials play, including one for Locovore: It has taken a revolution for healthful eating and fine cuisine to merge, and merge they have in the breathtaking landscape of the Maine seacoast and the ambience of Locovore. Marcus Deloitte sources the finest ingredients from seven certified organic local farms, fresh oysters and seafood from our local waters, and grass-fed beef. Gracious service and an extraordinary wine list, all the newest craft cocktails, and you are guaranteed an evening you will remember for years to come. Make your reservations on-line at locovoredining.com. We look forward to hosting you soon . . .*

Vivien: Well, that was nice.

Kathy: Austin and I have been twice. He mostly enjoys the craft cocktails. I love all the veggies off the wood-fired grill.

Marcus: Ah, you're remembering the greatest scapes. (laughs) We were going to put that on the menu, but thought better of it.

Vivien: It's remarkable how many wonderful things they're doing with Bourbon, don't you think? Can we take another call? Good morning, you're on.

George the Welder: That monastery down in Massachusetts, I think it was built for the Trappists by the Grace family.

Vivien: I think that's right. My friend who was there, I don't think I'm telling a big secret, he said that he saw that there were vaults in a wall for Peter Grace and his family when they died.

George the Welder: He was a good guy—Mr. Grace.

Vivien: Is he still alive?

George: I don't know. He headed up that Grace Commission that Reagan appointed to root out government waste.

Kathy: And poisoned the groundwater in a town down in Massachusetts.

Marcus: Woburn.

Vivien: I think the Trappists, which are actually the Order of Cistercians of Strict Observance—how do I know that—had a monastery in Attleboro, Massachusetts, that burned down, and Mr. Grace built them the new one.

Marcus: But the monks rarely speak of it.

Kathy: He is clever, isn't he?

Vivien: The vow of silence, right? That's the joke. My friend said that the only place the retreatants and the monks talked was in the kitchen.

Marcus: See, it is the higher power of food and cooking that promotes a sinful level of conviviality.

George the Welder: Am I still on?

Vivien: Of course.

George the Welder: I don't have anything else, just that the place is supposed to be really beautiful, all fieldstone, and that's where they're making the Trappist Preserves that they sell in Renys Underground. (click)

Vivien: You know, Marcus, I've had the pleasure of eating a lot of very nice food, in the homes of friends, but there is something different about a meal in a fine restaurant. What do you think that's all about?

Kathy: Probably, Marcus's hair. Oh, good, we've got a call. You hit the button, Vivien, and I'll beam them up.

Vivien: It's your radio station.

Kathy: Now you're talkin', Caller.

Woman Caller: Okay, thanks. I'd like to take a stab at your question. It's all about the ambience. I'm kidding. Aren't we a little sick of the ambience, and in real estate, the amenities? You know what amenities are? They're small niceties about a house that should make you pay thousands more than the place is really worth. Anyway, why do we like eating in good restaurants?

Vivien: Go for it.

Woman Caller: For myself, I would say that to start with, when I am going out, I have already primed myself for a treat. I've bathed—

Marcus: Too much information—

Woman Caller: You're right—gotten dressed up, and begun enjoying myself before I'm even in the car. Then you get there and they ask you if a certain table just like all the others suits you, and it does, as though it was put there just for you. Before you know it, you've got about two and a half dollars of wine in front of you for which you will pay twelve dollars, and the pretty waitress or waiter asks if it's alright and, of course, it is, because as I said, you're primed to have a great time. Should I go on?

Kathy: I don't know, maybe Marcus is mad you've blown his cover on the wine deal.

Woman Caller: Everyone knew already. I saw on the *Food Channel* that in restaurants with sort of a French cuisine, we like the food because it has more salt and butter than we use at home. That's pretty funny isn't it? But to be fair, that probably doesn't apply to Locovore.

Vivien: So, what is it, the magic of the restaurant?

Woman Caller: I think we just give in to a general feeling of well-being, an acknowledgment that we are lucky to be out, out and with the money to treat ourselves to an excellent meal prepared by someone else, in good company, and with people fussing over us. And there are other lucky people all around us that have brought the same positive energy to the place. In some ways, it's a bit of a fantasy. If we are smart, we will have avoided political arguments—we will have had a lovely time, and will go home to a clean kitchen.

Marcus: I think your assessment is fair and accurate. I would only add that your scenario could equally apply to your going to a sports bar and having good fish 'n chips. There are some patrons who possess a more discerning taste and for whom we strive to present a very special meal.

Woman Caller: Yeah, granted. It's just not me. I always ask for extra tartar sauce.

Marcus: It's a small percentage. We want them to come and not lord their epicurean knowledge over everybody else, and empty the room.

Kathy: And Marcus's discernment extends to knowing which fourteen-dollar wines to mark up. They're not all the same.

Vivien: That caller has gone, we'll take another one. You're on the air with Marcus Deloitte and friends.

Male Caller: Hi, am I on?

Vivien: Good morning, who's calling?

Male Caller: That last lady didn't give her name.

Vivien: Of course, you are right.

Male Caller: So, I don't have to give my name, right?

Vivien: Right.

Male Caller: Okay, I've got three things written down.

Vivien: You have a *list?*

Male Caller: No. Okay, here goes: Mr. Deloitte, inasmuch as monkfish has been referred to as the poor man's lobster, how can you justify charging thirty-two dollars for it? You can purchase a boiled lobster on the dock for about ten.

Marcus: Is this serious?

Vivien: Caller, do I recognize your voice from another occasion when you cast aspersions on the integrity of today's guest?

Male Caller: Are you going to cut us off?

Vivien: Do you have someone else there with you this morning, with your list?

Male Caller: There's no fu— Question two, do you sometimes purchase chicken from Hannaford's, or maybe that was somebody else with real cool black hair that I saw there checking out a whole cart of chicken breasts? It might not have been you. (click)

Marcus took off his headset, rose from his seat, whispered something to Kathy, and headed for the studio door. Vivien looked at him and Kathy.

Vivien: I've cut him off. I thought I recognized the voice.

Vivien looked past them and saw that Austin was in the lobby with the same upturned hands and the "what are you gonna do" expression that he had been kind enough to offer once before.

Vivien: (covering her mic with her hand) I'm so sorry, Marcus. Please don't go.

Marcus: (in a voice audible to the listeners on their radios) You guys finish without me, I've got wine to mark up.

Now Kathy snatched off *her* headphones, gathered up her coat, and followed Marcus out of the studio.

Vivien didn't think she could vamp alone to the news.

Vivien: Let's take a short break—

*. . . public service announcement . . .*

Through the glass Vivien watched a lot of flailing of arms and what appeared to be an argument between Kathy and Austin, then she played an ad for the big Ford dealership that she had already played once that morning, and did the math that she had by now mastered, relieved that ads would get her to the top of the hour.

# Chapter 19
# My Lost Son

The next day

*. . . and skipping over the ocean like a song. Good morning . . .*

Vivien: Good morning, and welcome to another edition of *Now We're Talkin'*. I am your host, Vivien Kindler. I can't get us started this morning without comment on yesterday's program. If you weren't listening, count yourself one of the lucky ones. We were having what I thought was a good discussion of the dining experience in a fine restaurant, and though I have not myself eaten at Locovore, I have no doubt that it is an excellent place. I let a young man on the air whom I might have recognized as a cynical and rude type for whom there is no place on this show. As most of you know, we have no producer or call screener for this program and we take the calls as they come, so I can only implore the listeners: if you've gotten up in a bad mood this morning and are thinking of making trouble, please don't phone the *Talk Show*. It would be preferable for Vivien to talk about the weather for three hours if that's all we have. You can hear that I am still rattled because I have referred to myself in the third person, something that I have pledged to myself that I would never do.

Okay, let's see how we do today. The weather: I am looking out the plate glass window of the WNWT studio and I see that a slow, cold drizzle has begun. That was interesting, but I think we have a call. Good morning,

George the Welder: You didn't do anything wrong.

Vivien: Is that you, George the Welder—a dependably kind person and a balm for a beleaguered radio host?

George the Welder: The kid was obviously a seminar caller and he got all that crap out before you had a chance to stop him, and eventually, you got rid of him.

Vivien: I don't know. What's a seminar caller?

George: That's what Rush calls the ones that he thinks aren't expressing their own view, but have been put up to calling with the agenda of an organized group.

Vivien: I'd never heard that. He was a seminar caller. Okay, no seminar callers. It's a rule.

George: I've got a very good ear and the phrasing of those questions were not his own. He was reading from notes somebody else had written for him. You can spot a seminar caller.

Vivien: Someone was lying in the weeds for Mr. Deloitte. I suspect you are right, but we can't know, can we?

George: I can understand why you can't, but I can. He was reading from a paper somebody gave him. Probably because I have listened to so much radio, I can spot a phony.

Vivien: And you think it was a young person, you said "that kid."

George: I know voices. Didn't you think it was a kid, like in his twenties?

Vivien: Yeah, I guess I did. Let's move on, we're giving nastiness too much prominence. What did you have for us this morning, George the Welder? Are you out in your wonderful garden? It's cold, isn't it?

George: Yes, sitting on a milk crate in a light rain. I could tell you were upset and I don't think you should be. You didn't do anything wrong. Is it because Mrs. Hudson was there and the station people are mad at you?

Vivien: No one has said so, and I wouldn't tell you that, anyway. That's their business.

George: So, then, forget it. You're too sensitive.

Vivien: I'm pretty tough actually. I suppose it's that I really like what I'm doing. I look forward to coming in here every day, sitting in this seat, punching the buttons, dialing the dials, not knowing what is going to happen next, and almost always being delighted by kind people with interesting insights, wonderful stories. I would hate for it to end. This seems to me a very special opportunity in my life. Maybe I'm selfish, George the Welder.

George: Maybe a little. You're giving them a lot of time and effort for not much money. If you are selfish, it's in your wanting to have things your way. You're steering the show the way you want. You are, you know. You know that, but I'd say you're entitled. Fred just opened the phone lines and that was fine. It's different now.

Vivien: I think that's fair—that I'm steering the show, and even if our motives are good, most of us probably just want what we want. Some people think that even when we do things that we think are generous or magnanimous or sacrificial, we are still just doing what we want to do.

George: I don't know.

Vivien: When I was a kid—a teenager—my dad bought me a stereo. It was a combination amplifier/cassette player thing with nice speakers. When I opened it—it probably was a birthday— he had included with it a whole bunch of Frank Sinatra tapes. I don't see how I could have been so ticked off by so small a thing—there must have been other history because I lit into my dad about the Sinatra tapes. I told him that it looked like he'd bought the stereo for himself, that he'd bought me what *he* wanted. That was so terrible. I'm still ashamed today thinking about it. I don't think I ever apologized. He's gone and I never told him I was sorry.

That was just one thing, there were others, all small by themselves, but we didn't enjoy one another very much. I'm haunted by it, well, that's overly dramatic. I'm disappointed—

disappointed that maybe I could have made him happy. He wasn't very happy and, now selfishly, I'm sad about what I missed.

George: Were you an only child?

Vivien: No, I had two sisters, have two sisters.

George: So?

Vivien: So what, George the Welder?

George: Have you talked to them about your father?

Vivien: No, not like that. They live pretty far away and we don't have much in common. That's fine.

George: Did they make him happy, in the way that you didn't?

Vivien: Well, Denise, yeah, on some level she probably pleased him. She wasn't burdened with my seriousness. I probably wasn't always fun to be around. If she had gotten the very same present, she would have tried to like the Sinatra tapes because Daddy liked them. Yeah, she was nice in a way that I wasn't. And she would have gotten all dreamy and romantic listening to the lyrics. She probably started smoking because Daddy and Old Blue Eyes smoked. Mom and I harped on my father to stop smoking while Denise was running to the store to get him another pack. Maybe I'm selfishly thinking that I was more important to him than I really was. I get it, George the Welder, he had Denise—lucky for him. Now we're talkin'.

George: So, you made your own way.

Vivien: I left his household in the normal way and got older, which required no effort, married and moved to new places. I think it's only recently that you could say I am making my own way.

George: No children?

Vivien: No, but it's not too late. You need a man, though, don't you? (long silence) You had a son. Was he your only child?

George: We don't need to go there. No one wants to hear that story.

Vivien: I told you mine, part of it, anyway. He was your only son, wasn't he?

George: Yes.

Vivien: And he's not dead, is he? No, I'll not use that word again with its horrible finality. (pause) I hope you won't either. (pause)
Think about this, George the Welder: what if you had had three sons, go with me on this, I've been thinking about it—or four or five? You like to watch baseball, so does son John. Eddie likes to dance and does tai chi, which you find effeminate and wouldn't be caught dead doing. Dickie likes to go out on his

property and saw stuff down with his chainsaw where you shrink at the thought of killing any living thing.

George: I don't mind killing most plants. I leave the pretty ones and trim them to my liking.

Vivien: Go with me. John who likes baseball studied law and is revered, and a little feared, all over town. You admire that and are happy for him. Eddie and his wife have a frame shop and do nice work, but are always strapped for cash, which causes you worry. Dickie invests in real estate and has probably made a fortune, but he has the first dollar he ever made. It rankles you because you are generous and open-handed.

George: Actually, I am.

Vivien: John is the most like you, and because we are all a little selfish, his similarities to you give you pleasure. Of course, it's probably not that simple. Part of why Eddie is strapped is because he's generous like you—did all that framing for free for the corridors in the new hospital addition. Dickie who fells huge trees for no good reason has a tender spot for children, all kinds of children, which most people don't even know about him.

George: I had one son.

Vivien: Have! I think this is my point. An only child may have all the parents' hopes and dreams concentrated on him or her. Isn't that bound to be unfair and disappointing—both ways—for the parent and the kid?

George: What if the father of Tom, Dick or Harry just wanted to help with what he thought were basic things, like education, contacts, a little position in the community. That's a good one—position in the community. Maybe that's less important now, but I can tell you when I was growing up here, there were boys who knew they were going to be running everything when they grew up, and they were right. And money, education, contacts: what's wrong with a foot in the door to a career so you could have money enough to avoid the stress and worry that poor people live with all the time?

Vivien: Years back I heard this funny line: What do you get from a Harvard education? The pedigree, the network, and the hubris. Look at how the Supreme Court judges all come from the same law schools. It can't possibly be that one can't learn all the same stuff at dozens of other places.

George: You see my point. You agree with me. Education and contacts and money matter in the real world, and a man, or a woman, is a fool to not see it.

Vivien: Are we talking about Tom, Dick, Harry?

George: Which one did the tai chi?

Vivien: I think Dick. I've never had children, so it's unfair of me to judge, but, as I've said, I've been a child in a big family. Maybe it's a question of sensitivity, of knowing when our best intentions are not helpful?

George: It would be nice if Dick had just asked his father to back off and given his father a chance to think about it, instead of just going off angry and stupid and chucking everything.

Vivien: This fellow, Dick, it sounds like he may have a stubborn streak—probably came down through the mother's line.

George: Smart aleck.

Vivien: We're up against the news, George the Welder. Hold your torch right there for another day.

*. . . ping, the top of the hour . . .*

# Chapter 20
# Oh, Volunteers

### A new day

A heated argument about the use of Roundup in which one caller used an obscenity to describe another caller who would not apply the herbicide to poison ivy in a driveway.

A local selectman explained the pros and cons of purchasing heavy equipment for the town as opposed to contracting for services.

A reminder about a ham and bean at the Odd Fellows, which briefly touched on some hurt feelings around the quality of the mustard they'd "been putting out for as long as anyone can remember."

A call that Obie Peckham is better from his heart attack and should have "a good assortment" of whirligigs and other colorful lawn ornaments "quite soon."

### The end of the first hour

Vivien: Good morning, now you're talkin'.

Caller: Is it me? I haven't said anything yet.

Vivien: I know. I was just being flip. It's the name of the show—
*Now We're Talkin'*. Go ahead, I'm sorry, who's calling?

Tom: Tom on the Sheepscot River. Your station comes in pretty
good down here, not always, but most of the time.

Vivien: Great.

Tom: I hate government. I might as well get that out of the way
up front.

Vivien: All government—everything they do—federal, state and
local?

Tom: No, I shouldn't have even said it, but it's getting worse all
the time, isn't it? Never mind that.

Vivien: Okay.

Tom: I have a small skiff with an outboard motor. I have two
three-gallon gas tanks that I swap back and forth during the
season. Anyway, every fall when I haul the boat, there's gas left
in one of the tanks and I don't know what to do with it.

Vivien: Can't you leave it in the can for next year?

Tom: You can, and people say to put fuel stabilizer in it, but that's
not foolproof, and if you mess up your carburetor with bad gas,

most people have to take their motor to a shop for an expensive repair.

Vivien: I don't know anything about motors and gas. What do people say? I'm sure you've asked around.

Tom: I know what most people do. They pour it on the ground, or light a brush pile with it.

Vivien: Everybody knows that's bad, right?

Tom: Probably most people. You can run it in your car, or your lawnmower, but the two-cycle isn't great for the car.

Vivien: Two-cycle?

Tom: The oil that you mix with gas for an outboard. The oil can foul your spark plugs.

Vivien: So, what's the answer?

Tom: There have to be hundreds or maybe thousands of people like me up and down the coast, and around the lakes, too, who have the same issue. It seems to me it would be a useful role of government to set up some kind of collection system. And while we're at it, here's another one. Have you got time?

Vivien: Shoot.

Tom: You know how they say that low tire pressure decreases the miles per gallon that your car gets, and so, contributes to global warming?

Vivien: Yes. I've heard that.

Tom: Have you tried to fill your tires at a gas station with one of those air vending things? You go inside and try to change a couple dollars into quarters and the clerk scowls at you, even though it's their damn machine, and lots of the time the machine doesn't even work, or you run out of quarters. Old people can't do all that. My point is, if it's so important, and the planet depends on it, why don't they make a drive-through place in every town where minimum-wage people can pump up tires all day?

Vivien: Thank you, Tom. Seems like a reasonable idea. You've given us two wonderful new roles for the government. (pause)

Tom: Touché. (click)

Vivien: Maybe other callers will have a thought. Okay, maybe this is one. Good morning, you're on the *Talk Show*.

Caller: The boat gas, I light my grill with it. (click)

Vivien: That guy rang off quickly—pants on fire. I've seen him up in town—no eyebrows. Gotta run, great guest in the studio for the second hour, all about assisted living, please stay with us if you can.

*. . . a new hour at 10:06 and the intro . . . skipping over the ocean like a song. Good morning, and thank you for tuning in to the WNWT Talk Show with host Vivien Kindler taking your calls and hearing the concerns of our listeners in Frost Pound, Maine. So, let's all in unison, and with great enthusiasm, say: Wow, Now We're Talkin'. Lines are now open at 207 . . .*

Vivien: I'm so excited—

In-studio guest: I'm just nervous.

Vivien: You'll have fun. We have with us this morning Deborah Henrichon, who owns and manages Boothby Cove Assisted Living. Some of you may have had a family member or neighbor who has lived there, so you may know of it by reputation, or from personal experience.

Why don't I just talk a little about what I know about assisted living, which is not much, and you can chime in and straighten me out.

Deborah: Good, maybe I'll have calmed down by then.

Vivien: Or snuck out.

Deborah: I'll stay.

Vivien: Excellent. We have an older population in this region, I think everyone knows that, and, so, there's lots of interest in the different kinds of places where our parents, and eventually we, may want to live as we get older and lose some of our mojo.

Deborah: Mojo, medical term, you're doing great so far, keep going.

Vivien: Am I right to say that this is a field that is evolving constantly to respond to the needs of an aging population? Some people just move nearer the hospital, some can live independently in houses or apartments that are part of a larger complex that may offer continuing care in other settings, and some folks choose to live in a place like yours where there is a dining room, and which offers a range of caregiving and nursing.

Deborah: That's all perfect, and we fall into that latter category. And even within that general definition, places may all be quite different.

Vivien: Good. Now I will rely on you. How would you describe what you offer at Boothby Cove?

Deborah: We have quite a mix of residents. Right now, we have folks recuperating from surgery that need some help before they can return home. Some folks have chronic health problems and need nursing care, others are from time to time confused, confused or distressed, and better off around people that can help and reassure them.

Vivien: Is that Alzheimer's or dementia?

Deborah: Yes, both, or either, I guess. Our staff knows everyone in the family really well, and, hopefully, how to be with them in the way that they need, so it's mostly unnecessary to put a clinical name to their challenges.

Vivien: I think I see.

Deborah: Yeah, all these things vary from person to person and sort of exist on a continuum, so the labels aren't very helpful. Others may disagree.

Vivien: You've told us about Boothby Cove in terms of the mix of folks living with you, but I was getting at something less tangible. It was a loaded question based on what others have told me about your place. What do you think people say distinguishes it?

Deborah: I hope that they say it's our staff. For one thing, to care for people really well just takes a lot of people. If we only dress the residents that need help dressing, and help with bathroom stuff, and bathing and cleaning, and getting everyone's daily meds, and paying attention that everyone is getting good nutrition, it takes a lot of people. Some of our family won't eat at all unless someone sits with them and helps them.

Vivien: One bite at a time?

Deborah: Yes, with some it's every bite, and that's a huge time commitment. So, I've only described the acknowledged essentials.

Vivien: And there's more, I know there is; people have told me.

Deborah: My years with our old friends have led me to one conclusion that is not clinical, but more important than the measurable medical things. It's about how we view the residents as people. Surely there are many other assisted living homes that have our same priority, but it's where we spend extra time and money because it works for everyone.

Vivien: What do you do?

Deborah: It begins with the paradigm, well, no, that's not accurate, it starts with hiring wonderful people. The young women and men who have grown up right around here, and who have attended our local schools, are terrific people. That's just something about Maine. We are so fortunate in that. So, early on, a new staff member understands from the veterans, that each resident, guest, is a unique and wonderful creature who must be truly known and understood—known and respected.

Vivien: Respected.

Deborah: Here's the thing. Even when a man or woman has lost some mental or physical skills, what you have called mojo, and has lost some ability to communicate verbally, and may appear a little worn out, every one of them still hungers for respect. Think about it: a woman may have lost her husband who loved her and was her best friend, and lost the prestige and satisfaction of her job, and lost her house that she had proudly fashioned and cared for, and lost her place in a community that she faithfully served. A young man working in our dining room, or a CNA, or a nurse at Boothby Cove may not at first know anything about that woman's history. The resident I am describing may not be exactly happy to be in a new place, and she definitely can tell if she is being treated dismissively. So, here's the paradigm: we need to start right out speaking and acting as though she is special and wonderful, even before we know her story. When we have learned her story, it will come more naturally.

Vivien: And will you know her story?

Deborah: Yes, most of the time. We make a good effort that way. Yes, we have learned a lot of great stories.

Vivien: And that has to take time, valuable time.

Deborah: Our professional caregivers are encouraged to put in the time, and we have volunteers that have become part of the family.

Vivien: I would think that might be challenging—not for everybody.

Deborah: Some of the volunteers are folks who were the loved ones of residents who have passed. One young man started out spending time with us as community service.

Vivien: Like court-ordered?

Deborah: Something like that.

Vivien: Deb, are you willing to take some calls? Someone's on the line.

Deborah: Sure, but I need it to be understood that I just can't talk about actual individuals, only generically.

Vivien: Good morning, who's calling this morning?

JJ's Mom: Good morning. Community service, I don't know. You have criminals roaming around the halls of that place. That doesn't sound so good to me.

Deborah: Actually, we've only had one such volunteer and he is still with us. He's someone I trust completely. All our people have had background checks and are carefully monitored. But a volunteer can give our friends lots of generous time. It's precious to us and we're grateful. And, of course, the residents' families will also have met the volunteers and given their approval.

JJ's Mom: But criminals, I don't know. What did the fellow do? The one that you've still got working for you?

Vivien: I think we should trust Ms. Henrichon's discretion, don't you, JJ's Mom?

Deborah: It's all right. The caller's concern is not unfair. I can only tell you that the man in question was never charged with having done any harm to another person, nothing of that kind at all. In fact, everyone finds him charming and great fun to be with.

JJ's Mom: I guess I'm just old-fashioned. It's a whole new world out there, isn't it, Deborah? I heard about a woman that was visiting some murderer in jail somewhere and she fell in love with him and married him right in the prison. I hope you won't let things go that far, Deborah. Anyway, that's all I wanted to say today. (click)

Vivien: Let's take another call.

Brownie:
    Hauling Alone
    This morning in the darkness before dawn he starts to move
    his traps onto Killick Stone Island shoals.
    He could use the help of his boy who
    he thinks stern-mans for him sometimes,
    but he can do this work alone.

He is happy.

When his wife was alive, she worried about his safety.

Better he didn't tell her how lightly he took her warnings.

A man could do worse than be hauled overboard,

tangled in the lines of a sinking trap,

a tasty snack for *locustam marinam*.

The pretty girl in the turquoise scrubs

has left his window open

and the sea air wafts gently over his paper-thin skin.

Across the dark harbor,

hushed voices from other boats speak of their rising,

and of coffee and cinnamon rolls.

On a boat just out of view Larry curses like a sailor.

He is the only other one who wakes at four.

Again today, Elliott will, in his mind,

fill several ninety-pound crates,

and keep shipshape his paid-for boat,

robbing the bank of their usurious profits.

Some people ask if he knows that he is cruising aboard a

hospital bed that his son has fashioned into a lobster boat?

But no one will ask: What would be the point? (silence)


Vivien: Thank you, Brownie.


Deborah: What was that?


Vivien: Have you heard that caller before?


Deborah: No, I'm sorry to say I only listened to you a little last
week when I knew I was coming on. The hours you're on are
very busy for me. I'm running around. Please forgive me.

Vivien: That caller is a poet. He only recites a poem and doesn't stay on to explain it.

Deborah: The making of a man's bed into a lobster boat, that's a real story from Boothby Cove. About a former resident of ours, a lovely man no longer with us. I want to remember the poem. It was really good.

Vivien: Do you know how the poet knows about your resident?

Deborah: No, but I'll surely be thinking about it—wow.

Vivien: We have another call. Good morning.

Caller: Yeah, sure. I'm on, right?

Vivien: You're on.

Caller: The poet guy wouldn't have needed to go to the nursing home to know about Darrin Long's father. Oh, yeah, I'm pretty sure it's Darrin Long she was talking about doing the volunteer stuff. (Vivien looks at Deborah to see if the caller blurting the name has caused a problem, but is met only with a smile.) Everyone around here knows about freakin' Darrin. He's definitely harmless, drug stuff, resisting arrest. Hid in the woods for months, maybe a year, before they caught him. Made his dad that lobster boat in the nursing home. Lot of people know about that boat. Old guy took people on rides—rides on his bed.

Vivien: Thank you, Caller. I'm going to let you go. It would be better if we didn't mention names of actual people. I hope you understand. We've got another call.

JJ's Mom: Good morning. It's me again. Maybe this fellow's not going to fall in love with the ladies you've got living there. Probably they're a lot older than him, but what about bringing drugs in, I don't know, isn't that a problem? It seems like these drugs are everywhere. Young people dying, I don't know.

Deborah: We should move on, as Vivien has suggested. The issue we started with was about knowing and respecting our guests. A volunteer who was smart enough to know what would make one old lobsterman happy might be able to sit and talk with others and bring out in them some special essence that we should know about. That's what a volunteer might do for us, and if he or she does, it's a blessing.

*. . . a commercial, weather . . .*

# Chapter 21
# Pay the Gov'nah

Weeks later, nearly Spring

*. . . and skipping over the ocean like a song . . . Good morning, and thank you for tuning in to the WNWT Talk Show with host Vivien Kindler taking your calls and hearing the concerns of our listeners in Frost Pound, Maine. So, let's all in unison, and with great enthusiasm, say once again: Wow, Now We're Talkin'. Lines are now open at 207 . . .*

Vivien: Good morning, good in most respects, still cold and gray outside, but it's nearly spring and I've been in my seed catalog. How about you? I find that ordering seeds and getting some things started on the windowsill cheers me up this time of year. And I seem to remember that my mower wasn't starting very easily in September. I thought that today we could talk about your preparations for the warmer growing season. We've got a call already. Good morning, now you're talkin'.

Caller: Yeah, good morning, yeah, it was definitely Darrin Long.

Vivien: I'm sorry, Caller. Who was definitely Darrin Long? I'm afraid I've lost the thread.

Caller: The guy that made his dad's bed into a lobster boat. It's a true story. Had red and green lights and the name painted on the transom, the footboard of the bed. Real slick.

Vivien: I'll bet it was. I think we left it with Deborah Henrichon that we wouldn't speak of people by name. Is there anything else you had on your mind?

Caller: Maybe taking care of the rototiller and the lawnmower and the chainsaw was your husband's department, but he's gone. I think you told us that. Anyway, you're probably up the creek on getting your mower serviced. You're supposed to take it in in the fall so they can work on it over the winter when things are slow. Lots of people like you that don't plan so good will be bringing in stuff now. You'll be lucky if they don't chase you right out.

Vivien: Should I try to get my husband back?

Caller: I'll leave that to you, ma'am, but if you've got the cash, you probably should just buy a new mower. They're not made to last nowadays. If you've gotten four or five years out of it, take it to the dump. (click)

Vivien: Here's another call. Good morning. Who are we talking with this morning?

Caller: Yeah, well, I think you'll understand why I'm not saying my name. I'll cut to the chase. I bought a garden tractor in, let's just say, a local power equipment place. It'd be better not to say what year—you'll just have to take my word for it that it was pretty recent—and the owner of the place says to me when I'm paying him, "Do you want to pay the Gov'nah?"

Vivien: What did you take that to mean?

Caller: What do you mean, what did it mean? He was offering that I could not pay the sales tax if I wanted. That was over a hundred dollars.

Vivien: Is it possible he was inviting you to tell him how you felt about paying the large amount of tax—not offering to let you out of it?

Caller: Forget it, sorry I called. I stick my neck out and you don't believe me, great. (click)

Vivien: That's regrettable. Perhaps that dealer was offering to let him out of the sales tax. Since we don't know the caller, we can't assume much about the veracity of his account and he's making a very serious charge. I don't know anything about the State of Maine's auditing of the tax filings of retailers, but it seems to me that routine shortchanging of the state in the way the caller describes would be hard to cover up. We have another call.

Caller: Hello, Vivien, am I up?

Vivien: You're up.

Caller: I'd say that fellow was telling the truth. Here's another one: the elver guys. (breathless pause)

Vivien: I'm fascinated with that whole elver story.

Caller: Yeah, I guess. Japanese eat them raw.

Vivien: I read about it in a magazine years ago, way before I moved up here. The author started with somebody catching an adult eel in Cooperstown, New York.

Caller: I was calling about the taxes.

Vivien: I got carried away. What about the taxes?

Caller: I heard a lotta kids back in 2012, 2013 got in big trouble with the Feds—not paying taxes on hundreds of thousands of dollars they got for the elvers.

Vivien: Seems like that would be hard to get away with.

Caller: They used to get cash for the baby eels, not any more, they get a check now, and the catch is regulated, just like everything else. I don't know when shrimping is going to open back up.

Vivien: Neither do I. Is there anything else, Caller?

Caller: No, but I guess everyone wonders about the blueberries.

Vivien: What about the blueberries?

Caller: All those ladies up and down Route 1. I doubt they're paying income tax on the money they get for them blueberries.

Vivien: Gosh, again, I'm afraid this is speculation that is unfair. Who knows? Me, I'm just glad they're still doing it. Think of what is involved in getting you that little basket of berries for your pancakes—the burning off of the fields, the raking, the boring sitting there on the side of the road hoping that the odd car that slows when he sees your hand-made sign doesn't wreck getting out of the fast-moving traffic. That's what I love about this place, this place that is your home. Somehow, you've kept it very special—special and wonderful.

Keep it up, blueberry people, and you clammers and eelers, too. I salute you all. We need to take a break. Please stay with us, if you can.

*. . . news, weather, commercials . . .*

Vivien: I'm glad you are along for our second hour this morning. As we left off earlier, your host was rhapsodizing about wonderful blueberries, but just before that I had begun to talk about eels. I think the story of the eel, the eel's life cycle is so wonderful, weirder than the salmon that finds its way back to the stream where her parents spawned and she first drifted to the sea. I'm going to tell what I remember. Correct me if I'm wrong on any of this. Somebody in the story I read caught an adult eel in Cooperstown, New York, a place known for something else. I've looked at Cooperstown on the map and it's on Lake Otsego, which is the headwater of the Susquehanna River. The Susquehanna watershed is really huge and the river drains a big chunk of the Northeast. It goes into the Chesapeake Bay in Maryland. So that adult eel, and every eel in North America, at some point in its adult life swims down, in this case, the Susquehanna, into the Chesapeake and to the Atlantic open ocean and to the Sargasso Sea. The Sargasso Sea is like the deepest hole in the North Atlantic near Bermuda, and the eels reproduce down there where it's so dark and deep that no one has ever observed their mating. Then the hatched babies drift northward in the Gulf Stream and swim back up the Susquehanna or into some little estuary on the coast of Maine where their parents once lived. And then they get netted and caught by a nocturnal fortune hunter, or evade his net and make it to a shallow freshwater pond where they live several years of lazy freshwater leisure, oblivious to the tax issues. That's what I think I know about the eels, which are elver when they are in the freshwater estuaries, and glass eel when they're in the ocean. Blessedly, we've got a call. Good morning.

George the Welder: Good morning, Vivien.

Vivien: How are you doing? I've been thinking of you as the days are getting longer and snow is melting, whether you are out in your Japanese garden.

George: Picture the old eel struggling his way to Bermuda, not on vacation, but because he has to. Never mind that, I'm calling in defense of the power equipment shops.

Vivien: Let's hear it.

George: We've all seen it, the rows and rows of gorgeous red and green and orange riding mowers and snowblowers in front of the big box stores. A lot of that stuff is junk.

Vivien: Seems like some of it is of a poorer quality than what you would get from the small local guy. People have called in about that before. It's complicated.

George: The big point is that people buy from Lowe's or Home Depot to save a couple hundred dollars and then when the stuff breaks, they bring it to the mom and pop place for service. Who wouldn't be mad?

Vivien: Of course. And now Vivien from the radio walks in to the shop in the springtime with a lawnmower that won't start and now they're really rippin'.

George: I'll call you off the air at noon and tell you a local place where they're really nice. You probably already know it. They'll just tell you what they tell everybody, that they work on the stuff that was purchased there first, but that they will fix your mower.

Vivien: Perfectly reasonable. Have you been in your garden? Sticks to pick up, right?

George: I'm out there right now, not much budding, just the buds on the magnolia that were already there in the fall. I haven't much pep.

Vivien: Because it's sort of gray?

George: I've had some issues connected to the diabetes—kidney stuff, that and my eyes. I can see fine, for most purposes, but they say it will get worse. Tired old eel finding his way home.

Vivien: Are you seeing people? Are there people whom you would like to see, George the Welder?

George: You know, it's a funny thing. I've told you that my hearing is good. Maybe when you are losing one of your senses, the other ones get sharper. I think I am hearing you, Vivien, hearing you quite well. And I have a very good radio.

# Chapter 22
# Aroostook County

The next day

*... commercials and a PSA ...*

The day started with a happy Frost Pound tapestry of calls:

The library is giving away remaindered books. (The librarian always finds the decisions very unpleasant, "but we've only got so much space."). It's five dollars for a shopping bag's worth.

Lobstermen ought to buy their new traps from local guys who build them over the winter—support our local people. Vivien didn't know that a lot of gear is lost every season.

A young woman offered workshops on scrapbooking at her home, where she also "can provide supplies at reasonable prices."

Vivien: And who is joining us this morning?

Paul the Piano Tuner: It's Paul with another story. It's still rough, but I'd like to try it out on you anyway. I know you admire the old ways of Maine, so I thought you might like this one.

Vivien: Shoot.

Paul: In 1947, when my father was seventeen, he set off with his friend, Waldo Prior, for temporary farm work in Aroostook County. Some kids from Frost Pound had found work the previous autumn in Blaine, near Mars Hill. Kendrick Lynn, my father, had not travelled down east beyond Thomaston, so for him it was a great adventure.

Kendrick had four dollars and twenty-five cents for the trip and his friend, Waldo, had a dime, a dime that Waldo thought a shame to break unnecessarily.

The cold, tired boys spent their first night in Blaine, asleep upright in the cab of Waldo's pick-up. In the morning, Waldo, being already near despondency, thought they'd better call on the Methodist Church where they had seen humans stirring. Upon learning the purpose of the boys' presence in their town, the minister led them to the home of a farmer of his congregation. By chance, a kid whom the farmer was expecting for the potato harvest had not arrived, so he hired and housed the two boys from Frost Pound—on faith you might say. One of the boys was tall and strapping, but the little one, Kendrick, the farmer feared, might not be up to the rigors of picking up potatoes in the hot sun, but he took them both into his employ.

There was no digging, no grubbing around in the dirt. A plow contraption running off a tractor PTO turned the soil in the potato rows and an abundance of uniformly medium-sized Maine potatoes were tossed loose upon the sandy loam.

In adjacent fields belonging to other farmers, migrant workers did the same work as my father and Waldo. My father told me that there were Indians from Canada and as far away as Mexico up there and that they gathered the potatoes on their calloused brown knees. Dad had done his share of clamming, so he felt himself more efficient standing bent over. The Indians lived in a Quonset barracks. "You can't have them in your house," the farmer told Kendrick, "they're paid cash, same as you, and those boys spend a lot of theirs on whiskey."

You may wonder if the farmer in my story had a daughter. No, he didn't, he had two daughters. My father thought they were ten and twelve—no temptation of courtship—just as well since Kendrick was always a little shy around girls, anyway.

As the days and weeks progressed Kendrick felt his muscles hardening and his speed in filling the bushel baskets increasing. Up, with the brimming basket, and into the barrel marked Lynn, which when full would go against Kendrick's tally. He thought, I'm the fastest now!

The farmer asked Kendrick and Waldo to attend church with his family and they always went, not having much choice, the minister having gotten them their jobs, and the farmer knowing that the boys had nothing else to do. One Sunday morning the minister preached from Matthew 20, the parable of the workers in the vineyard. Jesus tells of how the owner of the vineyard paid the exact same amount to the workers that joined the crew late in the day as he paid the ones that had toiled since dawn.

A big midday meal always followed Sunday worship. My father said that those folks ate great amounts of vegetables, cabbage and carrots and beets, but that on Sunday there was always fowl or beef. After the meal, my father's pal, Waldo, eagerly awaited a pause in conversation to express something he had been composing in his brain since church.

"I think today I realized for the first time that I truly am a Christian." He looked across the table and met the eyes of the older of the girls. "It was so wonderful that the farmer in that story paid everybody the same. I must say, I love that thought, was greatly moved by it, that our Lord wanted everything to be even."

The older of the daughters, not quite a teenager, looked admiringly at Waldo who was, and is still to this day, handsome by anyone's measure. A Christian man like her papa, she thought, and so good-looking, too. She imagined herself married to the young laborer who chanced to have come into their home.

At the end of two months the boys prepared for their return to Frost Pound. One evening at supper, the farmer, looking in the direction of Kendrick, said, "You boys mind you get that cash home safe." Kendrick had had the same thought and asked the farmer's wife if he could borrow a needle and thread. That evening my father sat in the straight chair in the room he shared with Waldo, and sewed his dollars, all but his share of the gas money, into the lining of his coat. Near bedtime, the younger girl paused at the doorway she knew she was never to enter, and spoke softly to Kendrick. "That's not what the scripture meant, Kendrick, everybody getting the same pay no matter how hard they work. I'm sure of it. Papa thinks it's about when we accept Jesus. You worked hard for that money. It would be so very wrong if you were ashamed of it." And she went on to her own room.

For many months my father's thoughts wandered back to that happy season in Aroostook County and he imagined returning there the following September and seeing the younger daughter. With the potato money he bought his first lobster boat, a sixteen-foot open skiff, the first of a succession of ever larger boats.

He was a fisherman now, hooked into the unbreakable rhythms of that life, and he never picked up another potato. But nine years later, Kendrick drove his own automobile to Blaine and claimed that little girl for his wife, and she is my mother.

Vivien: The end?

Paul: Yeah.

Vivien: Perfect pitch, Piano Tuner.

# Chapter 23
# Ratings

Another Day

Off-Air

On Monday after her show, Vivien popped her head in Austin's office. She had in mind a plausible pretext for their meeting, but she knew it was false.

Ever since the show three weeks ago when the restaurateur, Marcus Deloitte, and her boss, Kathy Hudson, had been her in-studio guests, she had been walking her three-hour shift on eggshells. On that day she had dropped her guard and let a malevolent voice attack Marcus for trading in grocery store chicken, and grossly marking up the wine. That and the clever, but irrelevant poor man's lobster gambit about the monkfish. Marcus had stormed out, and the segment had ended without any peaceful resolution. Peaceful resolutions were what she thought she was good at effectuating, and here she had failed miserably with her own boss and her boss's friend.

This morning she had had a good program that covered Frost Pound's approach to property assessments, the politics that may or may not be involved in the allocation of moorings in the harbor, and the bragging by new people about the properties they have bought from longtime residents. One such newcomer had been overheard in the diner saying, "Of course, everything had to be torn out for us to live in it. Everything needed updating." Right on the air, Vivien had been emphatic in expressing her dismay at the stupidity and tactlessness of such people.

"It was good enough for forty years for those dear people. God bless them," she had said before she finally blurted out advice for such new people. "Just do what you want and shut up about it." She could not remember that she had ever said "shut up" on her program, but this morning it was the only thing that seemed to fit. I am not a wimp, she considered. I am brave enough to ask Austin where I stand.

Austin Hudson was in his accustomed seat behind his big desk. Vivien thought that it was in a college course that she had been told that men sit behind a big desk for power over the other guys in a meeting whose legs must dangle from a straight chair in the middle of the room—the big oak desk an armor and symbol of status. Today Austin rose up and came right around and pointed Vivien to an upholstered side chair and hitched an identical one for himself opposite her.

"I'm so glad you stopped in. We haven't had a chance to talk for quite a while."

Actually, Vivien thought, they had a chance almost every weekday, but she appreciated the kind salutation and relaxed a little into her seat.

"How is it going for you? From the listening I've done, it sounds like you aren't having any trouble filling up the hours, and you're getting plenty of calls. When I'm around town people talk to me about you."

"They do?" Vivien replied.

"Mostly they just smile and shake their heads and say something like, 'That girl you've got on Fred's show is a little different, isn't she?' Kathy and I are both pleased that you are with us, quite pleased really."

Really, Kathy too? Vivien thought. Austin had been economical with his nurture of her and *Now We're Talkin'*, but praise or compliments from Kathy had been non-existent. She is pleased with me, Vivien considered; that's a surprise—a big surprise.

There was a long silence that she imagined any second the man-in-charge would fill, but he just rested in his chair. Austin was looking at her as though she were a friend whose company he could just enjoy without a lot of words.

His appearance seemed different to her. She thought there was light in his eyes and that he was letting her actually see him. His mouth was relaxed and she noticed for the first time his big, slightly crooked teeth. This is an appealing face, she realized, the face of a person content in the work he has found himself in, and something more. She thought that he was perhaps shorter than she might have thought—shorter, but bigger, stronger in his calm.

"I haven't asked you what you wanted to see me about, I'm sorry," Austin said.

"Oh, it's a small thing. We haven't had anyone from the hospital for weeks now, the *Focus on Wellness* segment."

Austin smiled, the teeth showing, and was not quick to respond. "I think we'll have to let that ride for a while and see what happens. Some things have changed. His eyes were still comfortably trained on her as he considered his response. "Kathy has quit the hospital board; she feels as though she should spend time with different friends. She wants to spend more time with *me*, actually."

"I hope—" Vivien started and hesitated, "I wouldn't be surprised if you told me that I've had something to do with it all. I confess I'm headstrong about putting my own mark on the program, but I've always wanted to do that without hurting your business. I admire what you guys are doing here, what you do for the community, and I'd like you to make money at it. Tell me the truth, boss, am I messing things up for you?"

"Do you know what ratings are, Vivien? We subscribe to a bare bones book, we could get a more specialized report, but we're cheap. We've known that your audience was strong and getting stronger from the calls from advertisers. Where in the past I've had to call on every shopkeeper and car dealer, regularly and in person, to sell ads, they're phoning us now. The ratings book just confirmed it. You have more than twice the listeners that Fred Boyland had. That's a huge increase in a market this small. We'd always figured that about everyone sitting at home on weekday mornings who would listen to a local talk show was already listening. We were dead wrong."

Vivien thought that she might be crying and put a hand to her face, but the hand was dry. "Thank you so much for telling me; you didn't have to." She laughed silently and said, "I could ask for a big raise."

"Forget it, no one's irreplaceable. Anyway, in the new friends department—Kathy and I are going away, leaving tomorrow for three or four days. We haven't gone anywhere but station owner conventions for years. We're going to Montreal. Rob Auclair knows how to keep an eye on the transmitter and has the keys to the place. He can fill out the logs and he'll know where to find us in an emergency."

"That's so great. Have a wonderful time."

"We will, you can bet on it."

# Chapter 24
# Please, Something lovely

*. . . opening and theme music and . . .*

Vivien: Good morning, Frost Pound and lovely places along the beautiful coast of Maine. Do you see the days getting longer? Oh, I definitely do. We're home free now, don't you think? Do I seem a little giddy this morning? I bet that I do. Someone has said the loveliest things to me just this morning, some things that I cannot share. Well, that is not very fair of me. It sounds like I am teasing you and I apologize. This much I can say. I was reminded this morning that things are not always as they appear, that sometimes things are way better, way more promising, way lovelier than what we think. I'm being preachy, yeah, I guess. Me, I'm a little dense—blind spots, you could say—and I probably can't help that. But I can choose to see the good, to pursue the good, believing that there is a big, whole forgiving goodness out there that I mostly cannot see. I confess I often fall short, probably most of the time.

Who will call this morning and tell us about something that is lovely and good? Indulge me today while I am floating ten feet off the ground. Perhaps I will have settled closer to earth by the time we return from these brief commercial messages.

*. . . Look for the orange flag on the giant tip-up one mile north of Route 1 on the Fossett Road. Fossett Road Bait and Tackle has the live minnows those brookies are craving this winter, and a great selection of augers in every price range. And, of course, where would we be without our wonderful maggots . . . open seven till noon, now till the end of the month . . .*

Vivien: We're back. What are they charging for maggots, anyway? It can't be easy breeding maggots this time of year, can it? I think we have a call, good morning, you're on with the very foolish Vivien Kindler.

Bobby: Yeah, nothing wrong with trying to concentrate on the good stuff. I'm an ice fisherman. Bobby from Whitefield. People call me Catch and Release Bobby.

Vivien: You catch the fish and let them go. Because you have to, because it's the law?

Bobby: No, you can keep a few a day—I just don't.

Vivien: Why do you think you do it? Why do you ice fish, Bobby? It looks cold out there.

Bobby: Hm-m-m. I just like it. It makes me happy. I drill a hole in the ice and set a tilt and then drag my sled to another spot. I may nod to another man on the lake, but none of us talk much out there. We know how to dress for it, so we can stay out there longer than we really need to. There's a lot of just looking around and enjoying being in the outdoors. Maybe somebody has to have taught you the ice fishing ways.

Vivien: Someone taught you then?

Bobby: My dad. Sixty years ago. I'm seventy. I think that's a part of it. I thought of Dad out on the lake this morning—like I was a kid still and he was there with me. He always told me to hush—said the frozen lake was not a place for a lot of talk.

Vivien: Unlike this program, Bobby. We're all about talk—and you called us anyway. How about that?

Bobby: You're all right, Vivien. You wanted to hear about something nice and fishing is the best thing I've come across in this lifetime. I don't think many children fish anymore. It's all old men out on our lake. I want to say to dads that might be listening, or grampas, or moms for that matter, go up to Fossetts and buy the bare basics, and take a kid ice fishing. You won't regret it.

Vivien: Thank you, Catch and Release Bobby. We've got another call.

Caller: Am I up?

Vivien: Yup, tell me something lovely.

Caller: You're not from here, Vivien, but maybe you know that we call lobstering fishin'. Well, we do because it is fishing—fishing for crustaceans in salt water with a trap, not a hook, but fishing just the same. I've thought a lot about something that I haven't figured out. A boy can sit for hours on the bank of a pond staring at a red and white bobber, thinking that any second a giant bass is going to pull it under, and that boy is contented. What is that all about, Vivien?

Vivien: You've been pondering it, Caller, as *Bert and I* would say. What do you think it's about?

Caller: This is what I've got so far: the imagination, the anticipation, the wonder.

Vivien: I like it very much—the economy of words. You must have heard Bobby a few minutes ago. Out on the lake sixty years ago, his father told him to keep quiet. A harsh teacher, perhaps, who knows. Do you think Bobby was indoctrinated with the silence principle or is something else going on?

Caller: Something else. The wonder part. Every year I go hauling, fishing, with a lobsterman friend of mine. Here's something that I have noticed. This guy has been doing this for about 35 or 40 years, right? Well, I have watched my friend. Every time a trap breaks the surface, is grabbed and brought over the side of the boat, there is the same expression on my friend's face. It's part anticipation, what will be in the trap, how many, how big, how many dollars does that convert to; but I think it's something else, the piece I call the wonder. It's the same as the kid staring at the red and white bobber—it's spiritual. I've got to go. (click)

Vivien: That's some fine ponderin', Friend. Call again. We have somebody else on the line. Good morning.

Brownie:
    This is a little rough, I rushed it. (pause)

Red Flannel Shirt

You were not angry any of the three times in one day that
I cast the mackerel jig into your new flannel shirt.
I held back tears in the bow where you had set me.
Yes—you had told me when to slide my index finger off the
line where I had it pressed against the cork of the rod,
And how to point the tip of the pole toward the sea
on the starboard side.
I couldn't do it; it was my fault—not yours.
It was not easy unsnagging all the little hooks from your shirt.
You kept giving me another try!
You were less tolerant about the keeping of the fish.
You made me stop at six because a man always eats
what he catches. "It's a rule."
I didn't mind at all: it's the way you were and
I believed you because I loved you so much.
When we got home, you demonstrated on mackerel #1:
"Okay, pay attention, Son. Forward from his anus,
stick in the knife and slit it open and scoop out
all the guts in one quick motion.
Here, Son, just behind this fin—chop his head right off.
You're lucky there aren't scales on mackerel—makes it easy.
If you can kill him, you can clean him."
I was seven and tender and crying again: I remember.
But I didn't mind because I loved you so much.
Maybe my hands were not strong enough for the
cutting off the head part, and I failed and
you said we just wouldn't go fishing anymore,
but you forgave me, and we went out in your little boat,
again and again.
It was a wonder.
We're alike: stubborn about the important things.

Forgive me, Daddy.

(Brownie hangs up, and Vivien is silent)

Vivien: Ah, Brownie, you never disappoint. Let's take a commercial break.

*. . . a Chrysler and Jeep spot . . .*

Yes, Vivien thought, we really are getting more and more ads—and I'm talking less—nothing wrong with that.

Vivien: We're back and we have another call.

Marie Scanlon: Yes, Miss Kindler. Just this, the poem this morning was a lovely thing. Your Brownie is a talented boy, to be sure. I am so glad he is still writing.

Vivien: As a teacher of poetry, what about it—oh, I think she rang off. Please call again, Miss Scanlon.

### Off-Air

Marie Scanlon turned off her radio and poured her fifth cup of coffee from a now-empty carafe as she sat at the kitchen table in her one-bedroom, in-town condominium. That poet, Brownie, was definitely a boy of this town, she thought, as to persuade herself of the conclusion at which she had already arrived. He knows our corner of the world.

When her school teaching abruptly ended, Marie had treated herself to this apartment with its long eastern view up the salt bay, and this morning, the March sun had not yet swung past her big window. Sometimes she suntanned there. She hoped that it worked, tanning through the glass, but no one had ever told her that it was possible. It felt so nice, anyway.

The syntax of his radio poems is the same, that and the childlike, always seeking and questioning free verse that endeared him to her twenty years ago. The gentle humility that caused her to fear for him; it was unmistakable. It was he.

Dare she see him now and risk upsetting a long ago, happy place in his imagination, a place that may have nurtured his lovely gift? Is it selfish, Marie asked herself, to think that it was special for any of them? It was for her—thrilling, Miss Scanlon and those boys, mostly in twos and threes—they unconscious of their power and beauty those afternoons they parsed the subversive lines.

She wasn't truly so very ravaged by age and drink. That was just a sassy device the anonymity of the radio employed for fun. I am an old woman, though, Marie thought. How will I look to him?

Marie daily dressed now as she did then, presenting herself Bohemian to dear Frost Pound, telling them in her way that she had been places that they had not.

She thought she could do it. She glanced at herself in the hall mirror. She had walked that way on purpose. Not gruesome, she judged. It won't be awful for him. He will not think meeting Miss Scanlon at her house a seduction. It will not even occur to him. At least I have not gone to fat.

The close-fitting shirts and sweaters from thrift shops have piled up, indistinguishable one decade to the next; and long slinky skirts, and the twenty silver bangle bracelets on her right forearm. "How can you teach with all that clanging and ringing?" other lady teachers had asked. They could not deter Miss Scanlon from the small ways she showed herself different.

Marie never bought anything by mail order. She had never expressed it to anyone, but she thought that buying things that way would in her subconscious, brand her a materialist—an indelible, itching sore. But the plan taking shape would require her to make an exception.

Wine, she decided. Order something I would buy anyway, but this one time delivered to my door. Perhaps treat myself to a case of sauvignon blanc, and a little pricier than my usual. Why not?

## On-Air

Vivien: We have another call.

Caller: You haven't said anything about the ad in the paper.

Vivien: No, I haven't seen the paper. Did you hear that lovely poem about a boy fishing with his father?

Caller: What's going to happen on Thursday? Can the sheriff stop it?

Vivien: I don't know what you're talking about.

Caller: There's a big ad, half a page, in the third section of *The Gazette*. You really don't know about it? I didn't mean to be the one to tell. I thought that's what everyone would be calling about today. I can call another time. (click)

Vivien: I am at a loss. Our news director, Rob Auclair, on the other side of the glass is holding up a folded section of newspaper. Do you want to bring it to me, Rob, yeah, sure, bring it in, let's see what all the excitement's about.

There are several seconds of dead air while Rob swings around the hallway and enters Vivien's studio with the newspaper.

Vivien: (rustling paper) Okay, this is today's paper, Section C, page 7, the whole half page above the fold. It reads: **Our sacred honor, if not now, when**, question mark. **If not us, who**, question mark. **For such a time as this**. A mixture of patriotism and Bible. Powerful stuff. **Come and join local icon Fred Boyland for a historic day in Frost Pound. Time: Thursday, 10:00 am. Place: the parking lot at radio station WNWT, Frost Pound, Maine.** That's all in big bold type, this really is a whole half page. And there follows what appears to be an unattributed quotation: Quote, *This abomination cannot stand. Our once honored local talk show has become a pathetic talent parade of corny stories and bad poetry. What was a lively and incisive discussion of the news of the day has become a vulgar and cringeworthy probing of the private thoughts and prejudices of vulnerable callers. War rages in the Middle East, spending explodes through the roof, all unnoticed by Vivien Kindler, an egomaniacal fill-in host, dangerously exploiting an ever-shrinking audience.* Closed quote.

Then this at the bottom in a smaller, italic typeface: *Fred Boyland will personally be on hand to meet with old radio friends.*

Well, I was having such a nice morning, egomaniacally chatting about fishing. So, it's to be this Thursday at ten. This will be interesting. I hardly know what to say. Oh, good, someone else may bail me out. Good morning.

Caller: Yeah, it's me again. I was the one that called before, and you hadn't seen the ad in the paper yet, so I hung up.

Vivien: And now you're back. (uncomfortable silence)

Caller: Am I still on?

Vivien: You are. Will you be coming to the party on Thursday?

Caller: No, maybe, I don't know. I asked what you were going to do, before, when I called before.

Vivien: To answer you honestly, which is difficult at the moment, the words coming into my mind are all nasty and smart aleck. I guess I will just do what they pay me for and do the show like any other day.

Caller: Really? I've never been to the station before. Will you be able to look out a window and see the mob out there? Can you just keep talking like everything's normal with an angry mob tromping around outside the station?

Vivien: Oh, my, they will be tromping? Yes, I think I can, unless of course I see them coming over the barricades with the sounds of angry men.

Caller: Really, are the guys that own the station going to put up barricades?

Vivien: (remembering that Austin and Kathy are in Montreal) No, I definitely think that they will not. Anything else, Caller? I fear I haven't drawn a very exciting picture of the horrible confrontation destined for Thursday—underestimating it, perhaps.

Caller: Yeah, one other thing: What do you think of Fred getting dragged into this thing?

Vivien: Regrettable, regrettable on many levels, Fred's unfortunate participation. Perhaps he'll think better of it. Thanks, Caller. Someone else wants to weigh in. Good morning.

George the Welder: You remain calm, Vivien. Something tells me that you won't be too scared.

Vivien: Good morning, George the Welder. A welcome voice. How are you, good friend?

George: I will not be mounting the barricades from either front, being more nearly in the condition of one who has already seen too many battles.

Vivien: We would not ask you to take sides, George. It's sunny today, are you in your garden?

George: Today I am dressed for easy access for the medical professionals who will be along shortly, followed by a visit from Father Murphy.

Vivien: Are you ailing today, George the Welder? None of my business?

George: No, it's okay. I'm dying, actually. Not today, but I am surely on an inevitable program.

Vivien: Oh, George.

George: I shocked you, of course. There was no avoiding it. I called because I was feeling so good about something and I want you to be my soldier-in-arms.

Vivien: I'm in. Sign me up.

George: Good, this is it: I am not afraid. It is vanity; there's no getting around that. Let me explain it to you. Just to you, and to Rob Auclair—I think he's there.

I have known for years that a common problem that comes with the kind of diabetes I have is kidney failure. For months I have experienced the worsening of that in symptoms you and Rob Auclair don't want to hear, and then the doctors explained to me the likely course of my decline—they didn't call it that—and that dialysis was an option. I have always thought about myself that I was a brave man, but to be confronted with death and to realize that I am not afraid, I am strangely happy about it. Do you see, it turns out I do have courage.

Vivien: I hear you, me and Rob Auclair in the news department, and I will think about it some more when I get home. You see, George the Welder, there are some callers that I stay engaged with even after we go off the air. Did you know that, George the Welder? So, are you having the dialysis?

George: No. That's part of it. No one said that I can get well or even ward off death for very long, so I am refusing all treatment. I'd rather not put the system to the expense. We'll see about the palliatives. I think that near the end, that ends up being out of my hands, right? So, Thursday, you're apparently going to have your own skirmish and I am here to help you while I still can.

Vivien: How will you help me, George? I know that you will.

George: Just this: Be not afraid. Have it ring in your head for three days, whenever you feel the uncomfortable anxiety creeping in. Hear it: Be not afraid!

Vivien: Be not afraid. I promise. You know you have taken my breath way. But you're okay?

George: I listen to this show almost every day, all three hours, and I have learned a lot and I thank you. I hear your voice and though we have never met, I see you in my mind's eye and have enjoyed you as a friend. I warm to the sound of your voice. I think I told you before that I am good with voices.

(long pause)

Vivien: (through tears) I have valued you, George, even if at first you pushed me away. How could I know back then how wonderful you are?

George: I'm brave, but still needing courage for some things that there aren't doctors for. That's for another day. My wife informs me that clergy are in the house. I'm going to go now. Another day. I'll be around for a while still.

Vivien: Another day, friend. Let's take a break.

It's not time for the weather, but Vivien hits a button for the same forecast that played only minutes before.

*. . . "Everybody's Talkin'" potting down . . .*

Vivien: We're back. You're going to have to help me this morning, friends. If you were listening before the break you know that I've had a shock. Good, we've got a call. Good morning.

Lorna Paige: Hi, you don't know me. I'm Lorna. I don't know if you remember helping me get the mums from in front of the town hall? Well, you did. They're resting in my cellar right now, but I know how to bring them back in the spring. I've done it before lots of times. They say I have a green thumb.

Vivien: Good for you, Lorna. I remember. That's a nice gift to have, isn't it, knowing how to grow plants and flowers? I'm no good at it.

Lorna: What part are you bad at?

Vivien: I'm good at watering and the application of small amounts of Miracle-Gro. If I get any bugs or fungus or any kind of wilting, I'm sunk.

Lorna: Just so you know—I'm not against Miracle-Gro. Everybody up here is against it. I don't care, I think it works pretty good. You just drive by my place and look at the flowers in my windows and you'll see.

Vivien: Good for you, Lorna. The proof is in the pudding. Why have you called the *Talk Show* this morning?

Lorna: Oh, I heard about the big thing Thursday that was in the paper. I didn't read it—I don't get the paper. I just heard about it on your show.

Vivien: Don't worry about it, Lorna. You just keep doing what you are doing, okay?

Lorna: What do you think I can do for you? You helped me.

Vivien: (a little laugh) I don't know. Maybe bring flowers.

Lorna: Sure, I've got tons of flowers. I'll bring some flowers. I'm gonna go now, if that's okay?

Vivien: Of course, thanks for calling, Lorna. And we have another call, too. Good morning.

JJ's Mom: Good morning to you, Miss Kindler. Good morning even if there's trouble in the world with people stirring things up for no good reason. I don't know, no, I really don't.

Vivien: Is this JJ's Mom? It's good to hear your voice. Are you coming to the big party on Thursday?

JJ's Mom: I think you're teasing an old woman, and that's probably a good thing that you can make jokes at a time like this. No, I can't come. I still have my car, but I don't drive too far from the house these days. To the market, mostly. There's so many young people going so fast out there nowadays. I don't need to tell you.

Vivien: And it's pretty cold out there, too. You stay cozy at home with that sweet dog. I'll be fine.

JJ's Mom: I'm praying for you, Miss Kindler, that's what I called for, just to tell you that I'm praying for you all the time. I've got your name written down right here at the kitchen table to remind me. Here it is: pray for Miss Kindler.

Vivien: Thank you. Oh, she's gone, the board is lighting up this morning. Good morning, you're on with Vivien Kindler.

Milt Fossel: Hey, Vivien Kindler. This is Milt Fossel, Frost Pound's First Selectman. You've presented our bare-bones local government with a whole new set of problems.

Vivien: Yeah, I've really done it now, Mr. First Selectman.

Milt: You know I'm kidding.

Vivien: Yes, I could tell.

Milt: I've been aware of this demonstration set for Thursday. A citizen came in late last week and inquired as to whether a permit was needed in Frost Pound for a demonstration. No, it isn't. We've never had a demonstration before and we have no ordinance governing such things.

Vivien: Pass one, quick!

Milt: (laughing) You know we don't move that fast around here. No. I just thought I'd drive by from time to time on Thursday and you can have someone phone me if anything comes up you need help with. I asked the young man that answered the phone at your main number if I could come by and have a visit this afternoon with Mr. Hudson, but I guess that's not going to work out.

Vivien: Thanks for that, we'll be fine.

Milt: I told the protest organizer that they can't rally on your private property, so they've agreed to stay down on the street. It's narrow, but there aren't many cars.

Vivien: They'd be safer here in the parking lot. I don't think we should expect chaos. I just wish they were coming today and getting it over with. I don't look forward to thinking about this for three days, if you know what I mean, but I guess they need time to make the placards and such.

Milt: Woman said it was a peaceful demonstration, First Amendment rights, will of the people, disruptive changes to our way of life, that sort of thing. Tell Mr. Hudson to phone me if you need help, and he can call the sheriff's office, too.

Vivien: Thanks for that. They should really use the parking lot— we'll be okay.

Milt: I expect you will. Stay in touch.

Vivien: We've got another call. You're on *Now We're Talkin'* with the disrupter of our whole way of life.

Caller: Good morning, Miss Kindler. I'm Shirley Brine and I'm a parent-volunteer at the middle school. My daughter is there, eighth grade. The kids are doing a unit on the Bill of Rights and some of us were talking about if this was a learning opportunity for the kids, to see a non-violent demonstration going on right in their own town, and if it might be a good idea for a group of us to come on Thursday, just as observers.

Vivien: No, Mrs. Brien, I don't think so. I'm quick with that reaction, aren't I? No, it's not a good idea. You'd be adding to the traffic congestion without much to be learned. I'll tell the kids all about it on the radio. Maybe the kids could listen from in class. I'll be watching it out the window. Yes, follow it on the radio— that would be up to their teacher and the school folks. Please don't bring the children here—not a good idea.

Caller: It's Brine, like salt water, not Brien. I'll tell the others, them and the teacher, what you said. Okay, I'm getting off. Really, I don't see what was such a bad idea about it. Actually, I think you've been kind of nasty to me. (click)

Vivien: Sorry, I usually am a better listener than that. I hope I am. I hope my first reaction was the right one. We've got more calls lined up. Now you're talkin', what have you got for us this morning?

Caller: Hi, am I up? I've been holding for a long time. I'll be quick, maybe you've got other calls. The food—could I bring sandwiches for Fred's people? Are they going to be out there for two hours or more with no refreshments? I could swing by the Quik-Mart and get some grinders. I'll spend my own money. It's nothing. Would that be good, you know, helpful, supporting the town and all?

Vivien: It's a free country, Caller, as they say. We're out of time for now, gotta run. Be with us again tomorrow, same time, same channel.

# Chapter 25
# Assist in Living

### After the show

Vivien was spinning. Fred's demonstration was the least of it, a ridiculous and undeserved anomaly; but she was pretty sure that composure and common sense would get her through it. But the thing with George was different.

Nothing ever said or done on her radio program had thrown her like that: George the Welder saying that he was dying. It wasn't a metaphor or a veiled cry for help. He would have needed to have made up the amputation of the missing leg and the diabetes and the kidney failure. No one would have kept up a story like that for all these months—right up to refusing dialysis to save the system the money.

Vivien got herself out of the studio and sat in the radio station lobby with her coat on and didn't know what she would do. She said to herself what she had only before considered transiently: her world of intermittent and brief contacts on the radio was an illusion. She had never even seen the face of JJ's Mom, or George, or Brownie—him scarcely real enough for even a radio family—little more than a cipher. They all dropped in at their pleasure, and at her pleasure, during the three hours Monday through Friday when she needed them. And if they should be dying, she did not have permission to find them or phone them.

Radio George was dying, not just from nine till noon, but twenty-four/seven, and for good, and there seemed no crossing into his world. And she loved him.

Vivien realized that she had almost no acquaintance with death or dying. What was that woman's name from the assisted living place who was so nice? Vivien snuck back into the studio where the young afternoon disc jockey was at the console queuing up his playlist.

"I forgot my notebook, Sean, it's there by your feet. Thanks." Back in the lobby she thumbed through the last pages. There it was, Deborah Henrichon, Boothby Cove Assisted Living. She was really nice, she won't mind, I'll call her from home.

When Vivien pulled in her long gravel driveway, she saw that there was an old gray Subaru parked in her dooryard. A young man in a coat and tie hopped out of the car to greet her. "Mrs. Kindler, I'm Anthony Pascarelli Jr. from Hughes and Pascarelli Realty. We talked on the phone."

"I'm late, aren't I, Anthony? Have you waited long? I'm so sorry."

She had forgotten the appointment. In a moment of self-pity the previous week, still dwelling on the train wreck with Kathy and Marcus Deloitte, thinking that she was hurting the Hudsons' radio station and might even be fired, the idea of moving away had crept into her head. She didn't have any close friends in Maine and if she had made a hash of the radio job, she'd have to do something different. Why not move?

Austin had put her at ease on that front and she'd laughed at the mental picture of herself alone in a café by the Champs Élysées, and another tableau of Vivien beside a giant fireplace in Colorado or Wyoming wearing an expensive new après ski outfit. She had been relieved that Austin had spared her this ridiculous flight, but she had forgotten to cancel the real estate fellow.

"Anthony, I owe you an apology. I don't think I'm ready to sell just now. I've wasted your time. I'm really very sorry."

"Hey, that's okay. You've got a full plate already. We all know that. How about you show me around, tell me where the land is and sort of where the boundaries are—do you go down to the river? It looks like it. Is that your frontage—wow!"

"Sure, come on in Anthony. I can offer you something to drink, what time is it, too early for wine and beer? I'm going to have a glass of red wine, Anthony. What would you like?"

"I would like the red wine, but you might tell my father and the Board of Realtors. I'm fine, just kidding, sort of. How many bedrooms are there, Mrs. Kindler, and baths?"

"I'm just Vivien, Anthony. Four bedrooms, three and one-half baths, a finished basement, two-car garage. And that little barn is ours, mine, over there. Can you see it? There's a ramp and float at the river, pulled up for the winter. It's tidal like you'd think. We have a little rowing skiff that will float for all but about an hour on either side of low tide. You have to time your outings, but I don't use it much. I'm alone."

"That's what I heard. It's a really nice place."

Still thinking about wasting the ambitious young man's time, she ventured an idea. "Why don't I contract with you to do me an appraisal of the property, then when I am ready to sell, I'll know what I have here. How about that?"

Anthony produced a pad and said, "I pulled the square footage and sketches from the town hall, and I have your assessment for taxes. You don't need to pay us. Your place is worth a lot of money, Vivien. These appraisals the town does are always way lower than the market—not just yours, mostly everybody's, so those numbers don't help that much, but the square footages and that stuff is good."

"Are you allowed to say how much it's worth, just ballpark?"

"Don't hold me to it, I have to research the comps and all that, but it's real nice. It's all about the riverfront."

"*How* nice? Anthony, if you can say?"

"Six or seven hundred thousand—I think; I'd ask my dad."

Vivien never poured her red wine in front of Anthony. This had all transpired quickly and the cute young man left, but she poured it now, fuller than was her custom. She'd left her work notebook on the counter by her purse and she quickly found the number for Boothby Cove Assisted Living. Deborah Henrichon—she could remember the woman's name, could picture her. She'd sat in the studio with this woman to talk about elder issues and had been struck by the woman's calm assurance. There had been the funny business about employing a volunteer who had had a scrape with the law, and Brownie had phoned with a poem about a hospital bed made into a lobster boat.

She dialed. After a long wait, Deborah came to the phone. "Hi, Vivien, sorry that you've held so long. A man from the state was with me and a new resident joined us today and that woman's family are just leaving—crazy."

"Let me know if I've called at a bad time, I just—"

"No, we're good, what's going on?"

"I need someone to talk to about something personal—well, some might say it's not completely personal—I'd have to explain. I know this is short notice, but can I buy you dinner somewhere—tonight, if you can do it?"

"I don't get many invitations. It would be fun. I usually am not free till about seven. Is that okay?"

"Sure, how about the Publick House in Newcastle? Do you go there?"

Deborah said, "It's a favorite haunt of my ex-husband, who has good taste—see you at seven."

"I have one too, an ex with good taste. We have something in common. This is great. Thank you, Deborah, bye-bye."

In the restaurant Vivien had gone ahead and ordered herself a glass of pinot noir and had finished half of it when a hostess led Deborah to the wide doorway into the back dining room. Vivien rose and before Deborah had even taken off her coat gave her a quick hug. "Is a hug all right? I just put my coat over that chair; the hooks over there are pretty full."

"Sure, here's fine." Deborah stuffed a scarf in her coat sleeve and sat opposite Vivien.

Vivien said, "I jumped the gun and got a glass of wine. I'm sorry, you're right on time and I'm ready for another glass—oh, well."

"You're distressed. I told one of our girls I was meeting you and she told me about the ad in the paper promoting a demonstration. Is that worrying you? I wouldn't blame you."

"No. It's something else and it made me think of you. I've been so cryptic, so, I'll just get it out, but we don't have to talk about it if you don't want to. I'm happy just for the good company."

Vivien caught the eye of her waitress. "Oh, good, we'll get you a drink."

The waitress came over and said to Deborah, "Martini, two olives, hold the vermouth?"

"Great," Deborah responded, "and another red wine for my friend."

When the girl departed, Vivien smiled and said, "They know you here."

"It's not as bad as you think. I come here about every two weeks to have something deep fried and a cocktail—or two. You may guess that we don't serve deep-fried fish to our folks at Boothby Cove. As for the martini—it's what Lawrence and I always had here, so it's just a habit, a habit and a pleasant association."

"Is Lawrence your husband."

"Yes, he *was* my husband."

"He's still alive? Stop me if I'm prying."

"You're trained by your work to get to the point quickly. No, I don't mind at all. No, he didn't die. He's splendidly alive. He could walk through the door any moment, actually, in his apricot scarf and all heads would turn. It's really something to see. We split up, it's all good."

"You're further along in getting it all figured out than I," Vivien said.

"I think you said on the phone you have an ex, too. Would you like to talk about that? Is that why you called?"

"Thanks, no. It's something rather more to your professional expertise. Here it is. I have talked to hundreds of people now on my radio program, the one you were on with me. You were in the studio, but mostly I speak with people who have phoned in. I think it would be fair to say that with some of them I have encouraged a kind of intimacy—if not intimacy, certainly transparency. I'm pretty confident that I am not intentionally exploiting anyone. I flatter myself that I am a good listener and that our conversations are positive—for the callers and even for people listening at home and in their cars."

"I'm with you so far, and I believe you. Oh, good, here's my martini, my first one," and she laughed.

"Over the months I've done the show we've attracted several of what in radio they call "the regulars." Today an older man that I have grown to care for, to care for awfully, a regular, told me on the air that he was dying."

"I see. And did you think he was in earnest?"

"Oh, yes, there's no question about it. He has diabetes and kidney failure and I sense that it's bad. He's refusing treatment."

"And you thought of me. I can imagine why. Would you like to ask me something about it?"

"No, I think I wanted to have a drink and sit with somebody who might know how I'm feeling. Selfish of me, perhaps, and you even showed up. I'm so grateful."

"At Boothby Cove we inevitably become experts at death, experts up to the limits of our human understanding. I know I still have a lot to learn. I can tell you some things I think I know—and what I don't know. There are mysteries for sure—some are wonderful."

"Tell me anything, Deb, I'm so sad about this and I'm sure I'm not supposed to just let it go, and I couldn't even if I wanted to."

"The first thing I'm wondering is, will you speak with him again, will he call you?"

"Yes, unless he dies before he calls again. I don't know anything about the specific progress of his disease. Nothing."

"At Boothby Cove, we are what's called "aging in place." I hate to say facility or institution. For the majority of our folks we truly are what used to be called a nursing home. Anyway, aging in place means that families can assume that, if at all possible, their mom or dad is going to die with us. Usually they're not thinking that far out. So, we take on quite a responsibility because we know that we will have tremendous power over vulnerable people. We might exercise that power wisely and kindly, or we could, as you say, exploit. I'll explain the power: our residents are locked within our four walls, we feed them, we bathe them, we control their contact with the outside world, we give them their medications, we talk with them, get to know them, and we sit with them as they are dying."

"I don't even know where George lives," Vivien said. "I can find out. My boss knows who he is. Do you sometimes allow yourself to love them, the people in your care?"

"It's more common that nurses and CNAs get to love them. Yes, all the time. It's what's wonderful and horrible about our work. Last week two such girls drove seven hours to a town in New York State to attend the funeral of a longtime resident. We set ourselves up for real relationship; it's the only way to do the work well, and sometimes what you and I call *love* grows—and we suffer. It's unavoidable, just like you're hurting now."

"Thank you for telling me that. I've just got one guy and your poor kids have it over and over."

"Sometimes they have to quit. I hope you won't. I think you are good at what you're doing on the radio and your vulnerability is one of your strengths. Sounds trite, doesn't it?"

Vivien said, "What should I do?"

"I bet you've made this George love you, too. If you think that you have, you probably need to consider whether you've taken on a responsibility. That's for you to know."

"I understand."

"I thought you were going to buy me dinner," Deborah said.

They laughed. Deborah ordered the fried haddock sandwich that she always had, and Vivien had some doctored-up, broiled oysters from a farm right in Frost Pound. To Vivien they felt like fast friends. The food having made a break from the discussion of death, Vivien dared return to the subject of George the Welder.

"I've wondered if there are legal issues about a radio personality, I'm sorry, that's obnoxious—"

"I haven't been able to listen much, I'm sorry. But the girls say you're a minor sensation."

"There may be a line over which an entertainer, which is sort of what I am, can't step. I will need to talk to my boss about it. I'm sure it's never come up at WNWT."

Deborah replied, "I have a friend who got involved doing volunteer work in a homeless shelter at her church. They never had any formal profiles of the people she and her friends were serving, but over time she concluded that most of them were drug and alcohol abusers, and some were schizophrenics. The church volunteers were full of religious zeal to help the dear souls who turned up in the dark at their door, but just the same, an experienced social worker met with them and told them that they should just tell the guests their first names, and certainly never tell them where they live. It's probably not exactly analogous, but there's the same issue about opening yourself up to strangers."

"No, you're right. It is the same thing. What happened to your friend working in the homeless shelter?"

"She quit it. Actually, they shut down the whole program. Some of the group had crossed the line they were warned about and were driving the men from the shelter around in their own cars, taking them on errands. Eventually they were doing the guys' laundry in their washing machines and even brought the guys home."

"And they thought they were doing the right thing and felt good about it, too, right?"

"Yup," Deborah answered. "It's a classic question which has implications for all kinds of things. Are we supposed to be kind and sacrificial, even when it is dangerous? I'm being heavier than I usually am. You tempted me by asking my opinion on something in my wheelhouse. I hope I won't have ruined your supper."

Vivien said, "You're terrific."

"Tired, and rambling."

"I sort of stepped over the line with you, didn't I, making a personal call to somebody I'd had on the show?"

"Maybe," Deborah replied, "but in our case, you'd actually been with me in person. Have you made an assessment of me on the whackiness scale? Safe for dinner, unsafe for taking laundry home?"

"Yes, I think I did. I assessed that in all likelihood you were too busy to be a stalker."

"Your instincts are excellent. I am a good person, whacky within a healthy range, and too tired to go out looking through people's windows. I walk the short distance from my office to my pretty brick house, and I crash."

Vivien said, "I have a lovely house with a beautiful river view. Alan gave it to me outright when he was going away. I stay up late. I take a nap when I come home from the radio station, so I'm not tired till ten or eleven. Sometimes I'm lonely. You didn't ask that."

"It's mostly how we're individually wired; I think so anyway. I'm not lonely—probably wouldn't be especially, even if I wasn't around lots of people all day, every day. Just me."

"I'm intrigued about Lawrence, Lawrence whose *scarf, it was apricot.*"

Deborah smiled and took the bait. "You're wondering, what happened to our marriage when I seem to still like him? I think this was the problem. I've had a little practice articulating it and this is what I usually say. He was so beguiling and cool that I was too easily tempted into following him. I followed him willingly in everything. It was a fun ride until one day it hit me that he had led me away from that which I wanted most."

Vivien thought she would let that hang, what that thing was. They had just met. "I wasn't beguiled, I was lazy. Alan kept giving and giving and I kept taking and taking—"

"Accepting, and accepting."

"You're kind. I accepted so much, so willingly, that I began to feel like I was just a pile of Alan's gifts. There must be a Vivien under there somewhere."

Deborah said, "Let's have another drink," and they did.

"The radio program has saved me."

With the help of the martinis, Deborah said, "And now you've dug old Vivien out. Have you considered whether you can have Alan back now?"

"It's been months since we've talked. He's in Rhode Island. I doubt that he's lonely, he shouldn't be, but I don't know."

There followed silly talk about whether either of them had girlfriends and Deborah said that if she even had been so inclined, she could not have found seven girls to put in long maroon dresses as bridesmaids. "Me either," Vivien said. "Do you know about these bachelorettes where the bride and her girlfriends go off before the wedding and get drunk at a tacky resort?"

Deborah said, "How's that different from what we're doing right now?" They laughed and ended the evening joyfully, and agreed they should meet again. "You need to phone *me*, Vivien. I'm usually too tired to take any social initiative. I'd enjoy seeing you again, I really would, but you need to phone me."

Vivien thought she had a lead on what to do about George the Welder. She would think about it more in the morning. Pulling into her driveway her headlights glimpsed the $700,000 house that Alan had given her, and Deborah's remark rang in her ears: "Have you considered if you can have him back?" Once indoors, with lights on in her fancy kitchen, she picked up the wine she had not finished with the real estate kid. She went in a drawer for her address book and found Alan's 401 area code, Barrington, Rhode Island, number on a file card. The kitchen stove said it was only 9:27 and he would be up, up even if not alone. She dialed—

"Vivien, what's up?" Alan's voice right away said.

"Hi, you knew it was me?"

"I've got caller ID and it said that it was me calling me and I was sure I hadn't called myself, so it must be Vivien. How are you?"

"Okay, I'd say. It's kind of late. Am I interrupting anything?" She thought she heard noises on the line, but thought they might just be in her own head.

"No. I was watching TV. Are you okay?"

"Yes, I'm okay. It's just this. Today somebody told me the house in Frost Pound, the house you gave me, was worth $700,000." After a silence, she said, "I didn't know."

"So, it's up a little. Good for you, Vivi. I'm glad. It's the waterfront; as they say, they ain't making any more of it."

"You knew?"

"Sure."

Vivien said, "Thank you, Alan. Thank you for everything."

"You're not selling, are you?"

"No, of course not, where would I go? I'll let you go. Good night, thanks for a lot of things, good night."

# Chapter 26
# Tuesday and Wednesday
# before Thursday

Vivien had been slammed out of balance by a remarkable confluence: Fred and his minions planned to lay siege on Thursday; George the Welder announced his imminent death; Deborah wanted to be her non-radio friend; Alan spoke sweetly to her on the phone. And now she needed to do her radio program as if it was just another day.

*. . . So, let's all in unison, and with great enthusiasm, once again* say: *Wow, Now We're Talkin'. Lines are now open at 207 . . .*

Vivien: Good morning, Frost Pound. (long pause) I have been thinking that when I sit down in this little studio and prepare to meet you at nine-o-six, I may wrongly assume a normalcy, a routine in your lives that is not true. It is a small vanity—not a horrific sin, I hope. I admit I am more the center of my universe than I'd like, so I just project the temperature and speed of my life onto yours. I'm okay, so you must be okay, too. That's ridiculous, of course.

I'll elaborate a little. It could be a fruitful start of a conversation. Every once in a while, in my life, I have had days so much longer and more consequential than most of all of the others. Wow, I may have said to myself finally in bed at midnight—bear with me—I'm making this up as I go along, as an example: This morning I was up at 4:30 to phone for the Uber to the airport, I flew from Portland to New York. From La Guardia I found my way to the shop in mid-town Manhattan where a friend said I could buy a smart outfit for the reunion lunch with the college friends. I made it to Lincoln Center for the ballet and had the drinks with the girls in a cool bar on the south end of the park—I think we were on 58th Street—and then I walked alone to the crazy expensive hotel where, blessedly, I now lie. Okay, I made that all up. Lying there in the hotel room, I may feel remorse that I have wasted a lot of other days in which I've accomplished nothing that I can remember, or I may marvel that I have had the stamina to stand up for nineteen hours and successfully walk through the darkness back to the strange hotel. Life is interesting. Some days more than others.

Do you see what I mean? You wouldn't have had to go to New York City or spend a lot of money to have a crazy big day. I'm sure these days happen right here in Frost Pound. I know because I had one yesterday. We have a call. Someone is saving me from myself? Now we're talkin'.

Caller: Good morning. Thank you for taking my call.

Vivien: It's my pleasure. I used to say it more often, but it bears repeating—It's your show, your radio station. I'm the referee. What's up?

Cynthia Moreland: We're doing the Three Town Garden Tour again this year—Frost Pound, Spindleboro, and Pinkham. It's been years. They used to have it every June, but there were problems and it sort of died out.

Vivien: Now you've teased us. What were the troubles? Let me guess so you don't have to be the one to tell: Some rich lady just hired a professional and spent a lot of money and created something fantastic very quickly and everybody was annoyed—

Cynthia: —and none of the plant materials were even remotely native. You may as well have been in Rhode Island or Connecticut.

Vivien: And forsythia. I've heard terrible quarrels over forsythia. The regular ones versus the newer ones with the stronger yellow—

Cynthia: —it can be so overdone, can't it? One gentleman had a fabulous garden, but he'd shorn his forsythia into a very severe hedge and it very nearly disqualified him from selection.

Vivien: Stuff like that—I get it. Anyway, water under the bridge and we're back in business. Forgiveness?

Cynthia: Well, maybe a couple of the more difficult ones are no longer with us?

Vivien: When will it be? June, I bet. I want to come.

Cynthia: Saturday and Sunday, June 9th and 10th. I'll call again with more information when we get closer.

Vivien: How many gardens will there be?

Cynthia: Usually about nine or ten—more in Pinkham than down here, but they don't have our delphiniums—sea air. I'll ring off.

Vivien: I'm definitely going on the garden tour. We have another call.

Caller: Am I up?

Vivien: You're up.

Caller: What happened yesterday that was so big, before the garden woman?

Vivien: Of course—natural that you should ask. It was special and mostly quite personal: I made a wonderful new friend, was caused to worry for another, and was reacquainted with another. I think that more than anything, I attach importance to relationship stuff—just the way I am. You may be different.

Caller: Isn't Thursday going to be even bigger with all Fred's people landing on you? I guess that'll be a day to remember.

Vivien: Well, that's different from what I was talking about. The affair of Thursday, if it happens at all, can only last two hours, right? Didn't the advertisement say that they would bivouac here at ten?

Caller: Yeah, we're coming at ten.

Vivien: What's your name, Caller? I'll give you a shout-out through the window.

Caller: Doesn't sound like you're taking this very serious.

Vivien: Oh, I am, don't worry. If nothing else it's very distracting. Now you've nudged me right back into the distraction again this morning when my mind had somehow briefly taken me to the ballet.

Caller: Aren't you scared?

Vivien: No.

Caller: Do you think the freshwater lobster guy will be there? I know that guy really hates you.

Vivien: I think we'll move on to something else. (She disconnected the call and played the commercials Rob Auclair had queued up for her.)

*. . . Everybody's Talkin' potting down . . .*

Vivien: We're back with more of the *WNWT Talk Show* with Vivien Kindler, and look, we already have a call. Good morning, you're on with Vivien.

Brownie:
    Todd Swallow's Big Day
    Todd Swallow had one crazy, eventful day.
    It was in June when his thoughts always drifted to the sea and the fancy boats of the summer people.

A Saturday, because the boatyard was open till five,
closed on Sundays,
so he dashed down there and bought
the big powerboat he had lately been visiting.
You think that it was just another Saturday,
but hadn't Todd's ancient mom died that very morning?
And on that very same June day, Todd's youngest boy
who managed Earl Johnson's bait shack
said he'd take another crack at college.
"Gram always believed in me,"
Todd's handsome boy had said.
What a day in June that Todd's pretty wife, Laurie Swallow,
came home to give Todd another whirl,
and the pastor called to talk about elevating
Todd to be Deacon Swallow.
"It wasn't your fault, Brother Todd,
that Laurie went away with that lothario Lonnie Wilson."
What a day in June, a wild confluence you might say,
on the very day Edith Swallow finally died,
and left the Two Million. (click)


Vivien: (a long pause) Hysterical, Brownie. And all fiction,
though who wouldn't run off with Lonnie Wilson? We have
another call.


Caller: Yeah, hi, am I up?


Vivien: Yup.


Caller: We were just wondering. Do you think that if there are
enough people there on Thursday, Fred will get his show back?

Vivien: Maybe. We have another call.

Caller: My husband and I saw Fred and his wife in the grocery store last week. He's in a wheelchair and is all tubed up with oxygen and everything. I don't know how he can do the show from that setup, Vivien, do you?

Vivien: He could. I think Charles Krauthammer was paralyzed from the waist down and in a wheelchair all the years he was on TV. We'll see.

## Off-Air

There were other calls in this vein, which ended in a consensus that the demonstration on Thursday would come off without violence. Just the same, no other topic had ever so captured the imagination of her audience.

It's true of humans, Vivien confessed. We can't turn away from a car crash. It's sort of discouraging.

When Vivien ended her shift at noon, she slipped into the newsroom to catch Rob Auclair while the national news was still playing. "Promise me, Rob, you won't call Austin and Kathy about the stupid demonstration. This trip to Canada is very special for them. You and I aren't going to ruin it for them, right? Promise me!"

On Wednesday the young editor of *The Gazette* came looking for Austin Hudson, and finding Austin unavailable, told Rob how sorry he was about the whole kerfuffle with the demonstration. He'd never had an issue like that before and still hadn't figured out what he could have done differently. Rob told the editor, "Thank you. Vivien is unafraid. You sell ads—that's what you do—so do we. Forget it."

When she left at the end of her shift, Vivien could not recall anything about the program just ended, except the repeated references to "Fred's people," and speculation as to their exact number. It was a blur. I had better be well prepared tomorrow, she thought, and she determined to deliver a strong monologue at the top of the nine o'clock hour to get the show off to a smashing start. Maybe that would roll her along till noon.

# Chapter 27
# D- (Demonstration) Day

*. . . Harry Nilsson potting down . . .*

Vivien: Who among us would not like to be skipping over the ocean like a stone, but alas, it is March on the coast of Maine, still cold, and still wonderful.

From early in my childhood the seed catalog has held a special place in my imagination. For most of those years it was Burpee's, more recently I'm getting Johnny's in the mail. I don't know how I got on their list, but I did and am glad of it.

I have to think that the seed catalog people understand some very basic things about us humans. They know that no matter how dinged up we are by life, the great design of summer-fall-winter-spring shapes each of us, just like it does the plants and trees. In mid-January there begins to be more light, and an unseen calendar in the human brain gives off little yellow-green pulses.

We will not be mocked. Tiny and fleeting fragments of hardwired renewal and rebirth pop and recede in our brains. Maybe we think we have grown too cynical to be shaped by them. But, knowing otherwise, the grandees at the seed companies descend the seed catalog staircase with great solemnity, come and stand among the hushed mailroom minions, and declare: "Mail them today!"

For me, spring is spelled L E T T U C E. Lettuce, I am in love with greens—all kinds. If I got a rescue dog, I hope he would be a mesclun mix. From this microphone I have talked about lots of things that I know almost nothing about. I think I usually confess my ignorance, but we've got to fill three hours. Here's something that I do know. Just as soon as you can turn the ground, you should scratch a row and cast half a bag of lettuce seeds. If you mix them in a tin can of sand, they'll distribute more evenly in your row. You need not even cover them. Just spread them on the surface and tamp down the ground with your foot or a short board. Water your row. If it snows and freezes, lettuce seeds are unharmed. They will grow when conditions permit. A side dressing of manure or compost will help. Easy as that, your own salad greens, weeks of them in May and June. I hope you will remember Vivien, the big mouth that finally told you something important. I think we have a call, good morning.

Caller: Yes, good morning. We got a rescue dog from down in Brunswick. I never heard of a muskellunge mix.

Vivien: It was a corny joke, Caller. What did you want to share with us this morning?

Caller: Are they out there yet?

Vivien: Who, out where?

Caller: The protestors.

Vivien: I don't think so. I'll keep an eye out, but in the meantime, let us talk about micro greens.

Caller: We just do zucchini. Some years the wife does tomatoes in a tub on the deck. When do you think they'll start to get there?

Vivien: The tomatoes? I think we have another call, now we're talkin'.

JJ's Mom: Good morning, Miss Kindler. You really can't beat a Jack Russell, no, you really can't. Maybe some men need a big dog for bird hunting or something, I don't know. I could never see the sense in killing those beautiful pheasants, can you, Miss Kindler? I don't know. Fred said the state grows them and lets them loose in special places where the hunters like to go. My husband has seen them standing on the side of the road, looking around confused because they were just dropped off. That's what he thought was going on. I don't know. Fred knew a lot about hunting. People liked that about Fred, that he liked the same things as them. Maybe that's why Fred called himself the voice of the common man. I don't know, it just never made sense to me, but who am I to judge? I don't want to be judged and I bet you don't either, Miss Kindler, no, nobody likes that, no they don't.

Vivien: How about you, JJ's Mom, do you have a green thumb?

JJ's Mom: A green thumb? No, I wouldn't say that. No. I do pretty good with African violets. I've got some in our living room. They look nice on my mother's lace doily in the parlor. Do you have antimacassars, Miss Kindler? I don't think modern girls use them much anymore. I guess when the arms on their chairs are worn through, they just go out and buy new chairs. That's the way now, isn't it? I guess it is. They call it a throw-away society.

Vivien: I'm sure your violets are beautiful. I bet there's a knack for taking good care of them. Good for you. No vegetables?

JJ's Mom: I was just calling this morning to make sure you are all right down there. Are there any of those foolish protestors there yet? It's not even ten, so I suppose it's quiet still. I'm going to go and just follow it all on the radio.

Vivien: I'm fine. A friend told me not to be afraid and I am happy to say it's working because I am just fine, JJ's Mom. We have another call. Good morning, you're on the *Talk Show*. Can you turn your radio down, please?

Shirley Brine: Miss Kindler, this is Shirley Brine. We spoke the other day about the middle school kids and their Bill of Rights project. We're down here in one of the portables and we've got a good radio set up and the kids are going to take notes. You said you'd look out the window and tell the kids what a real non-violent demonstration looks like, so we're all here. Hold on a second, okay, Miss Kindler, the kids have something special for you, okay, one, two, three—

The Middle School Kids: (loudly, the whole class)—Wow, Now We're Talkin'!

Vivien: Thank you guys. I guess I did promise a blow-by-blow, didn't I? Okay, I'm looking now, even though I wanted to talk about lettuce. There are two cars in the parking lot, and so far, the drivers appear to be staying in their cars. I'll keep you informed. Okay, this must be it, the beginning of the non-violent protest. A fellow is out of his car now and is going into his backseat. He's getting out what appears to be a sign. It's upside down, leaning on his car right now, and he's sort of standing in front of it, so I can't read it, but it's black magic marker on a big poster board nailed to a stick. We're going to break for the news and weather right now, but we'll be back. We're stuck here, right? So far, we're holding our own.

*. . . national news followed by the local news read by Rob Auclair, and the weather . . .*

It's 10:06 when Vivien returns to her microphone.

Vivien: We're back, as they say in radio. I may resort to hackneyed expressions this morning because of the unusual circumstances. I'll be a little off my game.

I hope, Frost Pound, Maine, you will phone me this March morning to talk about your seed orders, your seed orders or any gardening issues. We've not even touched on the difference between the leaf and the heading varieties. I really need your help in vamping through the next couple of hours.

The call screen is blank.

Vivien: I'll fill in with the play-by-play I promised the kids. It's overcast here as it likely is where you live, also. I think I've spotted random snowflakes flying, but not much. It's cold enough for the snow to stick if it amounts to anything, but I don't believe a serious accumulation is expected.

There are five cars now. The man with the sign on a stick is closest to me. He's out of his car and has been walking in a tight circle in the parking lot, sort of pumping his sign up and down, I guess to draw attention to it. We have a call. You're on with Vivien.

Student: Mrs. Kindler, this is Tammy. I'm an eighth grader at the Middle School and we're following the demonstration for our 1st Amendment unit—well, actually, the whole Bill of Rights, the whole Constitution—anyway, what does the sign say—what's written on the man's sign?

Vivien: I hoped you wouldn't ask. Uhhh, well, it's what you would call an epithet. It starts with a made-up word that's a combination of the state that Vivien moved to Maine from, the state that Maine used to be part of, combined with a common swear word that is a body part. Then after the vulgar epithet, the words, **go home**. So, it's blank, go home. That's the best I can do.

Student: Is that the only sign? (laughing and snickering in the background)

Vivien: No, there are three other men and they have signs that look more professionally made. One says, **Rip It From the Headlines**, and another one says, **The Fred Boyland Show.**

Student: I'm handing the phone to Marcie.

Marcie: This is Marcie. We heard you think people should say their name and we voted on it and you won. That was Dawn before, she forgot to say her name. So, okay, outside, are they shouting or anything?

Vivien: The man with the vulgar sign is shouting, sort of yelling into the sky to no one in particular, but I can't make out the words through the window, which is fine. (click) Marcie's off, we have another call.

Caller: Yes, thank you for taking my call. I was wondering, do you prefer the sugar and butter, you know, the multi-colored corn, or the all-white, or all yellow? I'm older than you, so I remember when we just had Golden Bantam—all yellow. Maybe that would be a good conversation starter. I thought I'd, you know, help. I'll hang up and listen on the radio. (click)

Vivien: Thank you, friend. Plain white for me, but the freshness is really the main thing, isn't it? Sometimes with the sugar and butter the kernels are so lush and deep that one ear is like a whole meal. Do you know what I mean? I like it fine, but isn't it a whole different experience?

I'm taking you outside again now. An older pink Cadillac, like you'd have if you were selling Mary Kay—it has pulled up now and has attracted the attention of the crowd. Crowd is probably an exaggeration. There are about eight people. They've all turned towards the Cadillac and put their signs down and are clapping and cheering. They really are full of enthusiasm. Okay, one man has gotten into his car and has turned his radio up very loud. I think I am hearing my own voice. Yeah, he's tuned to our frequency and is blasting *Now We're Talkin'* all over the neighborhood, except that there are no other buildings out here, blessedly, no actual neighborhood in which to have a beautiful day. Oh, my. He's approached my big window and is giving Vivien a sign with his hand. He's pulled down four of his fingers leaving one sticking up—perhaps you've seen this gesture elsewhere.

Rob Auclair has come into Vivien's studio and whispers to her, "Are you okay? I can call the sheriff."

Vivien: (Vivien shook her head) Everything is cool, kids. The 1st Amendment is alive and well. The woman driving the Cadillac has gotten out and she has gone around to the passenger side, which is out of my view, and opened that door. It looks like she is speaking to the person in the front passenger seat. Now she is going to the trunk. One of the other picketers is helping her. Oh, yes, I see. They have taken a wheelchair out of the trunk and between the two of them have gotten it spread apart properly and have wheeled it around out of my sight. (long pause)

Will anyone weigh in on the bi-color corn issue? I guess not? (pause)

Well, there is a man in the wheelchair now and they've put a small oxygen—I assume it's oxygen—but that's not very good reporting, is it, a tank, a canister of some kind, mounted on the back of the wheelchair, and the woman has pushed him a little closer to our building. The protesters are really whooping it up, now. They have formed a pretty tight circle around the man in the wheelchair and their signs are bouncing skyward in remarkable unison, and my voice over their car radio is blaring obnoxiously everywhere. I may be encouraging them, yup, I've just gotten another vulgar finger thing. I'd rather not be telling you that, but I promised the play-by-play. I think I'll drop it for a while, they're hearing everything I say, you know, to let the temperature drop a little. We'll be right back.

*. . . three car dealership commercials in a row . . .*

Vivien: We're back. This is what Johnny's says about the variety called Double Standard. "Open-pollinated bi-color sweet corn."

That's the term I couldn't think of, bi-colored. "Early maturing, with strong germination in cool soil. We developed this hardy corn for northern home gardeners, especially seed-saving enthusiasts. It is based on a nice yellow corn called Burnell that was grown in Maine in the early 1900s." Would any of our listeners like more information on the bi-color offerings?

I'm looking out the window again now, in case the middle schoolers are still tuned in. The protestors, all men except the lady manning the wheelchair, are all now holding something wrapped up in white paper, and one of them has unwrapped his and is taking a bite. There are some high fives and there is, I would say, from this safe distance, a general atmosphere of jubilation.

Another car has just pulled in. (long pause) It's an older American mid-size sedan, two-door, and a color you don't see often. Sort of a flat blue-green. Okay. Someone's getting out. It's a woman, small, older I would say, and she has a little dog on a leash. She is approaching the cluster of men. The dog, it might be a Jack Russell terrier, is straining at its leash and barking like crazy. Can you hear it? I can hear it through the glass.

Geez, she's picked up the dog which is trying to escape her grasp, but it's little and she's controlling it, but she's right on top of the men and is yelling at them, and the dog is barking furiously. The men have spread out a little, but she and the dog approach the men individually and the woman is waving one free arm at a man. Waving at each of them to get out, get going—that's what it seems like, like she's telling them to scram. She is insistent. The woman and the dog have backed one guy all the way to his car and he has shut the car door now. (pause) He's rolling, yup, *that* guy is leaving. She's right in the face of two more of them, and seems like she's letting the pup almost bite them. I think the dog did just nip that guy, but she has the dog under control, generally speaking.

The man in the wheelchair is just watching the show, and the woman who brought him is standing next to the wheelchair holding one of the subs. I don't know what people in Maine call them—hoagies, subs, grinders?

The woman with the snarling dog has attacked and rebuffed all of them now, fearless you would say, and they've almost all gotten in their cars. (a long pause)

I think the woman is getting back in the Ford Taurus, or whatever it is. Other than the pink Cadillac, the parking lot is empty except for where Rob and I park over on one end. She may be having trouble maneuvering her way back to the street. There she goes, wow! She's gone. That was interesting—Lone Ranger.

Okay, here are the cavalry, too late for the excitement. A white sheriff's vehicle, an SUV, is rolling through. He has slowed near the man in the wheelchair and his guardian. The officer rolls down the window, presumably to speak to the man in the wheelchair, okay, I think we have another call. You're on.

Caller: Hi, I'm one of the middle schoolers, Christine. Is the man in the wheelchair Fred Boyland?

Vivien: Do you think so? I can't say that for certain. I've never met him.

Christine: It must be. We all think it's him—Fred. (click)

Vivien: The sheriff or maybe deputy sheriff—he's rolling back to the street now. He's stopped at the street. (long pause) I think he's leaving, yeah, he's heading out. We have a call. You're on the air.

Caller: I have something. American bald eagle just flew over my farm.

Vivien: Wonderful. Where are you?

Caller: Up on the old Carter road.

Vivien: I've never seen one. I hope I will—maybe tomorrow.

Caller: You'll prob'bly see him. I think I only winged him. (click)

Vivien: I think that was supposed to be funny. It was to me. It has started to snow a little harder. The demonstrators have all left, kids. Maybe it's just as well, you probably need to get on to another class. I'm afraid the wheelchair couple are still out there and are getting snowed on. Okay, this is good. The woman has brought a plaid blanket from the Cadillac and is winding it around the man. I wish they would get back in their car, though. It's too cold to be out there. I think we have another call. Good morning, you're on with Vivien.

Brownie:
    Work, Work, Work
    Work, work, work.
    Of eating and sleeping and love-making, we will tire,
    But work: long hours of that, we creatures can surely do.
    Consider the ant hill that some laughing child destroys—
    just for the fun of it.
    Back to work the workers go, to put it right again.

The Queen must be served!
Or the hornets when the woman with the green garden hose
knocks down their perfect, silver orb.
Two of them swoop around and give her neck
a warning sting and tomorrow rebuild under the eaves
over the bathroom window.
Or the groundhog who finds her hole by the
squash vines filled with rocks.
No matter; did they think I did not give myself
an escape route?
Up and out I'll crawl this afternoon—
see my twilight shadow,
dust off my heels and go back to work.
Or the beaver when the uniformed men
from the State tear out his dam.
Don't they think at nightfall I will go to the soft alders and
begin to put it back?
I can work all night, can't I? And the next night, too.
But consider the wretched human whose work is to
Talk, talk, talk.
From his workplace, the man, they lock, lock, lock.
He only wants to work, work, work;
Talk, talk, talk, to his tiny Maine town
or the whole damn nation
Consider the grief, the frus, frus—tration.
(long silence)


Vivien: Oh, Brownie. We need to take a commercial break.

*. . . commercials . . .*

Vivien: It's snowing harder now, guys. Another car is pulling in, an older Subaru. It's pulling up close to our friend in the wheelchair, who some have speculated may be Fred Boyland who was briefly referenced in the big newspaper advertisement. The woman driver is getting out. She is going into her back seat to get something. (pause) I think it's flowers—a big bouquet of them. It is flowers. She is walking toward the old couple. She kneels to speak to the man in the wheelchair. The man reaches his arms out from under the plaid blanket to grab the woman's arms—the woman with the flowers—and he pulls her to himself for a small embrace. That's it. (pause) It looks like she is leaving—she is, there she goes.

Right over the air Vivien speaks to Rob Auclair, who has kept a close eye on her from the other side of the glass.

Vivien: Rob, I'm trying to get the attention of our news director. Rob, would you come around here and spell me for a few minutes? There's something that I need to do and we're not quite up against the eleven o'clock news. Yeah, right now, if you can, great.

## Off-Air

Rob comes around and takes the seat she has left to put on her coat. He puts on her headset.

"I'll be right back, I think, I'm just going outside for a minute," Vivien said. Rob, unprepared for talk, and with no callers on hold, decides to play *Daylight* by Maroon Five that will get him to the top of the hour.

Vivien was not prepared for the pathetic sight of Fred Boyland, close up, snow on his thin hair and eyebrows, his mouth sagging out of symmetry, a bouquet of geraniums in his lap.

Vivien looked into the eyes of the old woman and said, "Are you Mrs. Boyland?"

"Yes, come on Freddie, I think we need to go now, don't you?"

"Fred," Vivien said, "if it's okay with you, I've had an idea. Would you come inside for a little, get out of the snow. Our listeners all know you're out here, maybe some of them would like to hear from you. Come on inside, Mrs. Boyland," and Vivien began pushing Fred's wheelchair toward the station entrance. "Come on, this will be nice. You've come all the way down here."

The stuff that ran from the top of the hour till six past was playing now—almost on autopilot, and Rob had come to the front hall to meet the trio at the door. "Rob," Vivien said, "would you help me get Fred into the studio; we'll need to move some chairs out of there to get him close to a mic. This will be great. We'll make a seat for you in there, too, Mrs. Boyland."

"No, no. Freddie, do you want to do this, you don't have to? We can just go home."

Fred didn't answer. The furniture rearranging was accomplished to make room for a wheelchair, and Rob helped with the headphones, whose wires competed with the oxygen line. All this was accomplished barely in time as the *Now We're Talkin'* intro and music played . . .

## On-Air

Vivien: Good morning, Frost Pound and surrounding villages on the Mid-coast. We have a very special guest with us in-studio for the third hour of the *WNWT Talk Show*. Many of you were faithful listeners of the *Talk Show* during the years that it was hosted by our guest, Fred Boyland. I have surely taken the show in a different direction, but have always been conscious that I was walking in Fred's footsteps. Is that mic working, Fred? Say hello to our audience, your audience.

Fred: Yes, it's me alright, yours truly. (The idea of his own self going out over the airwaves again, has raised him up.) So, folks, are we ready to rip 'em from the headlines? (The voice was weak and faltering and she looked through the glass at Rob, who returned to her a shaking head and an ironic smile.)

Vivien: Oh, my, are we going to rip 'em from the headlines? Just kidding, Fred. Lines are open if you want to swap ideas with a familiar voice. We have a call. You're on the air with Fred Boyland.

Caller: Am I on?

Vivien: Yes, sir.

Caller: Fred, you don't want to sit down with the person who stole your job. We made our point. We did what we came to do. We can come and get you out of there if you want. Just say the word. (click)

Vivien: You probably know who that was. I am at a disadvantage.

Fred: Yes, I kn- kn- know the fellow.

Vivien: I hope that we can talk current events, because that is your wheelhouse. But I must say something important first, just to clear the air. I hope you won't mind, Fred. That man said that I had stolen your job. (She looked at Fred and he was impassive.) That's not what happened, is it?

Fred: I h- h- had a show th- th- that was going real nice; I had a big audience and they took it away. One d- d- day they just took it away. It's all the s- s- same thing.

Vivien: Maybe they did—just take it away. I don't know all the details of that. It's important to me, though, that we are clear about one thing. I came in here and applied for a job after it was announced on the air that you weren't coming back, so I'd like you to understand that I had no hostility toward you. There was a job opening, and I just pursued an opportunity. You understand that?

Fred: W- w- would you like it if out of the blue they t- t- told you, you were d- d- done?

Vivien had processed it all a dozen times: Fred had had a stroke, was in the hospital, and his speech had been badly compromised, but there was no point in her stating the obvious.

Vivien: I'm going to pot your mic up a little, okay, great. Let's move on to the headlines. Oh, I know. You saw this, I bet, Fred. Did you hear they were introducing oysters in the Medomak River?

Fred: P- p- probably not a great idea. That river is the best clam resource in the State of Maine. W- w- why can't they l- l- leave well enough alone? What do your listeners think—can we take calls, Vivien, it's y- y- your show?

Vivien: Yes, of course, Fred will take calls. It's not my show, though, no, I learned that from you, from you and the Hudsons. It's Frost Pound's show. We've got a call. Fred, you take it.

Fred: Good morning, you're r- r- rippin' with Fred.

Caller: Freddie, this is Lil Harding. Vivien, my late husband, Tom, and I used to run with the Boylands. We had some good times, didn't we, Freddie?

Fred: How have you been, Lil? It's b- b- been a long time.

Lil: You know we closed up the big house, sold it last spring? Got to be too much. I'm with Susie's family now. They're good to me—can't complain.

Fred: Yeah, downsizing, good.

Lil: Say, Freddie, do you remember the summer nights we ate clams down on the dock? Those were some of the best times of my life. You guys were awfully fun to be with back in the day. I bet you still are. (silence) I've grown to like oysters, though, can you believe it?—raw. It took me a while and I used a lot of cocktail sauce and lemon juice in the beginning. But I take 'em straight now. I even have my favorites.

Vivien: Me, too, Lil. I asked some marine science guys if there was, you know, any inherent incompatibility between the soft-shell clams and the oysters. I don't think there is, not as far as the culture of one affects the culture of the other. I guess it would be a problem if there weren't enough nutrients in the water to support both, but I don't think that's the case.

Fred: W- w- what would a d- d- dinosaur like Fred Boyland know about th- th- things like that?

Vivien: Everybody's opinion counts. No one knows that better than you.

Their conversation is interrupted by another man who has quietly slipped into the studio, Austin Hudson.

Vivien: Hey, look who's here? A day early, right? A nice surprise, isn't it, Fred? It's the big boss, Austin Hudson, the license holder of Frost Pound's terrific radio station. Mr. Hudson has been travelling out of the country and, I take it, has just returned?

Austin: (loud, over Vivien's shoulder) We have. Tuned in to the *Talk Show* when we got in range. Good to see you, Freddie. You look well. I got you a coffee, light and sweet, and a glazed stick. I hope that's right.

Fred: You remembered.

Austin: Of course, I did.

Vivien vamped through the next half hour with as much as she knew about the care and feeding of oysters: the differences that result from growing them in different parts of the river, differences in marketing, the popularity of Maine oysters in New York restaurants, the complete absence of pearls. Not many— but a few phone calls helped her out. Nobody asked for Fred

Boyland. JJ's Mom didn't call, George the Welder didn't call, but Vivien got through it.

When the 12:00 noon tone sounded, Fred freed himself from his headphones with the ease of a motion a thousand times repeated. Rob was busy now, so Vivien came around to help Fred and the wheelchair. Fred made no eye contact with Vivien and did not thank her. But in the lobby, when his wife had hugged him and bundled him up for the out of doors, she turned to Vivien and said, "That's a very fine thing you did today, Miss, thank you. We'll leave these geraniums with you if it's all the same."

# Chapter 28
# Extra Help

### Off-Air

Rolling slowly in his big van, Brownie spotted the black numeral **7** at a doorway of the Returning Tide condominiums. He parked his delivery van, hoisted a large, heavy box onto his right shoulder, and navigated the slush to Ms. Marie Scanlon's #7. As was his custom, he pressed the doorbell, but was immediately drawn to the large note, hand-written on a sheet of white copy paper and taped to the mailbox:

**Brownie**
**Please see me after class**
**at your convenience.**

He hit the bell again, but hoped that no one would answer. No one did. It was his Miss Scanlon. Failing to get the required signature, he left the box on the covered porch.

On the day the tracking said the box of wine might come, Marie had arranged to be out all day. Once home in the early evening, she found the heavy box at her front door and brought it inside. That evening, she did nothing out of her routine. Though living alone, she dressed up, put on lipstick, and rearranged her long black hair atop her small head. It was her routine and part of her rearguard defense against bag lady-ness. That first night nothing happened.

The next evening at six, the earliest Brownie could change out of his uniform and drive to Returning Tide, he pulled up to the guest parking in his own car. He was fearful in an unusual way and he wished it was not already dark. He did not ring, but knocked. Marie had determined she would answer on the second ring and come to the door with a relaxed and casual smile. She had even practiced. The thrill was there again. She had thought about this moment, her favorite student coming for extra help, handsome and youthful still after so many years. Nineteen years—she had checked it by the yearbooks.

"Brownie," she spoke, opening the door on a second knock. The name she had decided to call her guest exited her mouth without force of sufficient air, and right away her ruse of casualness was wrecked.

"Miss Scanlon, how have you been—I'm sorry—cross that out, trite, delete. I hope you are well—that's what I mean."

"Please come in. Are you alone, not with the other boys?"

"Yes, all alone, as I am most of the time these days. The others grew up. It's wonderful to see you, Miss Scanlon."

"And wonderful for me to see you, Brownie." She took his cap and reached for a sleeve of the coat he was taking off. She was certain this was the first time she had ever touched him.

"Please come sit, or stand, I'm having a drink," and he followed her toward the kitchen that was open on the dining and living rooms.

"I thought you were here," Brownie said. "I thought I saw you once, but you never get packages."

"Just that wine yesterday." She smiled and said, "Would you like some of that white wine. Maybe something stronger; I have a good cheap cab—or beer."

"The red wine would be great," he replied.

"I'll have that too. You won't be emasculated by my opening the wine, will you?" she said as she pulled a corkscrew from a drawer. They were quiet as she opened and poured the wine. "I bought myself these stemless goblets the other day. I've been knocking over the stemmed ones of late. I think these are very nice."

"Great."

"Are you still smoking, Brownie?"

"Oh, no, I've never smoked," he answered.

"I enjoy a cigar," she replied and walked to a pretty wooden box on the dining room sideboard. "I was remembering you and the Poetry Club in your cars smoking after school."

"We were just goofing around, waiting for you. I never inhaled. Eventually you would come out to your car, always carrying piles of folders and papers."

"English teachers bring home a lot of work. I never minded, but I did wonder if people understood it, that reading and grading papers required a lot of time."

"Were they worthy of your time?"

"Mostly not particularly worthy," she answered, "but you had to approach every paper as though it might be wonderful. There was no other way."

"And there were diamonds in the rough."

"Do you remember Chad Cushing?"

"He was a year ahead of me."

"His dad was in the legislature, a lawyer. Chad was cruising for first in his class his senior year when he gave me one of the best papers I'd ever had. Chaucer."

"I didn't like that kid."

"It just felt too good, the paper. I drove up to Waterville to the Colby library and found the book. Chad's father had taken it out two weeks earlier. Chad's essay was a lovely paraphrase of its third chapter."

"What happened?"

"It was a tricky negotiation for a layman. I hope I remember it accurately. Yale, where he had already been accepted, was not informed. The plagiarized essay was counted a misunderstanding of the rules of proper documentation and he got a do-over instead of an F. That tall, awkward Brewer girl moved up to valedictorian."

"Genius. Chad's in the legislature now," Brownie said.

"And I believe everything that comes out of his mouth," Miss Scanlon said. "I smoke with my wine. Will you join me?"

"Okay, but give me a cheap one. I might not finish it."

"It's not so very cold. Sometimes I smoke on the deck," and she led him that way. "Why did you wait for me in the school parking lot?"

"We were in love with you, Miss Scanlon."

Marie Scanlon's life was lived among words—tens of thousands of them. She read two books a week, but for this nothing suitable came to mind. After a long pause and wetness on her cheeks, she said, "Probably it was the poetry, or hormones."

"Some of the latter to be sure, but it was mostly you, Miss Scanlon. Marie."

Marie clipped both cigars. Brownie stared at Marie's veiny, silver-bangled forearm as she lit his with a lighter conveniently produced from her skirt pocket. "Did you marry, Brownie?"

"Yes, just after college. Do you remember Cynthia whose father was the president of the white bank?"

Marie said, "Yes, she was a great beauty."

Brownie said, "She still is, prettier now than then. Do you mind listening to this?

"I've got a full glass of wine," she replied.

"I started at the bank and was well-liked. I was conscientious and worked hard. After a while I began studying for the examinations to be a stock broker. I passed. The bank guys were going to throw me a lot of business. It was all strictly legal and I hated it. I never became a stockbroker. I made a wreck of everything, hard to explain, I still don't really know what happened, just that I hurt a lot of people."

"You are a writer, now, aren't you?"

"That's what I think I am, even if I haven't ever said that to anyone. I love writing. I love the organizing of words in my head and the challenge of expressing ideas and feelings with economy. It's fun."

"Lucky for you, you're good at it."

"Have you heard any of my contributions—on Vivien's radio program?"

"I think maybe three."

"And?"

"Very good, uneven. I gather you get them out quickly because you are responding to other callers or things you have just seen on the road, so there's not been much revision. But they are lovely—worthwhile—and you love doing it."

"Do you remember that when Tommy or Adam would come to Poetry Club without any new work, they'd say they had writer's block, and you pretended you believed them. After all, weren't we deeply pained little Dylan Thomases?"

"Their youthful suffering was so affecting. What else could I do?"

"I'm stuck in adolescence myself and I hate it. I have never wanted to write about myself. People and things through my lens, sure, but not poems with me as the unnamed principal character. It's pretty lame. So, I'm blocking, that's the point."

"And you know why, right?"

"The unresolved quarrel with my father—do you remember him?"

"Big handsome guy, worked at Bath Iron Works."

"Yeah. He didn't think much of the Poetry Club thing, but he thought that I was in love with Miss Scanlon and he approved of that—an indication that even if I liked literature, I was probably not homosexual, and he thought the crush would wear off. You reminded him of Mary Tyler Moore—that's what he said. He wasn't yet onto the insidious danger of the poetry itself—not then."

Brownie wasn't uncomfortably cold on Marie's deck. They had brought the wine bottle outdoors and had a second glass. His cigar was out. He continued, "But Dad gradually realized that I was not a breadwinning husband, or a local politician-in-waiting, or a teller of coarse jokes at the country club. He was very angry. He didn't have the temperament or the tools to quarrel with me civilly, so he resorted to saying terrible, cruel things. I'm generally pretty tough and can take a punch. He exiled me from himself and my mother, and from their home. He said that I was dead to him."

"So, you've put some of it in poems. It sounds like you have run up against the limits of art to reconcile flawed and broken people. Some would argue that there is no such limit. They are better artists than you and I."

"Yes, it's not working."

"As your teacher, I suggest you commit to choosing new subject matter. And, with your father, try something else."

Brownie did not stay very long. Marie told him that for her it had been lovely and that she hoped that the club could meet again. She felt young and beautiful and as though she had been thoroughly ravished, but she was sure that they had only touched that moment when she first took his coat.

# Chapter 29
# Plaid

A week had passed since the day of Fred's big demonstration and Vivien was just as happy for the show to settle back into a gentle routine. There was lots of boosting of school and church and civic activities. She even ripped a few things from the headlines when the well ran dry. She was exhausted and needed relief. It was fine.

On a Tuesday during the second hour, she took a call from a familiar voice.

Vivien: Good morning, you're on with Vivien.

George the Welder: I'm disappointed this morning, Vivien, to hear you just prattling on about the news of the day. You're really not very good at it.

Vivien: A vicious thing to say. You know I have to fill three hours.

George: Maybe you just don't like politics and current events, which is not your fault, but this is not the way I want to remember you.

Vivien: Thank you for the heads-up. I'm a little lazy this week. What's going on with you, George the Welder? This is George the Welder, I hope, and I am not speaking so familiarly with George the Socialist.

George: I have felt the need to do some important housekeeping. A couple things.

Vivien: I can grab a bucket and mop and come over right after the show. You'd have to invite me, though, and tell me where you live. Do you know I would do anything for you?

George: (his voice weaker than usual) You have had some wonderful callers. The fellow that writes the poems. He's kind of grown on me. I would very much like to meet him, today would be good, good for him to come here if that is possible.

Vivien: I hope I can help with that, George. (she raises her voice) An all-points bulletin for Brownie. I could give him your address off the air—would that be good?

George: That won't be necessary. Just find him if you can. A man with his background in deliveries can surely find me.

Vivien: We'll find him: (loud) Brownie, phone home—like ET, phone home.

George: And one other thing and I must go, the whole College of Cardinals will be in my kitchen before long. I think I should see *your* face in person, Miss Kindler.

Vivien: A face made for radio.

George: Of course. I need to go now. Austin Hudson knows where I live. Bye, bye. Please find him, Vivien—today would be especially good, I think.

### Off-Air

On that afternoon, two or three dozen different Frost Pound residents half-expecting package deliveries sat in their homes near front windows till dusk, hoping that they would be the one to see Brownie and relay the message that Vivien's caller, George the Welder, wanted to meet him. They had all prepared the same speech: "The old guy phoned the *Talk Show* a little after eleven. He didn't sound too good and asked Vivien's help in getting to you. The old guy, George the Welder, wants to meet the poet. Somebody at the station has the address."

It was the girls at the clam shucking operation that first spotted Brownie. The lead girl spoke for them all: "That nice old guy, George, was asking for you on Vivien's show this morning. He wants to meet the poet. You are the poet, aren't you? We all listen to the *Talk Show* and hear your poems. We can see why he would like to know you. You're a really good guy. He said *today*. It seemed like it was important that he see you *today*."

On-Air

Vivien: (surprised to see Austin coming into her studio) I'm joined in the studio by our boss, Mr. Hudson.

Austin had never done this before, pulled up a seat in one of the guest locations as though he wanted to be on Vivien's show.

Vivien: I think that mic is on. What's up?

Austin: I was thinking about your discussion with callers a while back, you remember, about the famous people that have vacationed around here.

Vivien made a funny face at him. There hadn't been any such discussion. She was sure of it.

Austin: You know there's a guy in Round Pond that says Don McLean and his girlfriend stayed in his barn. (Austin made a record spinning gesture with his index finger.)

Vivien: Apocryphal, no doubt. Great songwriter—we have *American Pie* in the rotation. Actually, we play it quite often. (Austin nodded his head, up and down, and opened his eyes wide. Vivien was on the computer display and Austin nodded again, and she hit a button. The eight and one-half minute song began.)

Off-Air

She pushed back from the board and said, "What's up? I don't need the bathroom," she laughed.

Austin handed a little piece of paper to Vivien and said, "Here's the address. I can cover for you for the rest of your shift."

"What, are you serious?"

"Yes, it might be important, you should probably go right now."

"Can you do this? All the bells and whistles?"

Austin said, "Pretty sure, Rob's right there."

"Okay, if you really think—"

"I can do this much for *you*, can't I? We're going to need each other, so I'd better start building up some credits."

"Why's that?" Vivien said.

"Because I'm all alone running this place now and I need you!"

Vivien said, "Alone?"

"Kathy's taken a job as hostess at a fancy restaurant. So, it's just you and me, kid."

"Oh, I'm so sorry."

"It's all right. Not really. Maybe we can talk about it some time. She's giving me the station—the whole kit and caboodle. There's plenty of other stuff for her from her father. I'll tell you more later. Get out of here, he's waiting for you."


Off-Air


George Dessert lived just about where Vivien had imagined. It was a small house with a fenced garden wedged in among much larger 19th-century homes from the shipbuilding boom. It was sweet, cozily embraced by mature trees and hollies. There was a closed garage and two cars in the driveway: an older red Jeep Cherokee and a span clean, shining black Chrysler. Vivien parked on the street to not block anybody in.

298

She had to make the familiar decision: knock at the front door or the kitchen door, and she chose the kitchen. A small, tidy lady—prettiness shining through sad eyes, met her at the door right away. "Please come in, I'm so glad you are here. You're Miss Kindler from the radio, aren't you?"

"Yes, thank you. I'm sorry, I don't even know your name. I call your husband George the Welder."

"Miss Kindler," Mrs. George the Welder said, "this is Father Murphy. He's been so wonderful to us through this time. Father wanted to be with my husband today—you understand? I'm Lena, Lena Dessert. Some people say dessert like something sweet after supper, some say de'-say, the French way. You're going to want to keep your coat on. He's out in the garden with Minna. Minna's my cousin, but hospice sent her to us and she's an angel.

"George said you would come. He called the station a few minutes ago. I sometimes listen in," and she pointed to a rectangular, yellowed, AM-only relic on her kitchen table. "He's talking to Mr. Hudson right now. They know one another. Come with me to his garden. He's going to be very happy. Get up real close to him so he can see you good when you're talking. He's very weak."

Vivien said, "Excuse me, Father. It's a pleasure meeting you," and followed Lena into a back hall that had been altered with a gentle ramp that led to a back door.

At the doorway, George's wife said, "You go, see him bundled up on that chaise. That's Minna. See how big she is? She carries him in and out by herself. She says that's why they sent *her*. I'll stay in the kitchen with Father."

The garden was as she had imagined it—the work of art a gruff old male human had fashioned by primordial instinct. All clean and simple, a meandering raked path, gently shaped forms of different sizes and textures, the largest a Japanese maple.

Under the trained, smooth, twisting limbs was a white and blue human nest that held George. From where Minna balanced her great frame on a teak garden seat, the cousin met Vivien's eyes. Vivien smiled, but did not speak.

It was a big shock: the high school football hero, the builder of Navy ships, the leader of the crew that would unify the temporary classrooms with the discount roof trusses. So tiny he was now, cocooned in Wedgewood quilts and a stocking cap under his maple tree.

"Hi, I'm Minna," the big woman said softly to Vivien. "He's on the radio. George is talking to Mr. Hudson on the *Talk Show*."

Vivien sees now what she had not at first noticed, that Minna's big red hand is cradling a phone near George's mouth.

Minna now craned her own face closer to the phone.

Minna: (into the phone) Someone has joined us, Mr. Hudson. George, look, a nice young woman has come out to see you. Do you know who this is?

Austin: Is it Vivien Kindler who hosts our daily *Talk Show* on WNWT, *Now We're Talkin*? If it's you, Vivien, speak right up so our listeners can hear you?

Vivien: (into the phone and out over the air) George the Welder, it's Vivien and I've come to see you. (He looked into her face and the corners of his mouth tried to turn up a little.) Hello, Austin. How are you doing filling in for me? It's not as easy as it looks, is it?

Austin: I think, damn well. Oops, I swore, George. There goes the station license. Vivien, George and I were talking about football in these little towns back in the day, and that's probably why I've lapsed into locker room language.

Vivien can see that George wants to speak and Minna holds the phone near his mouth.

George: They'll take that license from you over George Dessert's dead body.

Austin: Thanks for that, George, and for what you've done in your work life, and for being part of our Frost Pound radio family. I'm going to ring off, George, and let you visit with our Vivien.

George: Austin. She's beautiful, you know. Promise you'll take good care of her—maybe pay her a little better—she's so beautiful.

Austin: Okay, I promise. You cornered me on live radio. Not fair. So long, George. (click)

### Off-Air

George's head sagged over to one side, exhausted. "You're a tired boy, George," Minna whispered sweetly.

Vivien said, "Should I go?"

"No, can you just sit with him for a while? That's what he'd like. Take my chair. I'll go in for a cup of tea. He gets angry, don't you, George, if I try to put him back inside. He loves it out here in the cold. We'll all be in the kitchen."

Vivien wanted to touch him and she made some gentle pats at the comforters. "I think you really are warm under all this goose down, George the Welder." He was as small as she had at first discerned, and she tucked at the place where there should have been a leg. She had never been so near to death. That is surely what this is, she thought. It's why the priest is here.

This is the warmest part of the day, she thought, and with no leaves on George's big tree the sun is shining right on his face. She judges that she can stay awhile, that there is nowhere else she must be. She spots the barrier with the neighbor formed by the tall bamboos, some tan and dead, and others light evergreen. She sees that the chickadees and juncos and mourning doves coexist here happily with the man and that someone has kept up the raking of debris.

The peaceableness of it was broken by the noise of the metal storm door. Vivien turned and saw standing in the path by the backdoor, a tall uniformed man, all in light brown. He carried a package of sorts, a bag from Renys Department Store. Vivien stood and looked at him. She thought she was shaking and she said, probably inaudibly, "They found you."

George's face was still turned aside, protected in the covers, and his eyes were closed. The tall young man said, "Hello, Vivien, how is he?"

"No one has told me anything. We had a little talk before. I guess you saw Father Murphy. I'll leave you."

"No, don't go." He got on his haunches close to George the Welder and for a few moments just looked at him. "Hi, Daddy, I've come. I've come home."

At the sound of the voice, George awakened and turned, and life came into his eyes.

Brownie said, "I got you something. I was thinking about how I messed up your good flannel shirt out on the bay a while back. You remember, with the mackerel lures." He produced from the Renys bag a folded-up, new plaid Carhartt shirt with all the tags still on it. "I picked you up a new one this morning. It wasn't cheap, but they say it will last forever."

His father whispered, "For eternity—perfect. My son, my beautiful son."

Vivien backed away quietly, slowly at first, then more quickly. From the kitchen door she turned and saw the poet, silent, but for his whole self spread atop the welder.

# Acknowledgements

For love, mentorship, encouragement, affirmation, editing, and proofreading: Ed Ericson, Bret Lott, Scott Bolinder, David Joly, Chandra Lee, Hope Mahoney, Sherry Cobb, Brad Davis, John Martin, Alexandra Lyman, and Mary Coogan Martin.

# Note from the Author

The Dalai Lama said: "Be kind whenever possible. It is always possible."

If *Talk Radio* has made you laugh, or warmed a place in you, please leave a review online anywhere you are able so that others will read it too. Let Vivien's kindness ripple into a troubled world.

Thank you so much for reading one of our **Literary Fiction** novels.
If you enjoyed our book, please check out our recommendation
for your next great read!

*The Five Wishes of Mr. Murray McBride* by Joe Siple

**2018 Maxy Award "Book Of The Year"**
"A sweet...tale of human connection...
will feel familiar to fans of Hallmark movies."
*-Kirkus Reviews*

"An emotional story that will leave readers meditating on the
life-saving magic of kindness."
*-Indie Reader*

View other Black Rose Writing titles at
www.blackrosewriting.com/books and use promo
code
**PRINT** to receive a **20% discount** when purchasing.

BLACK ROSE
writing™